Aliatha
Romig

the
BOOKWORM
box

Helping the community, one book at a time

W E B   O F   S I N #1

SECRETS

Book #1 of the WEB OF SIN trilogy

Aleatha Romig

New York Times, Wall Street Journal, and USA Today
bestselling author of the Consequences and Infidelity series

COPYRIGHT AND LICENSE INFORMATION

SECRETS

This is a work of fiction. Names, characters, places, and incidents either are the product of the author's imagination

2018 Edition License

SECRETS – WEB OF SIN BOOK 1

Blurb

The twisted and intriguing storytelling that you loved in Consequences and Infidelity is coming back at you with an all-new alpha anti-hero in the dark romance series Web of Sin, by New York Times bestselling author Aleatha Romig.

I'm Sterling Sparrow. You've no doubt heard my name or read it on the top of tall buildings. There's more to my business—my realm—than what is seen aboveground.

Within the underbelly of one of America's largest cities lives a world where a man's word is either his most valuable tool or his most respected weapon. When my father ruled that world and that city, he promised me someone who would one day make my reign complete.

Since that day, long ago, Araneae McCrie has been mine.

She just didn't know.

My father is now gone.

The city and the underbelly are now mine.

The time has come for me to collect who was promised to me, to shred her life of secrets and make her who she's always been—mine.

Have you been Aleatha'd?

Secrets is book one of the Web of Sin trilogy.

WEB OF SIN: BOOK ONE

SECRETS

Fiction is like a spider's web, attached ever so slightly perhaps, but still attached to life at all four corners. Often the attachment is scarcely perceptible- Virginia Woolf

PROLOGUE

Araneae

 $\mathcal{M}$ y mother's fingers blanched as she gripped the steering wheel tighter with each turn. The traffic on the interstate seemed to barely move, yet we continued to swerve in, out, and around other cars. From my angle I couldn't read the speedometer, though I knew we were bordering on reckless driving. I jumped, holding my breath as we pulled in front of the monstrous semi, the blare of a truck's horn filling our ears. Tons of metal and sixteen wheels screeched as brakes locked behind us, yet my mother's erratic driving continued.

"Listen very carefully," she said, her words muffled by the quagmire of whatever she was about to say, the weight pulling them down as she fluttered her gaze between the road ahead and the rearview mirror.

"Mom, you're scaring me."

I reached for the handle of the car door and held on as if

the seat belt couldn't keep me safe while she continued to weave from lane to lane.

"Your father," she began, "made mistakes, deadly mistakes."

My head shook side to side. "No, Dad was a good man. Why would you say that?"

My father, the man I called Dad for as long as I could remember, was the epitome of everything good: honest and hardworking, a faithful husband, and an omnipresent father.

He *was*.

He died less than a week ago.

"Listen, child. Don't interrupt me." She reached into her purse with one hand while the other gripped tighter to the wheel. Removing an envelope from the depths of the bag, she handed it my direction. "Take this. Inside are your plane tickets. God knows if I could afford to send you away farther than Colorado, I would."

My fingers began to tremble as I looked down at the envelope in my grasp. "You're sending me away?" The words were barely audible as my throat tightened and heaviness weighed down upon my chest. "Mom—"

Her chin lifted in the way it did when her mind was set. I had a million visions of the times I'd seen her stand up for what she believed. At only five feet three, she was a pit bull in a toy poodle body. That didn't mean her bark was worse than her bite. No, my mother always followed through. In all things she was a great example of survival and fortitude.

"When I say your father," she went on, "I don't mean my husband—may the Lord rest his soul. Byron was a good man who gave his...everything...for you, for *us*. He and I have always been honest with you. We wanted you to know that we loved you as our own. God knows that I wanted to give birth. I tried to get pregnant for years. When you were presented to us, we knew you were a gift from heaven." Her bloodshot eyes —those from crying through the past week since the death of my dad—briefly turned my direction and then back to the highway. "Renee, never doubt that you're our angel. However, the reality is somewhere darker. The devil has been searching for you. And my greatest fear has always been that he'd find you."

The devil?

My skin peppered with goose bumps as I imagined the biblical creature: male-like with red skin, pointed teeth, and a pitchfork. Surely that wasn't what she meant?

Her next words brought me back to reality.

"I used to wake in a cold sweat, fearing the day had arrived. It's no longer a nightmare. You've been found."

"Found? I don't understand."

"Your biological father made a deal against the devil. He thought if he did what was right, he could... well, he could *survive*. The woman who gave birth to you was my best friend —a long time ago. We hadn't been in contact for years. She hoped that would secure your safety and keep you hidden. That deal...it didn't work the way he hoped. Saving themselves was a long shot. Their hope was to save you. That's how you became our child."

It was more information than I'd ever been told. I have always known I was adopted but nothing more. There was a promise of *one day*. I used to hope for that time to come. With the lead weight in the pit of my stomach, I knew that now that *one day* had arrived, and I wasn't ready. I wanted more time.

The only woman I knew as my mother shook her head just before wiping a tear from her cheek. "I prayed you'd be older before we had this talk, that you would be able to comprehend the gravity of this information. But as I said, things have changed."

The writing on the envelope blurred as tears filled my sixteen-year-old eyes. The man I knew as my dad was gone, and now the woman who had raised me was sending me away. "Where are you sending me?"

"Colorado. There's a boarding school in the mountains, St. Mary of the Forest. It's private and elite. They'll protect you."

I couldn't comprehend. "For how long? What about you? What about my friends? When will I be able to come home?"

"You'll stay until you're eighteen and graduated. And then it will be up to you. There's no coming back here...ever. This city isn't home, not anymore. I'm leaving Chicago, too, as soon as I get you out." Her neck stiffened as she swallowed her tears. "We both have to be brave. I thought at first Byron's accident was just that—an accident. But then this morning...I knew. Our time is up. They'll kill me if they find me, just as they did Byron. And Renee..." She looked my way, her gray eyes swirling with emotion. While I'd expect sadness, it was fear that dominated. "...my fate would be easy compared to yours."

She cleared her throat, pretending that tears weren't cascading down her pale cheeks.

"Honey, these people are dangerous. They don't mess around, and they don't play fair. We don't know how, but they found you, and your dad paid the price. I will forever believe that he died to protect you. That's why we have this small window of time. I want you to know that if necessary, I'll do the same. The thing is, my death won't stop them. And no matter what, I won't hand you over."

"Hand me over?"

We swerved again, barreling down an exit until Mom slammed on her brakes, leaving us in bumper-to-bumper traffic. Her gaze again went to the rearview mirror.

"Are we being followed?" I asked.

Instead of answering, she continued her instructions. "In that envelope is information for your new identity, a trust fund, and where you'll be living. Your dad and I had this backup plan waiting. We hoped we'd never have to use it, but he insisted on being prepared." Her gaze went upward. "Thank you, Byron. You're still watching over us from heaven."

Slowly, I peeled back the envelope's flap and pulled out two Colorado driver's licenses. They both contained my picture—that was the only recognizable part. The name, address, and even birth dates were different. "Kennedy Hawkins," I said, the fictitious name thick on my tongue.

"Why are there two?"

"Look at the dates. Use the one that makes you eighteen years old for this flight. It's to ensure the airline will allow you to fly unaccompanied. Once you're in Colorado, destroy the one with the added two years. The school needs your real age for your grade in school."

I stared down at one and then the other. The name was the same. I repeated it again, "Kennedy Hawkins."

"Learn it. Live it. Become Kennedy."

A never-before-thought-of question came to my mind. "Did I have a different name before I came to you?"

My mother's eyes widened as her pallid complexion changed from white to gray. "It's better if you don't know."

I sat taller in the seat, mimicking the strength she'd shown me all of my life. "You're sending me away. You're saying we may never see one another again. This is my only chance. I think I deserve to be told everything."

"Not everything." She blinked rapidly. "About your name, your dad and I decided to alter your birth name, not change it completely. You were very young, and we hoped having a derivation of what you'd heard would help make the transition easier. Of course, we gave you our last name."

"My real name isn't Renee? What is it?"

"Araneae."

The syllables played on repeat in my head, bringing back memories I couldn't catch. "I've heard that before, but not as a name."

She nodded. "I always thought it was ironic how you loved insects. Your name means spider. Your birth mother thought it gave you strength, a hard outer shell, and the ability to spin silk, beautiful and strong."

"Araneae," I repeated aloud.

Her stern stare turned my way. "Forget that name. Forget Araneae and Renee. We were wrong to allow you any connection. Embrace Kennedy."

My heart beat rapidly in my chest as I examined all of the paperwork. My parents, the ones I knew, were thorough in their plan B. I had a birth certificate, a Social Security card, a passport matching the more accurate age, and the driver's license that I'd seen earlier, all with my most recent school picture. According to the documentation, my parents' names were Phillip and Debbie Hawkins. The perfect boring family.

Boring or exciting, family was something I would never have again.

"And what happened to Phillip and Debbie?" I asked as if any of this made sense.

"They died in an automobile accident. Their life insurance funded your trust fund. You are an only child."

The car crept forward in the line of traffic near the departure terminal of O'Hare Airport. A million questions swirled through my head, and yet I struggled to voice even one. I reached out to my mother's arm. "I don't want to leave you."

"I'll always be with you, always."

"How will we talk?"

She lifted her fist to her chest. "In here. Listen to your heart."

Pulling to the curb and placing the car in park, she leaned my direction and wrapped me in her arms. The familiar scent of lotions and perfumes comforted me as much as her hug. "Know you're loved. Never forget that, Kennedy."

I swallowed back the tears brought on by her calling me by the unfamiliar name.

She reached for her wrist and unclasped the bracelet she always wore. "I want you to have this."

I shook my head. "Mom, I never remember seeing you without it."

"It's very important. I've protected it as I have you. Now, I'm giving it to you." She forced a smile. "Maybe it will remind you of me."

"Mom, I'd never forget you." I looked down to the gold bracelet in the palm of my hand as my mom picked it up, the small charms dangling as she secured it around my wrist.

"Now, it's time for you to go."

"I don't know what to do."

"You do. Go to the counter for the airlines. Hand them your ticket and the correct identification. Stay strong."

"What about those people?" I asked. "Who are they? Will you be safe?"

"I'll worry about me once I'm sure that you're safe."

"I don't even know who they are."

Her gaze moved from me to the world beyond the windshield. For what seemed like hours, she stared as the slight glint of sunshine reflected on the frost-covered January ground. Snow spit through the air, blowing in waves. Finally, she spoke, "Never repeat the name."

"What name?"

"Swear it," she said, her voice trembling with emotion.

It was almost too much. I nodded.

"No. I need to hear you promise me. This name can never be spoken aloud."

"I swear," I said.

"Sparrow, Allister Sparrow. He's currently in charge, but one day it will be his son, Sterling."

I wished for a pen to write the names down; however, from the way they sent a chill down my spine, I was most certain that I'd never forget.

KENNEDY

Ten years later

I gripped the arms to the chair, refusing to allow a decade-old warning to affect me. I'd tried to forget it, to move on, as I'd been told to do. Yet forgetting the reason you lost your second set of parents at sixteen years of age was not easy.

"Kenni, you know I wouldn't ask you if I had a choice," Louisa, my business partner, cofounder of Sinful Threads, and best friend said. "You've been very straightforward about your aversion to Chicago. I've handled that market since we started this business. It's the problem with our inventory. The distributor insists that it isn't their problem. The warehouse has the records for the merchandise. Somewhere in between too many things have gone missing. It's getting out of hand."

Sighing, I nodded. "And it has to be addressed—in person? Now? It can't wait for next week when Jason can go?" Jason was Louisa's husband. Sinful Threads wasn't his baby, but he'd been known to help us when needed. I trusted him. He knew how important our company was to Louisa and because he loved her, it was important to him too. If he could help, he would.

Louisa's lips pursed and pulled to one side. "If this were New York, would you let it fester?"

New York was my baby. I found the buildings to house our inventory. I even interviewed the managers and upper management personnel. I traveled to the warehouse and distribution center monthly to keep my eyes as well as my finger on the pulse of the operations. It was the same way Louisa felt about Chicago. "Maybe I could handle San Francisco for you?" I asked my suggestion more than stated. "Then you could take care of Chicago. I'm just thinking about the relationship you have with Franco. You can lay down the law with him. You can probably do it all from here."

Here was Boulder, Colorado, outside of Denver. Being not too far from St. Mary of the Forest where Louisa and I had gone to high school, met, and become best friends, it had sentimental value. But there was more. There was economic value to our location. All of our manufacturing occurred here under our noses. It kept our merchandise to our strict standards. Yes, we could produce cheaper farther away.

Sinful Threads wasn't about cheap—it was about quality.

"I hate to admit this," she said, "but that's part of why I think you should go."

My brown eyes narrowed. "Tell me what you mean."

"I want fresh eyes. Chicago's operations are my baby. I'm more emotional there, not that I'm not emotional everywhere, lately," she said with a half scoff. "I hired Franco almost four years ago, long before we grew into what we are today.

Sinful Threads is growing and outpacing our current infrastructure. The distributor's orders for our silk scarves have quadrupled in the last quarter. The expenses are killing us, yet the resulting sales are phenomenal. Franco is determined that Chicago is ready for a storefront."

I leaned back, letting that sink in. A storefront. It was our dream. At first, we considered starting with a few mom-and-pop-type stores. It was the exact opposite of what we ended up doing. Instead, with Jason's encouragement, Louisa and I took our baby to the web. We started with a few smaller distribution centers in Midwestern cities. The labor and overhead there were less expensive. We were discovered. No longer do we accept direct internet orders by customers. We were approached by the biggest names in fashion asking to be our distributors.

The stores wanting our products were well established and located in the high-rent districts throughout the country. We had to move some of our operations closer to them. Chicago and New York were two of our top hubs. Lately, the numbers in Chicago weren't adding up.

"Do you think he's manipulating the numbers? Is that what you're worried about?"

"I don't think the problems are operational, but I'm afraid there's something happening that he isn't telling me. There's no way that Chicago has suddenly started misplacing inventory when no other center is experiencing the same problem. I think your suspicious mind can get to the bottom of this faster than mine."

"Louisa, with what you just said, you win the suspicion contest."

"Kenni, you are great at reading people. I like Franco and

trust him. It will be more difficult for him to fool you. And then there's that dinner."

"What?" My stomach twisted with my one-word question.

"What?" she repeated. "It's a dinner. You eat. I know you do."

I shook my head. "You want me to go to a city I haven't stepped foot in for ten years and not only conduct private business but go to a dinner? Who will be there?"

"It's been planned for months. I told you about it."

"I guess I hadn't thought about it. I knew you'd handle it. Who will be there?" I asked again.

"Investors and potential investors interested in Sinful Threads. All you need to do is give them a face for the product." Louisa looked down at her ever-growing midsection. "I'm not being sexist, but I don't think an eight-month-pregnant woman with swollen feet says sexy the way we want to project for Sinful Threads."

"Is there more?" I asked.

"Jason isn't thrilled with me traveling, especially if the trip will be upsetting regarding Franco, and..." Her big brown eyes looked my direction.

"And what?"

"The doctor thinks I need to stay closer to home. If this could be handled over the phone—"

I lifted my hand. "Lou, I'm sorry. I'm a bitch to put little Kennedy at risk because of some old wives' tale from my childhood."

Louisa ran her hand over her growing baby and smiled. "You know we haven't settled on a name."

"But you have to admit it has a nice ring. And bonus, it works for a boy too."

She tilted her head. "All these years and you've never given me the whole story about this Chicago wives' tale. Is it like witches and spells?"

A giggle escaped my throat as I tried to ignore the way the subject prickled my senses. "You've been watching too many supernatural shows on TV."

"It's more like books. About old cities like Chicago, especially ones where tragedies occurred." She leaned back and nodded. "Yep. You know. You've heard the story of Mrs. O'Leary's cow? Over 300 people were killed in the fire. Those spirits have to go somewhere, or they don't and they stay. Places like that are perfect for covens and the such."

"Stop," I said with a grin. "You need to read lighter fare for the baby's sake."

Louisa took a deep breath before standing and coming around her desk to the side where I'm seated. My office was down the hall, but in her condition, coming to her was easier and usually faster.

Leaning back, she crossed her arms above her bulging stomach. "I'm serious, Kennedy. You're my best friend. You're intelligent and know our product as well as I do or better. The people at that dinner will love you as more than the face of Sinful Threads. They will love you for you. I haven't met most of the people on the guest list, but you've done this before in other cities. I don't mind doing it either. Heck, I like the wining and dining." She tilted her head toward her midsection. "It's that now, wining isn't possible, and well, I need you."

"You know how I feel. I have done it, but I've also left most of the public appearances to you."

"Yes. I also know that you're the brains and you're beautiful, in case you haven't noticed."

My cheeks filled with pink and warmth. "Thanks."

"No, I'm serious. You work too hard. You never relax. You also never get worried or upset, even when Sinful Threads' books were more red than black."

"Because I knew we would pull this off. The product is amazing. The manufacturing—"

"See," Louisa said. "All business. Yet the only time you pale is when the subject goes to Chicago. If it isn't a coven, it must be the mob."

"Jeez, Lou. Are there any other dark parts of Chicago you'd like to discuss? You know, I heard about this guy named Leroy Brown."

"Yeah, yeah, baddest man in town. But from my experience that isn't true. The underground is true, and there are some bad men involved."

My stomach dropped, recalling the last conversation I had with my adoptive mother. *These people are dangerous. They don't mess around, and they don't play fair.*

"I'm not making this shit up," she continued, completely unaware of the way this subject affected me. "I know. Do me a favor. If it's the mob, will you find out where Jimmy Hoffa is buried?"

"Seriously? You're all over the place with this."

"No, I'm not. In the middle of the night, I watch the History Channel. Sleeping is getting harder and harder."

I stood and gave my best friend a hug. "Fine, to prove that you're blowing this out of proportion, I'll fly there the first thing in the morning. If you can, make sure that Franco will be available, but don't tell him I'm coming. I'll check out the distribution center first, and then I'll surprise him with a visit at the warehouse. When's the dinner?"

"It's tomorrow night at the City Winery Riverwalk. Franco will be there, and my name is on the guest list. I'll call and have it changed to yours."

"No," I said, thinking it through. "Leave your name on there." There was a bit of comfort knowing that my name, no matter what it was now, wasn't on a guest list announcing my arrival to Chicago.

"Come with me," Louisa said as she stepped toward the door to her office. "I have something for you. You'll knock them dead tomorrow night."

"I think I'd like everyone to stay alive."

She shook her head as she walked a few steps ahead. "I want that story someday." She turned and grinned over her shoulder at me. "If you don't tell me, you know my imagination is going to make it ten times bigger than it is."

I wasn't sure that was possible.

I heard my mom's voice telling me never to return.

It's only one day and night, I reassured myself. No one will even notice.

I followed Louisa down the hallway until we reached a large office that she and I used exclusively to inspect new products. It was where we decided which designs would be produced and in what quantity. You would think it would be well organized because most of our business was. You'd have thought wrong.

This office was the exact opposite of organization.

I let out a laugh as she opened the door. Instead of orderliness, the room was chaos. By the way items and boxes were strewn about, it appeared more like a dressing room in a high-end boutique, one recently vacated by an exceptionally picky customer who had tried on every item in the entire store.

It was bedlam, and I loved it.

"One day we'll organize..." My words trailed off as my sentence went unfinished.

We both knew that this mess was our secret to success. It was how we worked best when it came to the hands-on part of Sinful Threads. We both needed to touch, hold, and smell. A silk accessory or garment was meant to be more than viewed. It was also meant to be inhabited. That couldn't happen in an orderly manner. When the days became filled with numbers on reports and conference calls, this room was my salvation.

Louisa was correct. I lived and breathed work. She had too until Jason entered her life. I didn't fault her for falling in love. I was happy for them and still am. She found that person with whom she could share her world. He's an interior designer, and while what he created was different, he understood her passion for Sinful Threads. They're a good team.

None of the men I'd dated knew what teamwork even meant. Louisa said I was attracted to assholes, and she might be correct. There was simply a type of man who caught my eye. I wanted an equal partner in life; in the bedroom, my desires were different. Apparently, that combination didn't exist. Therefore, at the ripe old age of twenty-six, I'd decided that the best way to avoid assholes was to not date at all. It wasn't great on the sex life, but that's why God created vibrators—or God created man and man created vibrators. The end result was that man wasn't necessary for a nice release.

For everything else, if I became stressed or needed a

break, I came to this room and wrapped myself in potential Sinful Threads merchandise. It was all the diversion I needed.

"Here," she said, opening a box I hadn't seen before. "This just arrived."

My gasp filled the room as I reached below the tissue paper and pulled the dress from the depth of the box. This was a new product and the first time I'd seen it in anything beyond a sketch.

"Oh my God. Why didn't you tell me this was here?"

The luxurious silk was like liquid in my grasp. The neckline was constructed of onyx-like jewels designed to surround the neck, while the halter bodice would accentuate a woman's curves. The waist had loops to hold the golden silk scarf that would wrap around, while the skirt contained extra material that would flow and swish as the wearer stepped or turned. It was a stunning prototype. If this concept went viral, Sinful Threads would no longer be limited to accessories.

The real-life version took my breath away.

"Because it just came about an hour ago." Her smile grew. "There's more. I think you should wear it to tomorrow night's dinner."

I held the one-of-a-kind dress against my chest, and for a moment, lost myself in the image of actually wearing it out in public. "It's not really me."

"It damn well should be. You're half of Sinful Threads. Make a statement. I bet those investors will be falling all over themselves to order these."

"What are the numbers on this prototype?"

"Let's just say that retail will be a four hundred percent markup." She tilted her head with a grin. "That is, if they order soon. It'll go up higher after that."

I used to wonder how much people would spend for quality. That was what Sinful Threads was about. It seemed that the higher the price, the greater the demand.

"I'm not..."

"It's your size. Take it. And when you come back Friday, I want to hear how it went. The hell with that, call or text me tomorrow night. I already know that it—no, that *you*—will be a hit."

KENNEDY

"I'm on the way to the warehouse now," I said into my phone, speaking with Louisa from the comfort of the back seat of the car I'd hired. "The distribution center's first-shift manager, Ricardo, is standing by his claim that the merchandise numbers on the arriving manifests are incorrect. I also spoke with the second-shift admin, Vanessa, and she also agreed. She offered to come in early tomorrow and show me some specific evidence."

"Will you still be there?"

I took a deep breath, watching the city where I was raised pass by the darkened windows of the car as my driver navigated the city. Being summertime, the streets overflowed with both automobiles and pedestrians. Not only were there the inhabitants of the windy city on their way from point A to point B but also vacationers, large groups with children in tow to see the sights of Chicago.

With the cloudless blue sky, breezes rustling the bright

green leaves of the trees lining the streets, and the sparkling waves of Lake Michigan visible from Lake Shore Drive, the ominous feeling I'd anticipated overwhelming me the second my feet touched Illinois soil was nowhere to be found.

"Yes," I said. "I'll stay through that meeting and then fly back tomorrow."

"Tell me you're going to wear the dress?" Louisa's voice raised an octave in anticipation.

My cheeks lifted. Out of the corner of my eye, I caught my reflection in the rearview mirror. The smile on my face was the opposite of what I'd expected to wear while in Chicago. Nevertheless, I embraced it. "I tried it on. Oh, Lou, it's stunning."

"No, sweetheart, you're stunning. With your blonde hair and that gold scarf as a sash, you'll wow them at that dinner. I wouldn't be surprised if we have thousands of orders waiting by tomorrow."

Since meeting her at St. Mary of the Forest, Louisa and her family have been my biggest cheerleaders. The Nelsons became my family as I'd been without one. With two daughters of their own, they didn't have to take me in and include me, but they did. From school breaks to family vacations and even holidays, Louisa and I became like sisters as well as best friends. That didn't mean we agreed on everything. It meant we were together even when we disagreed.

"First things first," I said. "I'm off to Franco."

"Call me as soon as the meeting is over. He has been..." She searched for the right word. "...evasive in our emails and phone calls. I can't thank you enough for making this trip."

"You know that I want you to stop worrying. Auntie Kennedy wants her niece or nephew to be stress free."

Louisa laughed. "I'm not sure what part of owning Sinful Threads you think is stress free, but fine. If only I could drink wine."

"One day and then we will each have our own bottle."

"It's a deal. Call me."

"I will."

After our call disconnected, I gave *stress free* a thought. I wanted that for Louisa, especially now. I wasn't confident I'd ever been completely without concern, not since the last day I saw my mom—my adoptive mom.

Through life, things happen. I had to learn that it was normal and not build each incident up in my mind.

There was the one time when I was skiing in Vail with Louisa's family. While out on the slope, there was an incident with a ski lift. Regular mechanical malfunction we were told, yet it seemed Lucy, Louisa's mother, was overly concerned. And then when we returned, we discovered the condo had been broken into.

I pushed those thoughts away. Things like that happen to everyone. I wasn't special. I wasn't a target. I was Kennedy Hawkins. That was all.

Taking a cleansing breath, I pulled up the latest Chicago manifests on my tablet. They were the up-to-the-minute reports from the distribution center where I'd just been. Ricardo had sent them to my secure email while I was still there. I hadn't gotten any vibes from him, other than he was unhappy that there were problems. As a matter of fact, he seemed overly confident that the problems were not on his end.

That confidence was contagious.

It was the first time I'd met him, but I wanted to believe him.

Comparing the numbers to the manifests from our corporate office that updated hourly, the numbers didn't make sense. The discrepancies varied by item. Ten off on one, sixteen off on another, exact on the next, and two off on yet another. Even our numbers from corporate didn't match.

I started to wonder about the computer program and made a note to have Winnie, my assistant, check with IT.

No matter how much I searched, I couldn't find a pattern nor a rhyme or reason to the discrepancies, scribbling more notes with each turn in the road or change of lane.

Numbers were my thing. I understood them.

There was no emotion in numbers. They simply were.

I'd learned too young to turn off feeling.

Sometimes, it was as if one side of my brain wrestled with the other. While numbers didn't have sentiment, our merchandise did. Louisa and I worked with our designers. Originally, we'd created the prototypes from sketch to fabric. It became too much. Either we could oversee the creative side and run the business or vice versa.

Having the fashion designers in Boulder, we were still hands-on. Trusting other people with our numbers, our business, the profits and losses was a bigger risk in both of our opinions. We still decided upon what creations became Sinful Threads—the emotional side of our business—and we kept our fingers on the pulse of the numbers.

The car bounced upon uneven pavement, pulling my attention away from my task at hand and back to the world outside the windows. The warehouse district was a far cry from the beauty of Lake Shore Drive. Large industrial buildings surrounded by chain-link fences filled the landscape as cargo trucks sat at loading docks.

"Ms. Hawkins, this is the address," Patrick, the driver, said as the car moved through an unlocked gate within the fence surrounding the facility.

Beyond the darkened windows, I noticed a tall man walking from my warehouse toward a large black SUV. There was another man in a dark suit, a step behind.

Curiosity? I wasn't sure what had drawn my attention, other than he was leaving my business and definitely not dressed like a worker or truck driver.

The vehicle reminded me of the kind used on television shows for law enforcement or important government officials, big and powerful as if it were reinforced. While the second man hurried to the driver's side, the dark-haired man in the expensive gray suit caught my eye.

If I were to believe Louisa, that probably meant he was an asshole.

His suit coat was unbuttoned, blowing back from the starched white shirt tucked into the trim waist of his slacks. He wasn't wearing a tie, and his collar was unbuttoned enough to show a small view of his tanned neck. An important man on a mission could be his description, and again, I wondered what he had been doing at Sinful Threads.

And then he turned our way.

With his hand on the passenger-door handle, his steps stopped as he looked our direction. Even from a distance, I was struck by his aura of authority. His features were granite as he studied our car, as if he had a say in who came and went from my warehouse.

His dark hair blew slightly in the summer breeze, and the

same color lined his strong jaw in a trimmed professional
style. Removing his sunglasses, his handsome face remained
creased as his eyes narrowed, and he continued to study
our car.

I thought to ask Patrick if he knew who the gentleman
was, but why would he?

Before my arrival in Chicago, Winnie hired an agency that
offered both transportation and security. I may have told
Louisa that this trip was no big deal, but I couldn't forget my
mother's words. My assistant's idea was a good compromise. A
few thousand dollars seemed a fair trade for my peace
of mind.

Our car stopped a few parking spaces away from the
large SUV.

"Ma'am, would you like me to accompany you into your
meeting?"

I'd said no at the distribution center, but the twisting of
my stomach told me to trust my instinct. After all, I'd hired
this company, I might as well utilize more than the transportation benefit.

"Thank you, Patrick."

A moment later, my door opened and what I'd been seeing
through the windows was now felt. The breeze blowing the
trees poured into the car with sweltering summer heat
replacing the air conditioning.

There were many things I missed when I was forced to
move to Colorado. The extreme weather of Chicago wasn't
one of them. It was difficult for people who didn't live in
climates like Chicago's to understand that while summertime
was scorching, the same area could easily be ten degrees

below zero in the winter. That didn't include heat index or wind chill.

If you didn't know what those terms meant, you haven't lived in Chicago.

Gathering my bag with my reports and tablet, I stepped out of the back seat, my heeled pumps landing on the soft asphalt as heat seared my bare legs and under my skirt. My blouse clung to my skin as the sun beat down. With my eyes covered by sunglasses, my gaze was drawn to the man I'd seen moments before.

I hoped that he wouldn't be able to see that I was looking his way.

I didn't know why I was concerned. He wasn't hiding the fact that he was still watching me.

With each step I took, his stare continued as his head tilted ever so slightly toward his broad shoulder. In the midst of blistering heat, his menacing demeanor appeared calculating yet calm if not downright cold as he scrutinized me from head to toe.

There was confidence in his disposition.

It was as if instead of the temperature radiating from the sun, it was the heat of his gaze penetrating beyond my surface to me—the *real* me.

KENNEDY

My skin peppered with goose bumps as the absurdity of the thought settled into the pit of my stomach.

He saw the *real* me.

That was impossible.

I didn't know the real me.

My back straightened, unwilling to allow this man to intimidate me with only his gaze. Yet if I were honest, that was happening. His stare alone was the impetus to the foreboding feeling now coursing through my blood. With my chin held high, I continued to walk toward my destination, pretending I didn't notice him.

Patrick moved in sync as we silently walked past the ogling man. I forced myself to keep going, step by step, up the stairs to the door near the loading dock. Once there, I recalled again that I was where the dark-haired man had just been.

Why had he been in my warehouse?

Once the door closed, I let out the breath I'd been holding and removed my sunglasses.

"Ms. Hawkins, are you all right?" Patrick asked.

"Yes," I said with a shiver. "I think it's the heat."

My eyes adjusted to the dim interior. While the inside of the building lacked the glare of the sun, there was little change in the temperature. The still air was sweltering, and yet the icy chill of the dark-haired man's stare had me on edge.

I pushed it away and surveyed my surroundings. The setup of the warehouse was similar to our others throughout the country. Nodding at men and women as they moved merchandise, I made my way beyond the rows of tall shelves to the offices near the back of the warehouse.

A push of a button and the door to the offices opened.

"May I help you?" a young woman asked. The name Connie was on a nameplate on the counter separating me from her desk.

"Yes, Connie, I'm here to see Franco Francesca."

She looked down at an old-fashioned desk calendar covered in scribbles. "Do you have an appointment?"

I stood taller. "No. Is Franco in?"

"Ma'am, if you don't—"

"Please tell him that Kennedy Hawkins is here to see him."

Her complexion paled. "Ms. Hawkins, I'm sorry. I didn't realize…" Her apology faded as the sound of ringing came from her desk phone. Just as quickly it silenced as she spoke into the handset, taking the call off speaker and only allowing me the ability to hear her side of the impending conversation. "Franco, um, Mr. Francesca, Ms. Hawkins is here to see you."

She nodded, agreeing with what I couldn't hear. "Yes, sir, Ms. Hawkins...Just arrived." She lifted her eyes back to me. "This second...I don't know...Yes, sir."

I'd met Franco twice, both times in Boulder. This was Louisa's territory, and no doubt, my unannounced arrival was both a surprise and possibly a shock. Yet, I wasn't sure it warranted Connie's clipped responses.

"Ma'am," she said, lowering the headset to her desk, "please follow me, and I'll take you to his office."

Nodding, I turned toward Patrick. "Please wait here." I tilted my head to a few rather uncomfortable-looking chairs along the wall.

He nodded, but instead of sitting, stood along the wall with his hands clasped in front of him. The stance brought a brief smile to my face. It was like the bodyguards on TV. I'd never felt the need to have one, but I liked the optics if nothing else.

Through the door, we entered the typical cubicle farm of a shared area. Men and women working on computers and talking on telephones filled each space. No one paid attention to us as Connie took me around the perimeter. We came to a stop at a closed door.

Though the sidelight was covered with small blinds and closed for privacy, I was certain I heard Franco's voice speaking as Connie knocked on the door. Within seconds, the door opened, and the man I'd meant to surprise was standing before us. By the way his eyes were opened as wide as saucers, I'd say my goal was accomplished.

"Ms. Hawkins, what brings you to Chicago? I hope everything is well with Mrs. Toney."

I didn't know Franco well enough to assess his frame of

mind—if he were truly surprised; however, intuition told me that perhaps nervous was a better assessment. Perhaps it was the perspiration dotting his brow or his clammy complexion. Then again, the warehouse was warm, and even the air conditioning in the offices was having trouble keeping up. Franco also didn't appear to be the type of man who worshipped the sun or worried about his physical appearance. In his mid-fifties, he was not aging well. With a receding hairline and soft, paunchy middle, his presentation led me to believe that the only weightlifting he did was twelve ounces at a time.

And yet I reminded myself that despite his appearance, up until recently, we'd had no difficulties with his facility.

I thought it best to wait on his first question—what brought me to Chicago—and concentrated on his second—Mrs. Toney. "Yes, Louisa is well. As you know, her baby is due soon so traveling isn't easy for her. She asked me to make Chicago a priority."

"Connie," Franco said, speaking past me, "will you make sure that we're not disturbed?" At the same time, he took a step back, gesturing for me to enter.

His office was plain, done in an industrial manner with OSHA regulations hanging on a poster on one wall as well as maps of the Chicago line of distribution. His metal desk was unimpressive, and the only window was the sidelight looking out to the cubicles.

"Yes, sir," Connie replied. "Do you want me to make that contact for you?"

"No, I've handled it."

I wasn't sure what they were talking about, but I could guess it had to do with whomever he was speaking to when Connie and I arrived to his door.

Once the door was shut, he went on, "Make Chicago a priority? Is there a problem?"

I took the seat opposite Franco's desk and pulled my tablet from my bag. "Louisa has been corresponding with you about some discrepancies, correct?"

He sat on his side of the desk near the front of his seat and leaned forward. "Yes, I thought we had it all worked out."

"Can you tell me what you think was worked out?"

I let him talk, nodding occasionally as he rambled about standard human error with the added factor of new employees. It was when his speech made a complete loop bordering on redundancy that I interrupted.

"Franco, who was the man leaving the facility when I arrived?"

"What man? We have different people coming and going."

"A tall man, dark hair, and well dressed. He didn't try to hide his interest in my car or me."

"Well, Ms. Hawkins, I wouldn't be surprised that you'd catch the attention of any or every man."

His inappropriate reply was not reassuring. "No, this was different. He was staring at the car before I ever got out."

Franco's thin lips formed a straight line as his head shook from side to side. "I don't know. We could ask Connie if he signed in."

"Is everyone who enters the facility required to sign in?"

"Yes."

"I didn't."

"No, but you're *you*. This is your facility."

"I'm glad you remember that, Mr. Francesca. I'd like to see the staging area for inventory. Let me meet some of these new employees."

"I'm sure it wouldn't be that exciting. It's most likely the same as in all of your facilities," he said dismissively as he stood.

"The difference," I said, my voice that of the CEO, "is that in our other facilities, we aren't having discrepancies between the warehouse and distribution center. When a valued retailer orders twenty-five golden scarves from Sinful Threads, is invoiced for said twenty-five scarves, and only seventeen arrive, you can understand how that is a concern." His lips flattened as his Adam's apple bobbed. "If that happened once, Louisa and I could overlook it. The scenario I described has not happened once. It has happened with too much frequency."

He rounded the desk, coming to a stop inches in front of me. "Let me look into this further. There was no reason for you to make the trip."

Standing, I met him eye to eye. Without my heels I was nearly five feet, seven inches tall. In my current shoes, I was approaching five-ten, possibly an inch taller than the man infringing upon my space. "I will take that tour now, and we can continue our conversation this evening at the Riverwalk."

His lips twitched before moving to a feigned smile. "That's great news. I'm certain you'll find the investors all interested in Sinful Threads. I'll be sure to alert Connie to have your name added to the guest list."

"That won't be necessary. It's been taken care of."

It hadn't—and that was on purpose—but it would be. Winnie had instructions to have me added moments before I was to arrive. There was no need to make my appearance public any sooner than necessary.

KENNEDY

I smoothed the silken fabric of the dress's skirt as I took one last look in the full-length mirror within my hotel suite. My long golden hair was piled on the back of my head in a French twist as spirals of curls dangled near my neck and around my freshly made-up face. The black onyx-like jewels glistened around my neck, making my light brown eyes pop. I would like to say my hair took me hours, but the truth was that the humidity of Chicago turned my usually straight hair to ringlets.

I had a memory of years earlier when my adoptive mother told me that one day I'd be happy with the curls. In this instant, her wisdom made me smile. I reached down and spun the gold bracelet upon my right wrist. The older I became the less often I wore my mother's old bracelet, yet there was something about being back in Chicago that made it seem right.

I could go days or even weeks and not think about her, but

when I did, the loss would be as staggering as it was the moment I boarded the plane for Boulder ten years ago, as if it were fresh and new. My eyes filled with moisture as I stared at the charms. When she'd given it to me, there was an old-fashioned key and a golden heart locket with a faded picture. Upon my high school graduation, Louisa's mother, Lucy, added what appeared to be a golden diploma. Then when Louisa and I cut the ribbon on the very first Sinful Threads manufacturing facility, Lucy added a small golden pair of scissors.

Though Lucy had helped me cope, I missed the woman I knew as my mom.

Was she safe? Would I ever know?

Did she know about Sinful Threads? And if she did, was she proud of what I'd created?

There were so many questions that would forever remain unanswered. I pulled the worn photo from my clutch bag and studied it for over the millionth time since I last saw her. It was the only picture of me and both my parents, Byron and Josey—my adoptive parents. I was nearly fifteen years old in the photo. That was the age where taking a picture with your parents was the last thing a teenager wanted to do. I'd do anything to go back and put a real smile on my face, one to match theirs.

The photo had been hidden, folded in half and stuck in a pocket within my purse. Besides my mom's bracelet, everything else connecting me to the Marshes had been taken from me before I even realized. When I entered the airport that cold afternoon, my purse was nearly empty. My phone was gone and so too all the pictures within it. Friends, family, and classmates were erased. My mother must not have known about this one picture tucked in a zippered pocket hiding amongst a tube of lip gloss and some dried-out mascara.

I sighed, looking down at the three of us. "You said to carry you in my heart, Mom. I do." A lump formed in my throat as I spoke audibly to the picture. "But Daddy didn't have the chance to.... I feel better when you're both with me."

Bringing the picture on this trip seemed silly. Yet I did it, taking it from the drawer in my bedside stand where it usually stayed and slipping it into my carry-on.

I smoothed the crease that would never go away. With my mom in the middle, it was ironic that the crease separated me from her and Dad, as if fate was saying we'd forever be separated.

As I tucked the photo back into my clutch, I stopped. Outside the large windows were the tall buildings of Chicago. I was back, being where she told me not to go. Quickly, I changed my mind, opened the small safe at the top of the closet, placed the picture along with some other jewelry in the small secure enclosure, and using the last four digits of my mom's phone number, set the code.

"You're with me," I said as I tested the handle and glanced at the bracelet I still wore. "I'm going to put your photo in here for tonight. It's my turn to keep you safe."

Going back to the mirror for one last assessment, I put on my figurative professional mask. I was the face for Sinful Threads, no longer a lonely, frightened teenager. With my chin held high, I looked the part.

The golden scarf wrapped around my midsection accentuated my waist. The color, as Louisa had expected, was the perfect counterbalance to my hair. A slight pitch to the left and then to the right demonstrated the quality and fullness of the skirt as the asymmetrical hem came between my knees and ankles. With the addition of stylish heels, my outfit was complete.

I was Sinful Threads.

With my shoulders straight, I made a quick call to my driver. An elevator ride later and I was seated in the back seat of Patrick's sedan as he pulled away from the curb and eased into traffic.

Even with the perfect outfit, there was a sense of unease that I couldn't shake. No matter what I had done or where I'd been, ever since the visit to the warehouse, my mind continually went back to the man in the parking lot. Without warning, the image of his dark stare twisted my stomach, setting me on edge.

My meeting tomorrow with Vanessa couldn't come soon enough. I was ready to go home to Boulder and leave that image—this whole city—behind.

Looking forward, my gaze met Patrick's reassuring smile in the rearview mirror, reminding me that I was protected. Though I didn't really know the man who was now my driver, there was something in his demeanor that calmed me. Probably ten or more years my senior, he was obviously fit beneath his dark suit. That and his almost-military-cut short hair gave him a distinguished and capable air.

"Are you stuck with me for my whole trip?" I asked, trying to take my mind off the man from before.

"Hardly stuck, ma'am."

"You're very kind, Patrick. You don't need to enter the dinner with me."

"I don't, but I would like to do just that. I'll stay out of sight, but, Ms. Hawkins, you are my job."

His determination comforted me. "Thank you."

My attention went outside of the sedan's darkened windows. Although it was nearly seven-thirty at night, the sky was still light and the sidewalks were filled with pedestrians as we approached Navy Pier.

Pulling to the curb, Patrick said, "I'll be happy to drop you off here, and then I'll slip into the dinner after I park. You can always reach me by phone."

Holding my clutch purse, I nodded. "Thank you again."

Lifting my chin and squaring my shoulders, I moved gracefully but determinedly along the walkway. This was my company—well, half—and though I didn't know the investors within the restaurant, my job tonight was to show them that Sinful Threads could handle any situation.

Walking toward the restaurant, I mentally replayed my earlier conversation with Louisa. Franco was accommodating in my requests, yet not enthusiastic. Everything that he showed me was accurate. I insisted on opening freight ready for departure. It was a useless procedure. The manifests matched perfectly. After hours of investigation and inquiry, there wasn't as much as one bangle, scarf, or woven brooch unaccounted for.

I nodded to the gentleman manning the entrance to the waterfront restaurant as he opened the door. Despite the large windows allowing in sunlight, it took a moment for my eyes to adjust to the dimness.

"Ms. Hawkins."

I turned to the voice coming above the din of the other guests and music seeping from speakers in every direction. Although she was dressed completely different from this afternoon, I recognized the person greeting me.

"Connie, thank you. It's good to see you again. You look lovely."

A far cry from the woman with a ponytail, polo shirt, and khaki slacks, tonight she was dressed for the occasion. For only a moment, her long tan dress reminded me of her khaki slacks—but only in color. The strapless dress with the fitted bodice was attractive, as was the Sinful Threads silk-spun bracelets on her left forearm.

I reached for one with a smile. "I see you're wearing Sinful Threads."

Her cheeks pinkened with a rush of blood. "I wish I could afford more." She took a step back. "Is that dress...is it...?" Her voice grew higher in excitement. "Oh my gosh. It's Sinful Threads."

I nodded. "It is. A new prototype. I thought it might be nice to show the investors."

"It's absolutely gorgeous."

"Ms. Hawkins," Franco said as he stepped closer. "My, you look, if you don't mind my saying, beautiful."

"Thank you, Franco. Please call me Kennedy, and hopefully very soon, you'll see dresses like this one as well as others coming through our warehouse."

"We have to let the investors see this."

I grinned. "That was my hope."

With a flute of champagne in one hand, I allowed Franco to escort me around the room, introducing me to both local and potential investors. Real estate moguls as well as politicians were all forthcoming with their praises of Sinful Threads. The discussion of a storefront in the Loop was brought up by many.

Remaining on the periphery, Patrick was rarely seen. Yet occasionally, his reassuring presence would come into view.

Before dinner, I spoke to the room, introducing myself to everyone, thanking them for their support, and vowing to keep Sinful Threads a viable contributor to the Chicago economy. Dinner was spent discussing our creative process and how important it was for Louisa and me to keep it in Boulder where we could oversee our operation.

During the meal, I was seated with Franco on one side and Mrs. Pauline McFadden, Senator Rubio McFadden's wife, on the other. Her husband was seated to her left. Mrs. McFadden praised Sinful Threads, certain the dresses would be perfect for the campaign trail as her husband tested the waters for the White House. I knew I should be thinking about the aspirations of the man across the table, but instead my mind was on the publicity a first lady could give to our company.

Just when I'd decided that this trip was most likely a success, my phone buzzed.

"Excuse me a moment," I said to the senator and his wife.

The screen of my phone said DRIVER. There was no reason to add Patrick's name.

"Hello?"

"Ma'am, I'm sorry to be the one to inform you that there's a situation at the distribution center."

My mind reeled. The distribution center had a first and second shift, no third. At this time of night, there shouldn't be anyone there. "What kind of situation? How would you know that?"

"When your assistant couldn't reach you, she called me."

I looked down at my phone, and sure enough, I'd missed

three calls from Winnie. "What kind of situation?" I asked again. "I need to get there. Do you have the car?"

"Ma'am, I slipped out as soon as I was notified. I'm already out on the street, ready to take you there."

My heart raced as I imagined fire and destruction. "Thank you, Patrick. I'll be right out."

Disconnecting the call, I began to phone Winnie when Franco approached. "Kennedy, you're not leaving already, are you?"

A situation.

Did Franco know what was happening?

I plastered a smile on my lips and nodded. "I'm afraid I am. It's been a very long day."

"Will I be seeing you tomorrow before you leave for Boulder?"

The tips of my lips turned upward as I decided. My answer depended upon the current situation. Depending on what it was, another unplanned visit could be possible. "I think that will be a game-time decision."

"Have a safe trip."

After quickly saying goodbye to many of the guests, I made my way out to the sidewalk. Night's darkness had finally fallen, yet the lights of Navy Pier created a false daylight. Beyond the illumination, out over the water, the black velvet sky dotted with stars reminded me of my love for the lake. There was something about the scent of the fresh water that revived my spirit.

Taking a deep breath, I hurried toward the row of cars. First and foremost, I needed to learn what was happening at the distribution center.

As I walked, I hit call on my phone, returning my

assistant's calls. Instead of answering, Winnie's phone went straight to voice mail. I debated about leaving a message, deciding to simply disconnect. She had tried to reach me. Seeing that I'd called would hopefully let her know that I knew about the situation.

I would have tried to call again, but my driver was in sight. He must have seen me too because in another step, Patrick's door opened, and he hurried my direction to open the back-seat door.

"Thank you, Patrick. I'm capable of opening the door."

His lips twitched. "It's my job, remember?"

"I might miss you after I go home tomorrow."

"Thank you."

I waited until he was back in the car and we started to pull out into traffic. "What situation is happening? Franco didn't seem to know anything."

His eyes met mine in the rearview mirror. "Did you tell him?"

"I didn't." Once my answer was out, I wondered if I'd made the right move. Was this like the warning we've all heard about going to another location without telling anyone? No. Patrick was with me. He knew. Winnie knew. And as he'd said, I was his job.

Patrick cleared his throat. "I was only told that your presence was imperative. The situation was crucial."

I opened my purse and looked down at my phone. It wasn't as late in Boulder. There was a good chance Louisa was still awake. With what she'd said about her restless sleep, there was a better than good chance.

Should I call her?

Chicago was her baby.

I closed the purse.

Stress free.

That was what I wanted to do for her.

There was no need to worry her until I knew more. I'd call her when I had news to report.

Besides, I was concerned enough for both of us.

I'd been given a card that allowed me entry to the distribution center's grounds for my earlier meetings, and I suddenly wondered if I'd brought it to the dinner. My pulse kicked up at the sight of the empty guard shack and secured gate.

Where was the night guard?

We didn't have a third shift working, but the building was to be secured 24/7.

Something in my senses was on alert. "Maybe we should call the police?" I said, my tone fluctuating, making it sound more like a question than a statement as the car slowed.

The tall lights illuminated the empty parking lot as Patrick lowered his window, inserted the card, and the gate moved to the side.

"How did you get that?"

His eyes met mine again in the mirror. "Ma'am, it's the one from this morning. You gave it to me."

I did?

I was correct when I told Franco it had been a long day. With everything happening and my unsuccessful detective work, I must have forgotten to retrieve it. "Well, I'm glad one of us is prepared." I surveyed the side of the building. Nothing appeared out of the ordinary. My earlier concerns of fire or destruction were quelled. "I was imagining fire engines and flames," I said aloud.

Patrick parked the car near the door we'd entered earlier in the day.

"It looks empty."

"Ma'am, I'd like to accompany you inside."

"I think I'd like that too."

As we approached the door, I stopped. "We can't get in."

Patrick held up the same card he'd used to gain us entrance to the parking lot.

"That will open the door, but each facility has a specific code to enter into the alarm system. They're changed routinely and only known by the top building administrators and security. Our system is top-notch."

My driver held up his phone. "Your assistant, Winifred, sent me the code."

I sighed. "She did? I wasn't able to reach her."

Patrick shrugged as he inserted the card. As we stepped through the door, the faint beeping of the alarm system alerted us to its presence. In another fifty-eight seconds the police would be notified of a break-in.

I started to wonder how Winnie was able to get the code, when all at once, the beeping stopped.

"I guess the code was correct?" I said.

"Yes, ma'am."

The dim entry and hallway had scant illumination with only security lighting. The effect was a shadowed tunnel as we retraced the steps I'd taken earlier in the day and made our way back toward the offices. Yellow light spilled from beneath the closed door to Ricardo's office, the same one I'd visited earlier. "Is Ricardo here?"

Instead of answering, Patrick reached past me, turning the knob and pushing open the door.

Taking one step beyond the doorframe, I froze. We were no longer alone. My mind reeled at the man behind Ricardo's desk. "What? Why are—"

"Patrick, you may go."

I didn't recognize the deep voice commanding my driver, and in the darkened room with only a circle of light from the desk lamp, I couldn't see the whole of the man behind the desk. However, as my knees grew weak, I knew.

I knew he was the man from before in the parking lot.

I didn't need to see all of him.

This man filled the office with an overpowering aura. In the circle of light, I saw large hands steepled beneath a strong chin covered in trimmed dark hair and a white starched shirt stretched over a wide muscular chest.

"And close the door."

His commands held no room for debate, yet that was exactly my plan. "Wait," I said, turning back, but Patrick was already on his retreat. The man I thought to be my protector wasn't looking at me, but nodding to the man behind the desk. He wasn't my protector at all. He was my traitor.

"Sir," Patrick said as he disappeared into the hallway.

As the door shut, I managed to make my feet move. Inch by inch I stepped. As I did, the circle of light grew, until my vision met the dark gaze and granite-like features of the man in the parking lot.

"Who are you?" My voice wavered, threatening to expose my unease. I looked back at the door, contemplating if I could escape, if Patrick would stop me, if this man would stop me.

"Don't even consider reaching for that handle."

Closing my eyes and taking a deep breath, I turned back,

my neck straightening. The spicy scent of his expensive cologne filled my senses as the small hairs on my arms stood to attention, and my skin peppered with goose bumps. Ignoring the fear that being alone with this man elicited, I feigned strength and demanded to know more. "Tell me what the hell you're doing in my distribution center."

The man stood, slowly pushing himself away from the desk as the small office chair rolled back. As he rose, his body passed through the light. The suit coat from earlier was gone and the sleeves of his white shirt were rolled up near his elbows, revealing toned, tan forearms.

Like a monster in a sci-fi movie, he grew, his presence towering above until he dominated the room. Though most of him disappeared into the darkness, I was dwarfed in his presence.

His deep voice came from beyond the light. "Araneae, you have no idea how long I've waited for this day. Welcome home."

KENNEDY

*A*raneae.

Araneae.

His pronunciation was different than the spider, a syllable less—*uh-rain-ā*. The name reverberated off the walls of the small office, drowning out whatever else he'd said. Or perhaps it was the rush of my blood coursing through my ears.

In the whirlwind of emotions, my mind filled with thoughts—my mother's warning, the name Sparrow—but voicing any of them wasn't possible. In a matter of seconds, my tongue had forgotten its role. Instead of speaking, the useless muscle became glued to the roof of my mouth as saliva evaporated.

No longer lost in the darkness, this mountain of a man walked around the desk, his movements graceful and preda-tory until he came to a stop before me, his prey. Lurking nearly six inches taller than me in my heels, the dark gaze from earlier in the parking lot shone downward as if I were merely a child under his admonishing stare.

Before my words could find their way out of my mouth, his large hand grasped my chin and pulled it upward. The room no longer existed. All that I could see was him—his gaze on mine. With each tilt upward, my pulse kicked up more and more, until under his stare my breathing slowed, and my knees grew weak.

I was going to faint.

No.

Taking a step back and away, I found my voice and demanded, "Tell me who you are."

The way his lips curled sent a chill down my spine. If he were smiling, his eyes hadn't received the memo. Again he lifted his hand, but this time it wasn't for my chin but to run a ringlet of my hair through his fingers.

"This is promising," he said.

Another step back.

My attempts at strength were failing miserably. In another step or two, I'd be backed against the wall. And while there was something about this man that had my emotions stirred in a way I barely recognized, the smarter part of me knew I needed to get away.

"Stop touching me." I sounded like a child, but I didn't care.

"Oh, Araneae, soon you will be begging for just that."

I lifted my palm to his chest. The gesture was meant to stop his forward progress, but it did more than that. Beneath my touch and despite his calm, calculating demeanor, his heart too was racing. Leaving my hand pressed against his solid chest, I tilted my face up to his. "Tell me who you are."

"I'll do better than that."

My hand dropped. "What's better than that?"

"I will tell you who *you* are."

I shook my head slowly as tears prickled the backs of my eyes, and emotions I'd kept suppressed for nearly a decade threatened to unfurl. I swallowed once and then again. I didn't know this man or even his name. He didn't deserve my tears. He hadn't given me any reason to believe him.

Or had he?

He knew my real name.

"Fine. First tell me who I am and then who you are."

This time as his full lips curled upward, his dark eyes shone, joining in his amusement. "In time. The most important thing for you to know is that you're mine. Tomorrow you'll travel back to Boulder and make the necessary arrangements to move to Chicago permanently. After all, this is where you belong."

"What? No."

His finger stroked my cheek. While I wanted to remind him not to touch me and explain what he'd just said, deep inside of me, I somehow knew the truth: what he was saying was right.

It wasn't *right* as in right versus wrong, good versus evil.

No, the man before me was neither right nor good.

It was the twisting in the pit of my stomach that told me that his words were accurate.

"You're crazy. I'm not yours. I'm no one's. I don't even know who you are."

The finger that had caressed my cheek, trailed lower to my neck and collarbone, each inch combustible. Like a match head being dragged across a striking surface, his touch caused a chemical reaction. The flame was lit as heat sparked within me, stealing my breath and twisting my insides.

I stepped back again. "Please."

His chiseled chin bobbed. "You like it. I can tell. I see it in the way the vein at the side of your neck pulsates and the way your breathing has grown shallower." His eyes scanned downward. "The way your nipples have grown hard. You want me to touch more than your regal, sexy neck." The desk light reflected as a shimmer in his eyes. "And don't worry, Araneae, I will. In time."

I pushed his hand away. "I don't know you. And I sure as hell don't know who you think you are, but you're wrong. I'm leaving Chicago tomorrow, and I'm not coming back."

This time he took a step back, lifted an envelope from the desk, and handed it to me.

In flowing script on the front was the name he'd called me, but there was more. There was also a last name: Araneae McCrie.

I couldn't stop the tears. "I-I've never been told..." I looked up at his face. If my emotions were affecting him, he wasn't showing it. "How do you know this?"

"The same way I know that you belong to me. Your father promised my father when we were both quite young that you would be mine. The day has come to honor his word."

What? An arranged marriage?

That was absurd.

"My father? A man with the name McCrie? I didn't know him. I never knew him. This isn't the Middle Ages and even if it were, his word means nothing to me."

"A man's word is either his most valuable tool or his most respected weapon. There is nothing more binding. Tonight,

I'm giving you *my* word. By this time next week, you'll be back with me, and you will be asking me to touch you." He once again caressed my cheek. "And I don't mean your face."

I didn't want to believe him. Yet he'd already given me more information about my past than I'd ever known. "Will you tell me more about my family?"

Shit!

Did that sound like I was agreeing? I wasn't. I was...curious.

"In time."

I let out an exaggerated breath. "Forget it. You gave me enough. I can search the internet with what you've given me."

"You won't."

My brow furrowed. "Why wouldn't I?"

"It isn't safe."

"And when I don't come back?"

"You will." When I didn't answer, he went on, "Because not doing so is also not safe."

"Are you threatening me?"

"Open the envelope."

As I turned the thick paper over in my hands, I had a flashback of an envelope in a car ten years earlier. I ran my finger under the flap. This time, the contents were sparser. I pulled the paper back to reveal a picture, the real kind with a glossy front that had been developed.

My breath caught as I stared down at the candid photograph of Louisa and Jason. They were dining at a restaurant in Boulder. By the look of her midsection, the picture was taken recently.

"Tell no one," he said, "about this. Only that you're moving to Chicago."

"She's pregnant and you're threatening her? You're a monster."

"Do as you're told and she will never know, nor will her husband. They will remain blissfully ignorant."

I opened the envelope wider. There was nothing else inside. "Tell me who you are."

"In time."

"Stop saying that!"

Again, his lips moved into a grin. "For now, all you need to worry about is arranging your move. Don't worry about a place to live. You're leaving on a red-eye tonight. And then when you return, Patrick will pick you up at the airport. The airline tickets are already in your app. Once you arrive back to Chicago, he'll deliver you to me.

"And that Google search or whatever search engine you think to use, don't do it. All of your devices are monitored. Believe me when I say, it's for your own good."

My mind swirled. It was too much, too unbelievable to comprehend. "I don't know you. And as for my own good, you're telling me to give up my dream and move to Chicago. No. This is preposterous. As for believing, I don't believe a damn word you say."

Maybe it was three steps, or with the length of his legs, it may have been only two. I wasn't sure. All at once, my shoulders crashed against the wall. His massive body pushed against mine, his hands capturing my wrists and pinning them to my sides. Chest to chest, he encompassed me, his heartbeat and even his words vibrating from him to me—all of me.

"Believe me," he said, his tone colder than before. "You don't know me yet, so we will let this one instance slide. In the future, remember that no one speaks to me like you just did. No one. And do not ever..." With each of his words, his hips moved toward me until his growing erection probed against my stomach. "...make assumptions about me."

Fear was a strange bedfellow. For all my life I'd done my best to keep it at bay, to avoid danger and ignore its power, its raw potential to be so much more than distress. As the emotion flowed through my coursing bloodstream, the excess was energizing and empowering.

The man's granite features from before had morphed. And that wasn't my only clue that I had an effect on this monstrous yet mysterious man.

I moved my hips ever so slightly his way.

His dark eyes hooded as his nostrils flared. "Araneae, you have no idea what you're doing."

I straightened my neck, raised my chin, and stared deep into his darkness. "Then tell me. Tell me what assumption I've made." Because most have been unspoken: *You're a bully. You're used to getting your way. You won't tell me what I need to know. And for some unknown reason, having you against me was the most turned on I've been in years—forget that. Not in years—in forever.*

I didn't say any of the examples aloud. Instead, I continued my unblinking glare into his dark gaze and willed my hands not to fight his grip.

"Your nipples are hard as rocks under that expensive silk." He took a deep breath. "And you're so wet my mouth is watering at the idea of tasting you, teasing you, and making you scream so loud as you come that Patrick will hear."

Pressing my lips together, I held back my retort, instead saying, "Those are not assumptions."

He loosened his grip and stepped back, his tone once

again cold and demanding. "Do as you've been told. Get on the plane tonight. Do what you need to do in Boulder and return next Wednesday night. Do not tell anyone about me or this arrangement, and your dream will remain intact. You assumed that I have a desire to take Sinful Threads away. You're wrong. I have neither the desire to take it away nor ruin it forever. That is, as long as you obey my instructions.

"The issues you've had here with merchandise will no longer be a problem as long as you behave. If there are any thoughts in that pretty little head of yours of disobeying, the demise of your business partner and your business will only be the beginning of your punishment."

He ran his finger once again over my cheek, now damp with tears. "For the first time, you have a choice in your future. The next step is currently in your hands. I believe you'll do what is best for everyone."

With his last word—his warning—hanging in the air, he turned, opened the door, and disappeared into the dark hallway. I stood motionless as his footsteps faded away, lost in my memory of his presence—his scent, his touch, and the way his body pushed against mine.

My mind spun and chest filled with the burden bestowed upon me.

A choice?

What choice was he giving me in effect—me in exchange for my best friend and our company?

How was that really a choice?

As the reality struck with the decision before me, dazed and bewildered, I bolted toward the doorway. "Wait! Stop. I have more questions. I need more answers. Damn you..." My voice trailed away in the silence. "I don't even know your name..."

My words echoed through the empty distribution center as more tears flowed down my cheeks. I leaned back against the wall with my arms wrapped around my midsection, trying to decipher what had just happened. In the distance new footsteps grew closer with each second.

A mix of panic and excitement washed through me. The instinct to run, to flee, pulled at my already-taut nerves. With my hand on the door, I contemplated closing and locking it, keeping him out, but reason took over. This wasn't my mystery man approaching. The new footsteps were Patrick's.

"Ma'am, your car is ready. Your plane is leaving soon."

KENNEDY

A noise escaped my lips, somewhere less loud than a growl, but nonetheless, an audible sign of my displeasure. This man who had been hired to protect me didn't. He'd betrayed me.

As Patrick continued to look my way, my head shook in disagreement. "No, I'm not sure where I want to go, but I'm most certain it isn't with you."

"Ma'am, as I said, you're my job."

My fist came to my hip. "Who assigned you that job? Not the company Winnie contacted."

"You're right; nonetheless, you are my job."

I let out another long breath. I could call an Uber or a Lyft. However, Patrick was here. Did I want to be left alone at the empty facility?

"Fine. I'm your job. No matter what, first I need to go back to my hotel room. And I have a meeting tomorrow. Vanessa is expecting me."

Patrick only nodded as we walked through the darkened hallway back out to the summer night's warmth. With a quick memorized code, Patrick secured the building.

Wracked with too many thoughts at once, as I sat in the back seat, I pulled up the app to my airline. The man had been right. Not being certain of my schedule, I hadn't booked a flight to return to Boulder, yet just as he'd said, I had one, leaving in an hour and fifteen minutes. I also had a return flight for next Wednesday, leaving Boulder at 6 PM and getting me to Chicago nearly the same time as tonight's situation at the distribution center.

Patrick remained silent as the car moved through the night streets. Near my feet was my carry-on bag. Maybe leaving was the best. Returning wasn't, but I'd work that out once I was safely out of this town. I looked again at my carry-on. "Why is my carry-on here? Where is my suitcase?"

"In the trunk, ma'am. Everything was packed."

A cold chill settled over my skin as I opened my clutch and pulled out my phone, lipstick, powder...no picture. "Shit! No! Patrick, we have to go back."

"I'm afraid that's not possible. You've been checked out of the room, and if we go back, you'll miss your flight."

"There was jewelry—"

"I believe you'll find everything in the carry-on."

Pulling the bag up onto the seat, a new panic surged through me. The continuing changing emotions created a whirlwind set on bringing down my defenses. If the man at the distribution center was one of the people my mother had warned me about—one she was afraid of—and if Patrick found the picture...

My skin prickled with a cold perspiration.

I didn't even want to think about it.

Byron and Josey had kept me safe. By returning to Chicago and delivering that picture, I may have done the one thing to risk her safety—if she could possibly still be alive ten years later.

The illumination within the car strobed between light and dark as we passed beneath tall streetlights. My cosmetics were all contained within their appropriate bags. It was as I dug that my fingers brushed against the soft silk of the Sinful Threads jewelry roll. It had many different-sized pockets and rolled closed, securable with a delicate tie.

Swallowing, I held my breath as I unfurled the roll.

Within the zipper pocket were the earrings and necklace I'd placed in the safe.

I continued searching.

It wasn't until the last pocket that I found the picture, once again creased but safe.

"Oh, thank goodness."

"Ma'am, is everything accounted for?"

"How did you...? The combination on the safe?"

I started to put the picture back when I realized it hadn't been alone. Pulling out the second picture, I saw it was the same as the one in the envelope—the one of Jason and Louisa. No longer relieved, my stomach twisted and temples throbbed.

Seemingly unaware of my turmoil, Patrick answered my ill-articulated question. "I was not informed of any particulars. Remember, I was with you. You are my job. Your bags were brought to me."

My picture was safe, and for the moment so were Louisa and Jason. The fact that both photos were found in a Sinful Threads product was part of my warning.

I laid my head against the seat and closed my eyes. Hadn't I already been the one to lose at every turn in life?

My birth parents...McCrie. That was all I knew. More than I knew yesterday but still not much.

The loving people who raised me...Bryon and Josey Marsh. I was present when they closed his casket. What about her? Would I ever know?

And now, to save the only family I currently knew and to save my hard work and business, I was expected to lose more?

That wasn't a choice.

My eyes prickled as more tears came to the surface, streaming down my cheeks.

I should be terrified of the man at the distribution center. My common sense told me that. Yet I was more afraid of losing Louisa and Sinful Threads.

The man...intrigued me.

Sniffling, I found a tissue and dabbed my eyes. From the surroundings, I could see that we were getting close. "Patrick?"

"Yes?" he answered, his gaze again meeting mine in the mirror.

"You work for him?"

He didn't verbally answer, yet his head bobbed.

"Can you please tell me his name?"

Side to side his head moved.

The small hairs on my arms stood to attention. "He can hear us, can't he?"

"Ma'am, your boarding pass is on your phone. I do recommend you hurry. You don't want to miss your fight."

The car came to a stop at the terminal.

Once I was out of the car with my purse and carry-on and gripping the handle of my suitcase, I laid my free hand on Patrick's arm and spoke in a whisper. "If you were me, would you come back?"

For the first time, I paid attention to the blue of his eyes as they softened, and he contemplated his answer.

"The decision has to be yours."

"*If* you were me..." I repeated, emphasizing the first word.

"In your position, with what you know and understand, I admit it would be difficult. If I were you with *my* knowledge and understanding, I wouldn't leave Chicago. Be careful, Ms. Hawkins. I hope to see you next week."

It was after midnight on the airplane, a glass of much-needed wine on the tray beside me, when I finally got the courage to text Louisa. We hadn't taken off yet, and this would be my last chance for a while.

"All your devices are monitored."

My teeth clenched as his words replayed in my head.

"LOU, ON MY WAY HOME. THINGS UNDER CONTROL. DINNER WAS A HIT. I'M BEAT. WILL PROBABLY SLEEP ALL DAY. SEE YOU SATURDAY."

Immediately my phone buzzed.

"Miss, you need to turn that off," the flight attendant reminded.

"I will."

Quickly I read:

"YOU DIDN'T CALL. I WAS ABOUT TO SEND OUT THE NATIONAL GUARD. I CAN'T WAIT TO HEAR. YOU AREN'T STAYING TO TALK TO VANESSA? ARE YOU SURE IT'S OKAY? WHAT CHANGED? AND I NEED PICTURES OF YOU IN THE DRESS. YOU BETTER HAVE THEM."

"Miss?"

Ignoring the flight attendant, I hammered back:

"CAN'T TALK. PLANE TAKING OFF. LOVE YOU. TELL LITTLE KENNEDY TO LET YOU SLEEP."

I added a heart emoji before making a point of turning my phone to airplane mode and putting it in my clutch.

I'd moved both pictures to my purse also, unwilling to let them be in the overhead away from me.

I thought about Louisa's question: was I sure everything was okay and what had changed?

I was most certain that everything wasn't okay. How would I tell her I was moving away?

Was I?

There was too much.

After we were in the air and the lights were dimmed, I reclined my seat and closed my eyes. Thankfully, the seats that had been booked for me were in first class and luckier still, this one had no one beside me. Holding my purse on my lap, I said, "I'm sorry, Mom. I should have listened. Tell me what to do."

KENNEDY

I woke with a start, bouncing in my seat as the plane touched down. I'd been dreaming...or maybe it was real. Whatever it had been left my breathing erratic and hands gripping the large arms of the seat. As consciousness seeped through my brain, my nightmare was forgotten, replaced with the terrifying reality of the last few hours. Images—so real that I still smelled his cologne and felt his warm touch on my skin—of the scene from hours earlier at the distribution center held me mute and captive as the plane taxied forward toward the gate.

"Tell no one about this arrangement."

"You are mine. Your father gave his word."

"Araneae McCrie."

"Do as you're told and she will never know, nor will her husband. They will remain blissfully ignorant."

My stomach twisted as the picture my recollections created became complete, including the mystery man's deep tenor and unforgiving granite features. In another light, in another instance, he could be handsome with his solid, tall build, muscular arms, and devilishly striking face. His chiseled jaw, high cheekbones, and dark eyes caught my attention in the parking lot. Yet recalling his looks filled me with dread instead of warmth. Those features weren't welcoming; instead, in my mind they belonged to a statue, cold as stone and just as unyielding, except for when he pressed himself against me.

As the plane taxied closer to the gate, the memory of him, the wall, the intensity of his gaze, and his body against mine came back with a vengeance. Looking down at my traitorous breasts, I wished for not the first time that I'd worn a bra under the silk dress.

After turning down the air vent from above, I crossed my arms over my chest.

Outside the small window, the airport was alive with lights. Men and women scurried about with orange vests and red wands, directing planes as small vehicles pulling trailers filled with or ready to be filled with luggage rambled around the tarmac.

It was still the middle of the night, or should I say early Friday morning. I wasn't sure of anything other than that the sun was still asleep and I wanted to be too.

How could I?

It was Friday, and in a week, I was supposed to be back in Chicago.

"Miss Hawkins, are you all right?" the flight attendant asked from her perch near the exit.

Her question using my name startled me. And then I remembered that I'd confirmed my name with her after boarding. "Yes, I'm surprised we're here. I guess that's what happens when you sleep for most of the flight."

"It's only been two hours."

"Two? I thought it took longer to get to Boulder."

She shook her head. "I'm sorry. Didn't you hear the announcements?"

"What announcements?"

"We have a traveler with a...situation. I really can't divulge any more, but we had to make an emergency landing in Wichita."

"Wichita? As in Kansas?"

"Yes, we'll all need to deplane. The customer service desk is working on helping everyone make it to their final destinations."

"No, I need to be in Boulder."

"This wasn't in any of our plans," she said. "I'm sure they'll be able to help you."

I sighed, thinking how I should be asleep in the hotel in Chicago, or even still on my way to Boulder. What I should not be was in Wichita, Kansas. Through the window across the aisle, the walkway moved like a giant snake, its mouth open as it came close to the door of the plane.

I pulled my phone from my purse and turned off the airplane mode. It was barely two in the morning in Boulder and yet I still wasn't there.

One advantage to flying first class was being one of the first to deplane. That was after the airline staff assisted the traveler with the *situation*. I was beginning to distrust that word. As the older man was escorted from the back of the plane, everyone stared. He didn't appear ill or belligerent.

After he passed onto the walkway, the bell dinged and like

the trained animals we all were, the cabin filled with the unclicking of seat belts as we all stood to retrieve our carry-ons. I turned to the man from the row behind me. "What's wrong with him?"

He shrugged. "All I know is that I need to be in Denver for an interview. Boulder was the closest I could get, and now because of him, it's not going to happen."

Immediately, I felt bad for the young man with blond hair and a slight but solid build. His shirt was rumpled as I was certain was my dress. The Sinful Threads prototype was not meant to be traveling attire. Once again, I had been left without a choice.

"Going to a party?" he asked with a grin, scanning me from my head to the toes of my high heels.

"Coming from one, I suppose."

"Yeah, well, this won't be one." He turned toward the rising crowd of sleepy travelers behind us.

"You're probably right."

A few minutes later, my new friend and I were in line for the customer relations. I held his spot while he comman-deered two cups of coffee. Step by step, I moved toward the one attendant at the desk, the one who appeared less than thrilled with her new assignment of helping a planeload of disgruntled passengers.

"Cream, no sugar," he said with a smile as he handed me the paper cup and slipped into line with me.

"Thank you."

A second agent came to the counter and nodded my direc-tion. "Thank you, again," I said as I moved to the counter to explain my dilemma.

Looking at her computer screen, the agent said, "Our first nonstop to Boulder is at 6:45. In less than four hours."

"I'll take it," I volunteered.

She shook her head. "I can put you on the standby list; you'll be number thirty-four. The 8:25 and 12:58 flights are also booked. For certain, I can get you on one at 5:30 tonight."

I looked at my phone. "You can't guarantee me a flight for over fourteen hours? How about to Denver?"

She shook her head.

I couldn't help but hear that my new friend was having the same problem.

All at once he turned my way. "You're going to Denver, too?"

"Boulder, but it's near."

"The only way for me to make my interview is if I rent a car. I could get you to Denver if you can go the rest of the way."

I looked to the attendant. "No chance of a flight until five tonight?"

"Five-thirty. Landing at six-nineteen." She shrugged. "There's always a chance. Everyone in this line is in the same situation. Please decide what you want to do."

What I wanted to do and what I was doing were polar ends of the spectrum.

I wanted to wake in my bed in my apartment in Boulder and have the last twenty-four hours be a dream—nightmare.

"Excuse me," my new friend said. "How rude of me to ask you to share a car without offering you my name."

Immediately my mind went to another man, a domineering man, who had done more than offer to share a car without the luxury of his name.

"I'm Mark," he went on, extending his hand. "I just pulled up Google Maps. It's a seven-and-a-half-hour drive."

Even considering this stranger's offer was craziness. Then again, everything was. If I accepted, I could be home before eleven instead of spending the day in the Wichita airport. "I could rent a car myself," I volunteered.

"You could," Mark agreed. "Two cars heading the same place. Two tired drivers." He shrugged. "Let's head on over to the car rentals and see what we can get."

"What about my luggage?" I asked, turning back to the agent at the counter.

"It will need to go on to Boulder. You can fill out a claim form, and it can be delivered to you."

"Can it get an earlier flight?"

"Ma'am, I don't know." She handed me the form and another slip with a web address. "Once that form is completed, you can track your luggage using the number from the tag when you checked in."

I sighed. "Okay."

"Kennedy," Mark said, tilting his head toward a wall. "I'll be over there while you do that."

"All right. I also need to call my friend and let her know what's happening."

"Hurry, we probably aren't the only ones thinking about a car."

It wasn't until I was nearly done with the form that I considered that Mark had just called me by my name. Had I introduced myself? I was most certain I hadn't.

My phone buzzed: DRIVER on the screen.

Seriously?

Every stubborn bone in my body bid me to not answer.

After all, Patrick had betrayed me by handing me over to that person. On the other hand, my driver was the only real connection I had to what could be my future—to the mystery man.

Handing the agent back the form, I stepped to the side and answered my phone.

"Patrick, why are you calling?"

"This isn't Patrick. Why the fuck are you in Wichita?"

Equal parts indignation and apprehension rose up inside of me, the bubbling concoction fueling my exasperation. "Why I'm in a damn airport in Wichita instead of in a nice bed in a hotel in Chicago is because of one person. Venture to guess who's to blame?" I didn't give him a chance to answer. "You."

"The picture of your business partner wasn't motivation enough to entice you to follow my instructions? I overestimated your empathy. The next photograph will include her family. I hear her little sister is lovely."

I fought back the nausea as I pictured Lindsey, Louisa's younger sister. Nevertheless, I wouldn't allow that fear to come through my voice. "If you think I'm here of my own doing, you're crazier than I thought. And believe me, I think you're as fucking crazy as they come. It wasn't like I could just say *hey, let's change the course of this flight.* Someone on the plane became...well, I don't know why, but the airline had to make an unplanned landing. I didn't choose to disembark in Wichita. Who would do that? And I'm working to get to Boulder as soon as possible. Just to make it clearer for you, I haven't willfully *not* done as you asked. Okay, asked isn't the right word. Nevertheless, my being here isn't my doing. It's yours."

"Stay there. I'll send a plane."

"Wait. No, you aren't sending a plane. And you still don't understand the asking part of a request. Don't tell me what I'm doing. I'm renting a car."

"And driving alone for eight hours? No, you're not."

"Fuck you. I'm doing what you said—or at least considering it. I won't be driving alone. I met someone heading the same direction."

The mystery man's voice cooled to below freezing, the icy tone coming through like a killing frost through the phone. "Araneae, there is more that you don't understand. Coming back to Chicago put you on the radar. Who is this person?"

I hesitated. Should I say it was a man?

"Araneae, answer my fucking question."

"Just a man, a kid really. He was seated behind me on the plane."

"Can you casually take his picture?"

I looked up to see Mark standing against the wall, looking at his phone. "Yes. Why?"

"Stop asking questions and do it," he said, restraint keeping his words clipped. "Send the picture to this phone. Then make up an excuse or don't. Just get away from this person. Now. Patrick will call you back with instructions. You'll have a private plane shortly."

I switched my phone to camera and snapped the picture. "Before I send it, tell me your name."

"In time."

"Why should I believe you?"

"Because you know I'm right."

As I let his answer sink in, the call disconnected.

"Kennedy?"

I looked up at Mark.

"Are you ready?"

With the softest boy-like features, there was nothing about this young man that appeared dangerous. My mystery man on the other hand—everything about him seemed dangerous.

I hesitated, looking back down at my phone, expecting some sort of new information.

"Because you know I'm right."

My instinct told me that I hadn't introduced myself to Mark, and yet he'd used my name twice. I hit send on the picture to the number I had marked DRIVER. Somehow Patrick and this man had pulled me into a web I didn't understand.

I'd let them figure out that Mark was not a threat.

"Yeah, I'm ready," I said, feigning a smile. "I'm sorry, but first I need to use the restroom."

"I've gone ahead and rented a car. It'll be waiting for us."

"How did you do that?"

He held up his phone. "Rental car app. They have an app for everything."

"May I ask you something," I asked as we walked toward the restrooms. "How did you know my name?"

His cheeks reddened. "I noticed you when you boarded, and I was one row back. I heard the attendant verifying your name. I was working up the courage to talk to you, but you fell asleep."

"It's been one of those days."

"Well, now we're talking."

I laid a hand on his arm. "I'm kind of..." *What the hell was I?* "...it's complicated."

We continued walking and talking, dodging the few other travelers wandering the Wichita Eisenhower Airport in the middle of the night. "That's all right. I'm just happy to talk to you and not drive to Denver alone. I'm a little nervous about this interview." He tilted his head with a grin as we stopped walking. "Here's the ladies' room."

"You didn't fill out the form for luggage."

"No." He held up his carry-on. "Everything I need for my interview is in here."

"You can go on without me. I'll meet you at the rental cars."

"And let you walk around by yourself in that party outfit? My father raised a gentleman. Maybe my good deed will help the karma for my interview."

Nodding, I went into the bathroom.

KENNEDY

*T*his was crazy.

Everything since last night had been unbelievable. I had to stop my overactive imagination. But was it my imagination? Why did the mystery man call? How did he know I wasn't on my flight? Was Mark really a threat? What kind of threat? I was on whose radar?

Questions came faster than answers.

It seemed like the person I shouldn't trust was not the nice young man waiting for me but the one who ambushed me last night or Patrick, the one who led me like a lamb to the slaughter.

The bathroom was uncharacteristically empty, nine stalls all available. That never happened. Then again, this was a night for firsts. As my high heels clipped over the tile, I pushed each door, half expecting someone to be waiting inside. Every mystery or thriller movie I'd ever seen ran a reel in my head. All I needed was a scary soundtrack to play behind the echo of my footsteps.

Wheeling my carry-on into the stall, I let out a relieved breath. Maybe they were wrong. After all, I still wanted to know how my mystery man knew I had an unexpected stop. He'd said my devices were monitored. Did that mean they were also being tracked?

A moment later as I washed my hands and splashed water on my face, my purse again buzzed. I recognized the tone as a text message. I wanted to ignore it, but curiosity was a strong motivation. If only it could give me strength too.

DRIVER: *"ANDREW WALSH, 24. CONSIDERED ARMED AND DANGEROUS. DO NOT UNDERESTIMATE HIS ABILITY TO CARRY SIMPLY BECAUSE HE WAS ON A PLANE. WEAPONS ARE MISSED BY TSA MORE OFTEN THAN THEY ARE FOUND."*

Second text, from same number.

DRIVER: *"PRIVATE HANGAR LOCATED AWAY FROM TERMINAL HAS WAITING PLANE. SENDING CAR."*

None of this made sense. I was tired of taking commands. This deserved conversation. Instead of texting, I stepped back into the stall and hit the call button.

"Ms. Hawkins?" Patrick's voice came through the phone.

The familiar tone shouldn't have disappointed me, but it did. "I thought I would reach...Never mind. Listen, his name is Mark, and he's waiting outside the bathroom."

"Ma'am, that's not his real name and he's dangerous."

"He sure doesn't look or act—"

"Do you remember how I answered your question?"

I thought back. Just before I entered O'Hare, I'd asked Patrick what he'd do if he were me, if he would return to Chicago. He'd said that if he knew what he knew, he wouldn't leave Chicago. "Yes, I remember."

"Car rental office is in the parking garage. Wait five minutes and the car that has been sent will be on the street between the airport and garage. Do not go into the garage."

"This is crazy."

"The optics in a parking garage makes it dangerous. Threats can be everywhere. More than likely there's a car waiting there for you, too. Not a car you want to be in. The driver's name you should be expecting is Scott. He'll be driving a black Suburban, and he won't be alone. His helper is armed."

"Where will they take me?"

"To the hangar where your plane is waiting."

I was afraid to ask the next question. "Where will the plane take me?"

Please don't say Chicago. I wasn't ready for Chicago. I needed to see Louisa.

"Boulder, ma'am. That was the boss's word. He keeps his word."

I sighed. "I still don't know."

"Please get in Scott's car. Any other decision could have deadly consequences."

I took a deep breath. "If anything happens, keep Louisa safe...and her baby...and Sinful Threads. Please."

"Nothing will happen if you follow these instructions. You'll be in Boulder in less than two hours."

"This wasn't me. Tell him that. Louisa shouldn't be punished."

"Ma'am, get to that Suburban."

"Patrick?"

"Yes?" he answered, no doubt impatient with my apprehension.

"How can I trust you or him after last night?"

"How can you afford not to after right now?"

"Black Suburban?"

"Kansas plates."

I didn't say goodbye or anything else. I simply ended the call as I heard a woman and small child enter the bathroom. From the crack beside the door, I watched them in a mirror until they disappeared into another stall, the small child asking a million questions.

This night had me mistrusting everyone, even a mother and child.

Walking out of the stall, I took one more look in the mirror. The reflection was nothing like the woman at the hotel last night. She'd been confident and in control, the CEO of a growing company. This reflection staring back at me was of a tired woman with a paling complexion, smudged makeup, falling hair, and above all, fear in her brown eyes.

It was then that I remembered that there was a change of clothes in my carry-on. I hadn't had the chance to change in Chicago, but if I did now, it would buy me a few minutes.

How long had Patrick said?

Five minutes.

Three minutes later, no longer in my dress or heels, I exited the bathroom wearing jeans and a long top. My heels were replaced by a pair of Toms. I figured flats would help me run—if I was given that chance. Besides, I didn't have any other options. The pins were out of my hair, and now it was in a low ponytail.

"I wondered what took you so long," Mark, aka Andrew, said.

I tried to smile but was certain it came out looking more like a grimace. "Like I said, it's been a long night. I figured this would be more comfortable for a seven-hour drive."

He shrugged. "More like seven and a half. Are you still planning on renting your own car? We could split the cost, and you could help me forget for a bit about this interview."

"I suppose I need to see what's available."

Four minutes had passed.

"Let's go."

Mark smiled his boyish grin as we started walking toward the escalators. "Car rental is in the parking garage." He stopped and turned. "There's a walkway over there on this floor, so we don't have to cross the street."

What?

"Umm. It's the middle of the night. I think I'd like some fresh air." Did I sound as stupid as I felt? Lying at the drop of a hat was never my strong suit.

"Then the escalators it is," he said, placing a hand in the small of my back and leading me toward the moving staircase.

At that moment, I knew.

I knew that despite Mark's childlike charm, Patrick and my mystery man were right. A shy, nervous young man who was scared to introduce himself and worried about an interview wouldn't have the confidence to guide me with his hand on my back. I took a step away from his touch, my nerves on alert.

They had been right, and I was misled.

We walked toward the outside, toward the wall of glass. First, the inside doors automatically opened, and then the outside. Fresh air filled the breezeway as a large black Suburban pulled to the curb. Despite the early hour, the breeze was warm. The sidewalks were sparsely inhabited.

The passenger door opened, and a stocky man dressed in a black suit stepped out. His suit coat was unbuttoned, revealing a holster strap. Momentarily, I thought about how airports were supposed to be gun-free zones. Remembering Patrick's warning about Mark, I didn't care.

"Ms. Hawkins," the man from the Suburban said.

I turned toward Mark. "I guess I have a ride. Have a safe trip."

He looked confused as he reached for my arm, his grip tightening. "Wait."

"Don't touch her," the man from the passenger seat said with his hand under his coat.

"Kennedy?" Mark's tone didn't match the grasp he had on my arm.

"I said to let go of her."

As soon as he did, I hurried away. "I'm sorry." I shook my head as my heartbeat quickened, and I neared the Suburban, another pulling up behind.

The driver was now around the automobile, opening my door. I refused to turn back to see what was happening with or to Mark as a commotion erupted.

"Scott?" I asked.

"Yes, Ms. Hawkins. We'll alert Mr. Sparrow that you're safe."

The weight of my unknown past landed heavily upon me as I collapsed in the back seat of the promised SUV. After the two men joined me, the doors shut. The slams echoed in the silence of the interior, reverberating with my mother's words: *Allister Sparrow is in charge. One day it will be his son, Sterling.*

The man at the distribution center couldn't be the father.

My mystery man now had a name.

STERLING

*M*y jaw ached from the damn clenching.
What the fuck happened?

"How did the plane get stopped? They don't just fucking do that," I asked aloud to myself as well as Patrick and Reid, my two most trusted employees. We'd been together since basic training. My father had all the money in the world to send me to college, but he thought the army was a better use of my time, making me respectable in the eyes of the law and the big money crowd in Chicago and beyond. The three of us ended up in the same recruiting class. Our backgrounds couldn't have been more different, but we each knew one thing. We knew how to survive.

Not just in combat but in your bunk at night.

It took brains, muscle, and guts. It took going it alone to prove you were worthy and watching your brother's back whenever he might need it. One eighteen-month tour in the desert turned to two. There was no reason to hurry home. My mother was busy with her life, and I sure as hell wasn't interested in coming back to my father.

Eventually, I did.

He knew I would. Well, if I didn't get killed before I was given the chance.

The prodigal son.

I was the sole heir to the dynasty he'd secured over the years with an iron fist. My time in combat was not only to hone my skills as a fighter, marksman, and sharpshooter but to instill in me his thirst for blood.

I wouldn't say it worked the way he planned.

Each day in the desert, the thirst grew. However, the blood I desired wasn't random. It was his.

Coming back to Chicago didn't last long. Perhaps he saw the threat he'd created. Upon my arrival I was moved away again. This time it was to Ross School of Business, a short drive to Ann Arbor, Michigan. Four years later, a Ross graduate and ex-military, my résumé to lead the Sparrow realm was almost set. What the great Allister considered the final step was doing my time in the trenches of South Chicago, learning to navigate both sides of the Chicago business.

That meant deciding men's fates one minute and smoking cigars with the old money the next. Hell, sometimes it happened simultaneously. In the world of technology, a man can play poker and order a death at the same time. If he wins the pot too, it's a hell of a night.

The night my father's body—minus the fourth finger of his right hand—was found, I took my rightful place at the helm. The Sparrow realm was mine, and so was the gold ring engraved with the family crest. Since that time, I had only one thing missing: the woman worthy to share my name.

That choice was made a long time ago.

In this instant, it wasn't a choice I minded. I'd known that Araneae was mine since my early teens. Born almost seven years after me, I've known her future since she was just a girl. I've watched and followed her. While my father instilled my belief that Araneae was mine, my mother didn't agree. More than once she'd warned that uniting our families could be my end. Perhaps she was right, and as in sending me to war, my father's ultimate plan was for my demise. No matter what the future held, I found comfort that Allister Sparrow could only watch that future from inside the gates of hell.

Though I knew since that fateful afternoon that Araneae and I were meant to be, with too many factions at work, the timing was imperative and her ignorance of her fate necessary.

Araneae couldn't comprehend how through the years her mere presence on the earth had been the light getting me through my darkest days.

Getting her to Chicago was the first step in revealing her existence. The process was easier than I imagined. I admitted that I expected more resistance in getting her here. She'd avoided it most of her life.

But then she was here, in my fucking grasp, her beautiful, velvety eyes looking up at me, and my disappointment quickly faded. She came to Chicago of her own free will, and her return will be the same. That didn't mean I held illusions that she was eager. Her conflict was palpable. It glistened in a spark that more than intrigued me.

Whether I was in uniform, on campus, or within the Sparrow realm, women have fallen at my feet, willingly bending to my desires. I admittedly used them to bide my time. They weren't worthy for anything more. The woman who was, who had been born for the position of my wife, didn't bend. In her tone and gaze was a challenge. Though that was new to me, I liked it.

When I thought about our call a few minutes ago, I couldn't decide if I was pissed at her smart mouth and wanted to punish her for the way she spoke to me, or if I was fucking turned on and wanted to punish her just to watch her round ass turn red under my palm before pleasuring her in a way she'd never known and would never forget.

My light, my sunshine, had the audacity to blame me, as if I'd arranged for the damn plane to stop. If I had, I wouldn't have questioned it.

I regained my focus to the present.

Both men were fully engaged. Reid was pounding away on keyboards—yes, plural, moving between multiple ones—looking into the airlines. An extraordinary hacker, there wasn't a system he couldn't penetrate. At the same time, Patrick held two phones, coordinating Araneae's escape.

"Do we know it was them?" I asked Reid.

"Andrew Walsh has been on the radar for a while. There have been rumors. I know for certain that the kid started a few years ago as a grunt, working the streets. He quickly moved up the ranks of the McFadden outfit. They called him Baby Face because his looks got him access where others failed. Apprehending McCrie's daughter would move him up the outfit faster than any other assignment."

My neck throbbed as I imagined her in his sights. She wasn't fucking in his sights. He was with her. "I thought the plane manifest was vetted. You're telling me he was on the same flight by coincidence?"

"Fake ID," Reid replied.

"Scott has her," Patrick said, speaking over our conversation before Reid had the opportunity to explain further.

"I want someone staying in Boulder until she's here," I said, my mind a mix of relief and rage.

"I'll get it arranged," Patrick volunteered. "Do you want her to know?"

I ran my hand through my hair. "No. Tell her to contact you if she thinks anything is wrong—any misgiving, any feeling of unease. Otherwise, tell the eye to stay back and watch from a safe distance." My fist pounded the large wooden desk. "Unless she's in danger. Then he steps in. No hesitation."

"He? I have an overly qualified woman," Patrick said.

Fuck me.

"I don't give a damn. As long as Araneae is protected."

Reid looked my way with a stupid look on his face.

"What?"

"Any misgiving? Any feeling of unease? You mean regarding anyone but you."

It made me scoff. "Yeah, that's what I mean." It was a good thing I liked these two assholes. Otherwise, at times their candidness bordered on insubordination. I supposed that was what happened when you'd been through life and death together.

"They're on the plane," Patrick reported, his updates like a play-by-play radio announcer. I wanted visual, but audible was going to have to do for now.

"What about Walsh?" I asked.

"The second team arrived, but he made it out," Patrick answered. "They're looking for him."

"How the fuck did they let him slip through their fingers?" Reid asked.

"Track him down," I said. "The Sparrows are making a statement: no one fucking touches her."

"No one?" Patrick repeated with a grin.

"No one but me," I specified.

KENNEDY

I watched suspiciously out the windows as Scott and his partner drove me through unfamiliar streets. I'd placed my faith in someone I didn't know, someone who sure as hell hadn't earned it. It wasn't until we pulled up to the small airport that my pulse attempted to resume a normal cadence. It finally found its rhythm as I boarded the private plane.

It seemed like with each passing minute the questions continued to mount with no answers in sight.

Had I made the right choice?

Who was Mark? Was he really someone named Andrew, and why would he have wanted me?

For that matter, who was Sterling Sparrow?

Was it reassuring that I knew his name?

No.

His name gave me no more information than I'd had before, with one exception: my mother had warned me about him. And then a new question came to my ever-churning mind.

Was it his family that had killed Byron, my dad?

Was that what she'd told me?

The thought turned my stomach.

I couldn't recall her exact words from over a decade earlier. Time changes memories, enhancing some while taking away from others. It's why my picture was so important to me. Even visual recollections fade and blend.

From the brief time that I was in the dark office with Sterling Sparrow, it was difficult to gauge his age. How old would he have been ten years ago? Could *he* have killed my dad? I didn't know anything about his capabilities. I knew he'd threatened Louisa and Jason, and he expected me to move to Chicago to be with him.

The thoughts sent a cold shiver through me, ice filling my circulation until I wrapped my arms around myself and rubbed my exposed skin.

What he'd described was an arranged marriage.

This wasn't the fifteenth century.

I wasn't bound to anything like that.

"Ms. Hawkins." The older lady's voice pulled me away from the dark vortex of my thoughts. "I'm Janet, your attendant for this quick flight."

"Hello, Janet."

"You look frightened. There's nothing to worry about. This plane is very safe."

My head moved from side to side. "I'm not, well not about this flight, as long as you can confirm that we're headed to Boulder."

"That was what I was told." Her kind eyes sparkled as she

told me about the refreshment center and stocked bar. "May I get you something after we're in the air?"

"No, thank you. I think I'd like to rest." Other than the fact that it was still very early in the morning, I feared that the twisting and churning in my stomach would keep my appetite at bay for hours or maybe weeks. There were too many things I didn't understand.

"Janet," I asked, "is this plane privately owned?" Maybe she could tell me more about the mysterious Mr. Sparrow.

"No. We're a charter service. We fly anyone who books us."

"So you don't know who booked my flight?"

Her head tilted to the side. "You don't know who booked your flight and you're here?"

I shrugged, realizing how pathetic that sounded. "It was booked by..." I stopped. "I know by whom. I was hoping for more information on my contact's employer."

"I'm sorry. I was on standby and your request came in as a priority. That's all I know."

"No need to be sorry."

A few minutes later, a tall gentleman entered through the still-open door, ducking his head as he stood in the cabin. "I apologize, Ms. Hawkins. I was away from the airport when I received the call." He looked to the attendant. "Hello, Janet, are we ready?"

"Yes, sir, we're all set."

"Then as soon as I complete my checklist, we'll be on our way to Boulder."

Both his and Janet's verification of our destination untied one of the million knots in my stomach. Only 999,999-plus to go.

Boulder.

I was going home. There had been a small part of me that was concerned; despite the promise made by Patrick, after what he'd done, I wasn't sure I could ever trust him again.

Taking a deep breath and settling against the plush white leather seat, I shut my eyes as the door closed and the aircraft began to move. Within no time we were effortlessly off the ground. I took one last look out the window, shook my head, and said goodbye to Wichita, Kansas.

Had it been fate that landed me there?

Sparrow had warned me not to tell anyone what was happening. I wasn't certain I could find the words to explain the last twelve hours to myself much less Louisa.

"How was your trip?"

"Eventful. You see, my last-minute commercial flight was detoured, leaving over a hundred passengers without the means to reach their destination. I happened to be sitting in front of someone who offered to rent a car and take me to Denver. Oh, and apparently he was armed and dangerous and had nefarious plans for me. And then there's this man, one whose name I'm not supposed to know. Well, he told me that I must move to Chicago to be with him to honor a decades-old promise my birth father made. No, I don't know my birth father's name. However, I did learn that his surname was McCrie. Or...is it McCrie?

"Anyway, that man somehow knew my flight had taken an unexpected landing and saved me from the malicious intentions of the man from the plane. Or maybe it had all been innocent and I'm a fool."

I wouldn't believe that story, and it happened to me. It would probably be best to not mention any of it to my best friend.

Yet I had to tell her something. How could I explain a sudden move?

Answers weren't coming.

I woke as the wheels touched down.

Unbeknownst to me, I'd fallen asleep. Maybe it was the privacy or the gentle sway of the aircraft? Maybe it was the sense that for the flight's duration, I was safe. Or maybe it was that despite sleeping on the first flight, I was exhausted. No matter, when my eyes opened, the sun was still barely under the horizon and thankfully behind us.

As I turned my phone from airplane mode, a number of text messages appeared. The two from Louisa reminded me that I hadn't messaged her from Wichita. She assumed I was home and settled.

I'd already decided this ordeal wasn't something she needed to know about. In her condition, I didn't want to add unnecessarily to her stress. Besides, there was too much to comprehend, and I was too tired to do it. All I wanted was to get home. And then my phone buzzed with a new message.

The screen read DRIVER.

My first thought was that I might as well enter his name into my phone—at least he'd told me his. My second thought was that *of course* he knew I landed. He seemed to know more than I did. I read the text:

"CAR WAITING TO TAKE YOU TO YOUR APARTMENT."

I should have been upset, yet in my current sleep-deprived, recently-awoken state, I was almost relieved. Could I trust an

Uber driver? Could I trust anyone? I didn't know. What I did know was that I was finally back in Boulder, where Sparrow had promised I would be.

The reality of my relief was short-lived.

I may be back, but according to him, it was temporary.

"Ms. Hawkins," Janet said as I unbuckled my seat belt. "I received a call saying there is a car waiting for you."

"Yes, I just received the same message."

"I hope you know who booked it," she said with a sweet smile.

I smiled. "I do. Same person who booked this flight."

"Well, maybe someday you'll learn more about his employer."

"In time," I said, remembering Sparrow's repeated phrase.

"Thank you for flying with us. Hopefully you'll use our service again."

I didn't have an answer. Sinful Threads couldn't afford private charters and neither could Kennedy Hawkins. Our company was doing well, but that meant that most of the profits went back into it. We had rent on facilities. We had shipments of silk.

That reminded me that I'd meant to visit the Port of Chicago, where most of our silk entered the United States. Louisa had been there before, but I hadn't. I supposed that if I followed the instructions I'd been given, that opportunity was still in my future.

The popping sound filled the plane as the entry door was released, opening forward and creating the stairway to the tarmac. All at once cooler, fresh Colorado morning air filled the plane, reminding me why I loved where I'd been living.

"Ms. Hawkins," Janet said, "let me show you to the office and where your car is waiting."

Stepping to the edge of the plane, I stopped, taking in the beauty. From the clear blue skies to the mountains, I was awed. Could I leave all of this for Chicago? My heart told me no.

"Ms. Hawkins," an attractive woman with dark hair said as Janet and I entered the small office off the hangars.

"Yes, that's me."

"I'm Shelly, I'm here to drive you to your apartment. I've also been instructed to get your luggage from the Boulder Airport after I take you home."

"You were? The airline said they'd deliver it to me. Is it in?"

"Not yet, but it will be soon."

"And you know that...?" Before she could answer, I shook my head. "Never mind, I know how you know."

"I'm just doing my job."

"It's fine. I'm very tired. I'd like to go home and to sleep."

Once we were in the car, I asked, "How long am I your job?"

"Just until I deliver your luggage. I would be happy to give you my card, and you're welcome to call me anytime."

I didn't need her card. I was beginning to understand that one text to Patrick could get her or anyone else to my door in record time.

When we pulled up to my two-story apartment building, the driver stopped at the curb. "I've been asked to accompany you to your apartment."

"It's all right. I've never had a problem."

Though she tried to convince me otherwise, I remained

resolute, refusing to allow what happened in Wichita to frighten me in my everyday life. That didn't mean I didn't think about it, listening to the quietness as I entered the building.

The secured door opened to four apartments, two on each floor, and a staircase to access the ones above. I glanced to the downstairs door on the left, the apartment below mine. Mrs. Powell had lived there longer than I had. While the other two apartments seemed to have renters come and go, Mrs. Jeannie Powell had been living there for over ten years. She and her husband moved in when they decided they were too old to take care of their home. He passed away less than a year later, and while I've tried to convince her to move to one of the new senior communities, she refused. I often worried about her being lonely, yet with her two cats, she always had a smile on her face. About once a month I accepted her invitation to dinner. We always ate the same thing: salmon patties and peas with a white sauce.

My lips curled upward, thinking how I'd grown accustomed to the routine. There was something about her I found comforting. Her stories were as repeated as her menu. I supposed not having family or a grandmother of my own, I enjoyed her company more than another woman my age would.

My chest hurt as I imagined telling her I would be going away. I wasn't ready to do that as I tiptoed by. Within a minute, I was atop the stairs and unlocking my door.

Pushing open the door, I peered inside the darkened apartment.

Everything was just as I'd left it.

Collapsing on my bed, I typed out a quick text to Louisa.

"HOME NOW AND OFF TO SLEEP. HAD A SLIGHT DELAY, BUT ALL IS GOOD. I'LL FILL YOU IN TONIGHT IF YOU HAVE TIME FOR DINNER. LET ME KNOW YOUR SCHEDULE."

Did I need to tell Patrick I was home? And why did I even think of that?

I'd met Sparrow less than twenty-four hours ago and already he was affecting my everyday thoughts. Since Patrick had been the one to hire the driver who'd delivered me to my apartment, my guess was that not only did he know that I was now safely home, but so did Sparrow.

I turned off my phone.

KENNEDY

I wrung my hands under the table as I stretched my lips into a smile. Across the table, staring intently my direction was Louisa, her back periodically arching and tummy protruding as she tried to make herself comfortable. The fact that she'd asked me to meet her at the same restaurant where she and Jason were dining in the picture Sparrow had given me made this all the more difficult.

"You know, I keep craving this restaurant," she said. "They need to keep a table open for me until this baby arrives."

"When was the last time you were here?" I asked.

"Jason and I were here..." She hummed in thought. "...I think it was Wednesday night."

I'd been right that the photograph was recent. It had been taken the day before it was given to me.

"So you got a weird vibe from Franco?" she asked, her brow furrowing as she lifted her water to her lips. "I'm always so thirsty. I hope that's normal."

"Honey, I don't know what's normal. Are you feeling all right?"

"I wish I could sleep better."

I knew the feeling. I'd fallen asleep on and off on the planes, and then when I first made it back to my apartment. That was until a few hours later when the driver—I couldn't recall her name—knocked on the door with my luggage from the flight. I couldn't wait to look inside to ensure that nothing had stayed behind in my hotel room. Since even the safe had been emptied—which still freaked me out—I hoped I wouldn't be disappointed. As it turned out, everything was present and more. In the pocket inside my suitcase was another photograph, this time of Louisa's parents with her younger sister, Lindsey. They were walking together on a sidewalk in front of buildings that I didn't recognize.

"Hey," I asked, hoping my question sounded casual, "how is Lindsey doing?"

"Oh, you know, busy with college, her job, and guys. I think most of her time goes to guys—plural, settling down isn't her thing—rather than the real work. Her classes don't start again until fall term."

Something about the picture in my suitcase came to mind. Lindsey was about to start her junior year at Boston College. Their parents lived in a stately home in Superior, Colorado, halfway between Boulder and Denver.

"Gosh, she hasn't been home since Christmas."

In the picture, the three of them were all together. They were wearing short sleeves, and on the sidewalk, there was a tree with leaves. Definitely not Colorado in the winter.

"No," Louisa said, "but she plans to come back before classes start to meet her niece or nephew."

"That's great. I know you miss her. From December until now seems like a long time for Lucy." Lucy was their mother and had stepped in as my surrogate on needed occasions. Sometimes it's nice to have a mom, even when you don't. I always wished I'd told her that before I got out of the car.

"Didn't I tell you?" she asked.

"What?"

"Mom and Dad went to Boston. They're there right now."

A spittle of tea flew from my lips as I choked on my drink. Louisa went on, "Jeez, Kenni, are you all right?"

"Sorry," I said, reaching for my napkin and cleaning the table.

"Yes, they've been there for a few days. Mom wanted to go see Lindsey before the baby arrives. I'm sure you know she won't be leaving..." Louisa rolled her eyes. "...probably *my house* for the next ten years after the baby's born."

"She just wants to help." I couldn't stop thinking about the picture as my blood chilled. Sterling had people watching everyone I loved.

"I'm sure I'll appreciate it," she said.

"You know, I told you everything was good in Chicago?"

"Yes, but now you're saying you're worried about Franco."

"I am. I think I might need to go back there for a little while."

"What? You always said you'd never go there. I figured that was why you came home so fast. And now you're saying you're going back?"

My lower lip momentarily went between my teeth as I contemplated the million different stories I'd tried to concoct. I didn't want to go back. I sure as hell didn't want to stay in Chicago and definitely not with him. However, Ster-

ling Sparrow was making it abundantly clear that my compliance had a direct correlation to the safety of the people I
loved. Protecting them, perhaps at the risk of my own safety,
wasn't even a choice as I looked at my eight-month-pregnant
best friend. Besides, there was more. He had something I
couldn't forget. He had information about me—secrets I
thought disappeared when my mother drove away.

My decision to comply had dominated my thoughts since
our impromptu meeting and what happened in Wichita. The
tone of his voice on that call, even the memory of it, sent
shivers down my spine and through my entire body as the
small hairs on the back of my neck stood to attention. In one
short meeting, I'd assessed that he had power and had no
problem wielding it.

His power had the ability to direct or influence those
around him. And yet it seemed by his tone on that call that
his power could also be unstable and volatile, like a volcano on
the brink of eruption when pushed the right direction. In that
call, for no reason that I could surmise, he sounded worried
about my safety. At first. I didn't realize the insight he'd given
me. The pictures were his way of capitalizing on my weakness
—my love for Louisa and her family.

I would go back to Chicago.

Not to stay but to learn.

And while I was there, I would capitalize on what seemed
to be his weakness—me.

"I don't want to worry you," I said. "The move won't be
for forever or even for a long time for that matter. I love
being here with you. I just think that for Sinful Threads we
can do more with division. You know, divide and conquer."

Her nose scrunched. "But what about the designs? I'm going to be a little preoccupied..." She rubbed her midsection.

I lifted my hand.

Although I was not certain how the future would work, I did know that Sparrow wouldn't be the only one to make demands. I had them too. "We will Skype or FaceTime. I'll be in contact with our designers. The only thing I can't do from Chicago is run the silk through my fingers. However, as long as everything is well with our material shipments, the designs will be fine. The prototypes can be overnighted to me. It will work."

Louisa shook her head. "I don't understand your change of heart."

"It's not a change of heart. It's about what's best for Sinful Threads."

Her eyes grew glossy. "What about me? I want you here with little Kennedy."

I forced a smile. "You won't be able to keep me away."

My list of demands was growing. Mr. Sparrow and I needed to have a talk.

KENNEDY

*T*he call rang twice before the growingly familiar voice answered. "Ms. Hawkins."

"Patrick," I said into my phone. "I need to talk to him. I *want* to talk to him—now." I'd waited two days since my dinner with Louisa to call. I wanted to be certain of my demands before I wasted my chance to voice them.

"Him?" Patrick asked.

"Are you really going to act like you don't know to whom I'm referring?"

He cleared his throat. "I'm certain I know. He's not available at the moment."

"He's not available because he's not with you or because he isn't used to having someone tell him what to do?"

"I will inform him of your request." His tone sounded amused.

"No, Patrick. Inform him that I'm waiting for his call, and I expect it this evening. This isn't a request."

"I will relay the message."

"This evening," I repeated before disconnecting the call and letting out an exaggerated breath. I tossed my phone onto the couch, watching it bounce over the cushions.

Did I hear Patrick smile? Is that even possible?

I didn't find my demand amusing.

Infuriating was what this was. Sparrow actually expected me to submit to his orders and move across the country and live with a man I didn't even know?

Yes. That was what he expected.

He expected more—my compliance to his every order.

Don't search for more information. All of your devices are monitored.

Tell me your name. In time.

Well, fuck you, Sparrow.

I knew his name. And since learning that, I'd learned more.

On Saturday, I'd gone to the local library and using one of their computers, searched Sterling Sparrow. While I was tempted to search McCrie, technically that was the search he told me not to do. He never said I couldn't search for information on him.

The picture that filled the screen confirmed his identity, complete with the dark stare I remembered and was now seeing in my dreams—or were they nightmares? I found myself falling down a rabbit hole of information, not at all what I'd imagined. I expected mobster or mafia, as Louisa had alluded to before I left. That wasn't what I found. Then again, I don't think that information was something people listed on their LinkedIn page.

Sterling Sparrow: kingpin.

Nope.

The information that popped up surprised as well as intrigued me.

A military veteran and University of Michigan graduate, Sterling Sparrow was listed as CEO of Sparrow Enterprises, one of Forbes list of richest people in America, and one of the top real estate developers in Chicago and beyond. Sparrow Enterprises was built by Sterling's father, Allister, reportedly beginning with family money from Sterling's mother. One article mentioned speculations of Sterling's political aspirations, yet from all I read, those were unconfirmed rumors. According to another article, those speculations were because of his father. It stated that Sterling was following in his father's footsteps. The older Sparrow had not only owned property all over the world, but prior to his death had begun a campaign to run for the mayor of Chicago. With his money and connections, the columnist believed that Allister Sparrow would have been a shoo-in, until his unfortunate accident ended his life. There were rumors of a hit by his political adversaries; however, the official investigation ruled his death a tragic mishap, occurring at a construction site on one of his many properties.

The death of her husband hadn't stopped Sterling's mother, Genevieve, from maintaining her newsworthy, elite Chicago status. As a member of numerous influential boards and commissions, as well as an alderman on the City Council, she was well-known for assisting the family business by influencing everything from planning to zoning. She and Allister had been considered to be among the city's uncrowned royalty. Sterling was now well-established in that rank.

All of my research confirmed my suspicions: Sterling

Sparrow was wealthy, influential, and powerful. What I couldn't understand was if that were true, why the hell couldn't he find a woman the normal way? Why did he want me? What was I to him?

Basically, my research gleaned information that instead of bringing me answers raised more questions.

In my mind, as the days passed, my agreeing to his demands had less to do with his threats of people who I loved and more to do with the realization that Sterling Sparrow was the only person capable or somewhat willing to give me answers. He'd already given me more than I had previously known.

I stared down again at my phone. Something told me that he wasn't accustomed to being told what to do. Would he call? "Come on, Mr. Great and Powerful Sparrow. You like giving orders. Can you follow them as well?"

I paced the length of my living room, taking in the familiar four walls and the closed curtains keeping the rest of Boulder from seeing inside. I'd lived in this apartment for over two years, moving in after the breakup of my only long-term relationship.

The walls were dotted with art and photographs. The leather sofa was worn where I usually sat. This was my home. I didn't want to leave it. I scoffed. Obviously, I hadn't made any attempts to do so. After all, it was Monday night, and I had nothing packed. I'd spent more time at the office than I had at home. My work would need to travel with me, not my personal belongings. It was as if packing were an outward sign of surrender.

Sterling Sparrow didn't know me. I wasn't the white-flag type of woman.

My decision to go ahead with this ridiculous plan was temporary. I would be back. There was no need to pack all my possessions. Each day I'd received another message. Yesterday's was a bouquet of flowers delivered to the office with a card devoid of the sender's name. It only read two words: In time.

I'd wadded the card in a ball and thrown it into the trash just as Louisa peeked her head around the doorframe. "Secret admirer?"

"Funny."

"Well, it's not your birthday."

"The card didn't have a name. I bet it's one of the companies trying to get our business."

"Probably from someone who was at the party in Chicago."

"Why would you say that?" I asked.

"Maybe because the orders for the dress you wore are through the roof. I can't wait to showcase the other styles our designers are dreaming up. There's another design we both liked about to be sent."

I was glad to hear something good came from my trip to Chicago.

And then today, there was the special delivery of a Sinful Thread scarf. That wouldn't have seemed odd except that particular scarf had not yet been launched. The only inventory was in our chaos room.

Sparrow's packages and messages kept him forefront in my mind. Over and over, I replayed the meeting in the office. Each time, the threats faded as I recalled the way my insides twisted when his hard body pressed against me and the aura of control surrounding him, hiding him in a fog of mixed emotions.

I shouldn't find that attractive, yet I did.

No. Attraction was not the reason I would return to Chicago. What made his proposal even consideration-worthy was not the idea of what it would be like to be with him. It was his promise that he could tell me about myself. At twenty-six years of age, I was being offered the chance to learn my own secrets.

I poured myself a glass of wine and resumed my pacing.

A million questions cycloned through my thoughts when the ringing of my phone brought me back to reality, causing me to jump. For a moment I stared, shocked that it was ringing, wondering if it was really him.

The screen glowed, but Patrick's name wasn't there. Instead it read BLOCKED NUMBER.

Taking a deep breath, I answered, "Hello."

"Araneae."

The sound of that name and the tenor of his voice rumbled through me.

"I-I wasn't sure you would call." Damn nerves.

A deep chuckle added thunder to the rumbling within me. With only his voice, he could brew a storm of emotions.

"I have questions and demands," I said, attempting to assert some control.

"Interesting. I would expect questions. We'll have plenty of time to answer those once you're here."

"That's the thing. I'm not going to be there, not without the answers first."

"It isn't that easy."

"Yes, it is," I said, falling back onto the couch. "I decide if

I get on that plane or not. I need more than threats before I make that move."

"The safety of your friends and business is no longer your concern?"

"Of course, it is. That's not what I mean."

"Then by all means, explain."

"I need more."

"I've already given you more," he said. "I've given you your name. Now it's my turn to receive, and I will on Wednesday night."

The confidence in his voice twisted my insides, almost enough to convince me that he was right. Almost.

"I have demands." I didn't wait for him to respond. "First, I will be in daily contact with Louisa. This may be by phone or FaceTime. I will not give up my best friend and business partner. I will also be involved in the day-to-day operations of Sinful Threads, and lastly, I will not be held prisoner. I will come and go as I want, including returning here as needed."

I waited while the phone against my ear remained silent. Finally, I asked, "Are you still there?"

"Is that all?" he asked.

"All?"

"Is there more?"

"Those were..." I said. "...well, will you honor those?"

"You see, I was right." His voice had changed. No longer a storm, it was now smooth as Sinful Threads' silk.

"About?"

"You, Araneae. Your concerns are centered on others instead of yourself. That flaw is beautiful and selfless and why you need to be here."

"It's not a flaw to think of others."

"It is if it's at your own expense."

"So I should tell you to go fuck yourself?" I asked, my indignation growing as I sat forward. "Maybe I should go on with my life as if you didn't turn it upside down."

"You're close. However, you should know, myself is not who I plan to fuck."

I sucked in a breath.

He went on, "I thought you may have demands in regard to your housing, such as a room of your own."

Oh shit!

I hadn't even thought of that. How could I not think of that? "I-I..."

"How does that make you feel to know I have plans for you?"

I snapped my chin up and sprang from the couch, my grip tightening on the phone with each step as I walked the length of the room and back. "For your information, my making this move is not and should not be considered an invitation for you to carry out those plans. I will have my own room. And the only fucking that will take place is with your own hand, so get used to it."

Again, the deep chuckle floated through the phone. "Your housing will be provided. The details are mine to decide.

"You know, Araneae, your words say one thing, but your body another. I remember the way your nipples beaded under that silk dress. If it hadn't been a prototype, I would have ripped it from your sexy curves. Soon, I'll see what I couldn't the other night when I had you against that wall. My imagination is vivid, but I want more, more than seeing. I want to touch, suck, and lick. I want to hold those luscious tits in my hand as they grow heavy with need and your nipples turn a deeper shade of red."

My pacing stilled as his words and breathy tone sent shock waves to my core. "I-I don't even know you."

"You will. And you'll want my hands on you as much as I want them there. You've been plagued with insufficient lovers for too long. I would surmise that right now you're wet. Your body knows what your mind is having trouble understanding. You want a man to take control, to quiet your smart mouth with his, and show you how satisfying it can be to let go. I'm that man. I always have been, and soon your mind and your body will come together."

"How do you know anything about my past?"

"It should be clear by now. You're mine. It's not debatable. It was decided years ago, and it's now time to make that happen in more than principle—in reality. I know everything about you because I make it a point to know everything about what belongs to me. You, Araneae, belong to me. I'll consider your demands while you consider mine."

"Tell me your name," I said, ignoring how twisted I was on the inside and the fact that he was probably right about the state of my panties.

"You know my name. Scott has been dealt with for his slip of tongue."

"What do you mean? What happened to him?"

"You know my name and you searched me." He chuckled, yet I didn't hear amusement on his side. "Which while technically was not a direct violation of what you'd been told, should warrant reprimand."

"I'm not a child."

"Then don't act like one. Also, be aware, not all information is on the internet. Only what I want public."

My pacing resumed. "Stop following me."

"My sweet Araneae, I'm in Chicago. You're in Boulder."

"Then quit having me followed."

"I also protect what is mine. You take unnecessary chances with what is most precious. It's clear that you won't be safe until you're here with me."

I stopped walking, my toes buried in the area rug as I asked the question that had been plaguing me since I decided to follow his demand. "Will I be?"

"Will you be safe?"

My mind said I wouldn't. Being with Sterling Sparrow may protect me from outside forces—he'd shown that in Wichita —but the man on the phone was likely more dangerous than whatever or whomever was after me.

"Yes," I answered.

"Time will tell." By the tone of his voice, I got the feeling that our discussion was nearly done. "You'll receive instructions regarding Wednesday. Patrick will retrieve you from your apartment and accompany you on the flight. We're taking precautions to avoid any air emergencies on Wednesday's flight. I don't want our reunion delayed."

"Sterling?" I couldn't describe the way saying his name affected me.

"Hmm."

"My friends and company?"

"Their fate is in your hands."

The phone went dead, and in that moment, I knew beyond a shadow of a doubt that I would talk with him again. However, the next time I wouldn't only feel the rumble and silk of his tone, but I'd also see the dark of his eyes.

KENNEDY

I left the office a little after one, promising to call Louisa as soon as I landed in Chicago. I'd meant what I'd said about staying in contact with her. That thought alone kept me sane as I drove to my apartment, fighting tears.

Taking a deep breath, I knocked upon Mrs. Powell's door.

"Kennedy, it's so good to see you," she said upon opening the door, her cat Polly doing a figure eight around her feet. "Come in before Polly decides to make a break for it."

I followed her inside. "Jeanne, I wanted to let you know that I'm going to be out of town for a while. I-I..." I took a deep breath as I looked around her apartment. Nearly every surface was covered in knickknacks, small figurines, vases, all sitting upon doilies.

She reached for my hand. "Are you upset about this trip?"

I shook my head, though the truth was yes. I swallowed as tears pricked the back of my eyes. "No, not at all. I just wanted you to be aware. I may not be back in time for our next dinner."

"Oh, I hope you are."

That brought a smile to my lips. "Me too." I leaned down and gave her a hug.

She reached for my hand as I began to back away. "Don't you worry. I'll look after your place."

"Thank you."

With each step up the staircase to my apartment, I cursed Sterling Sparrow. Once inside, I walked into my bedroom and did nothing. I had nothing packed. I had no idea how long I'd be gone or what I needed. My flight was leaving in four hours, and I was completely unprepared.

When the doorbell rang, though it was too early, I expected to see Patrick. Instead, I was greeted by a deliveryman holding a large white box with a red bow.

"Ms. Hawkins?"

"Yes."

He held out a small handheld device. "Please sign here."

I let out a long breath and did as he asked.

"Have a nice day."

I smiled and nodded, though with everything in me, I doubted that *nice* would be my description when I finally fell asleep at the end of whatever today would bring. Carrying the package to the sofa, I noted that it was lighter than it looked.

I'd read stories where a man would send a woman a dress or an outfit. Was that what he was doing? While I disliked the idea that he would tell me what to wear, I couldn't hold back my curiosity as I eased the bow from the Garbarini box. Garbarini was a high-end boutique located in Denver. I'd shopped there on a few occasions but rarely found anything in my price range.

With building anticipation, I lifted the lid and pushed back the tissue paper.

The only thing inside besides the tissue paper was an envelope with Araneae written in elegant swirls.

Araneae,

All that is in this gift is all that you need to bring with you.

Your every need will be met. Even though what is in this box is my attire choice for you, your closet here is filled.

Until our reunion,

Sterling

Like the note to the flowers, I crumpled this one in a ball, throwing it into the nearly empty box. Asshole.

Taking large strides, I went to my room and pulled my suitcase from the shelf of my closet. I may be moving to Chicago—temporarily—but he wasn't calling all the damn shots. Ripping clothes from their hangers, I tossed them on the bed until the pile was much too large for the one suitcase.

He could take his closet of clothes and stick it up his ass. I had my own clothes. If he thought I'd leave my Sinful Threads accessories and the dress I'd worn to that party in Chicago, he was crazy.

In less than an hour I had three suitcases filled with clothes and accessories, cosmetics and jewelry, and even a few pictures in frames from around my apartment. I made sure to have my hidden picture of my parents as well as the charm bracelet. The cheap gold-covered charms may not be what Mr. Sparrow had in mind for my jewelry, but I didn't care. Crossing my arms over my chest, I looked down at the luggage. "There you go, asshole. Fuck you and your closet."

I turned back toward my closet, taking in all the empty hangers. My bedside stand was empty, my Kindle and the picture that usually sat there, packed.

Shit.

Did I just play into his hand?

I'd planned on leaving things here, and now I'd packed everything that mattered.

As I lifted the larger suitcase back onto the bed to unpack, my doorbell rang again.

"Oh, wonderful," I said to no one. "Maybe another empty box."

I pulled the door inward to be met by Patrick's smug grin. "Ms. Hawkins."

My fist came to my hip. "What are your instructions if I tell you *no*, if I say that I've changed my mind?"

"I don't think you will."

"You don't know anything about me. I've lived in this area for over ten years. I'm not going to just leave it all behind." My protest came out louder than I intended.

"May I help you with your bags?"

My lips came together as I exhaled through my nose. "You should know that he told me not to pack."

"I do. Would you like me to carry the luggage to the car, or will you?"

"Are you always so fucking smug?"

His eyes shone, the only answer my question would get.

From what I saw, his answer was yes. "Ms. Hawkins, our plane is waiting."

I took a step back and gestured for Patrick to enter. "Fine. The luggage is in my bedroom."

As I reached for my purse, I slowly spun, taking in my apartment, my home.

I will be back, I vowed silently.

Patrick came toward me with one of the three suitcases and my carry-on bag that contained my laptop, tablet, copies of all my work files, and a backup supply of essentials. After what happened in Wichita, I wasn't taking any chances. "I'll be back for the rest," he said.

Hurriedly, I went into the kitchen and pulled a piece of paper from a drawer. As I reached for a pen, I listened for Patrick. His footsteps had disappeared down the communal staircase and out the door.

Louisa,

If you don't hear from me or I go missing, search for me through a man named Sterling Sparrow. I believe he lives in Chicago.

I love you.

Kennedy

Quickly I folded the paper in thirds, slipped it into an envelope, and as Patrick reentered the apartment I came up with another lie. "I'm getting some water. Would you like any?" His footsteps moved past the kitchen and echoed toward my bedroom.

"No, thank you."

I opened the freezer and tucked the envelope under a box of frozen cookies, knowing that if Louisa came looking, she'd find it. I also hoped that no one else would.

When Louisa and I were in college, we used to leave each other notes in the refrigerator or freezer, on the other person's favorite food. It sounds silly, but it was our thing, our way of ensuring that the other would find it.

As I closed the freezer door, Patrick came into view. "Are you ready, Ms. Hawkins?"

I looked down at my outfit. It was what I'd worn to work today: a black pencil skirt, white blouse, thigh-high sheer stockings, and black pumps. Around my neck was a black and gold Sinful Threads scarf. My hair was pulled back in a messy bun and my makeup was minimal. I hardly felt like I was dressed to be delivered to a man, but fuck him.

I wasn't going on a date.

"I'm coming back here, Patrick."

He didn't verbally answer, but his head bobbed. It was as close to an agreement as I would probably get and at this moment, I took it.

When we reached the curb, I was surprised to be met by the driver from before, the woman who'd brought me my luggage. "Ms. Hawkins."

"Hello." I turned to Patrick. "You aren't driving?"

"I'm only here for you." He opened the door to the back seat. It was the same car she'd driven before, the interior dark and cool.

I huffed as I settled into the seat and Patrick took the copilot's seat in front.

My mind continued to swirl with thoughts and questions, ones I knew would only be answered by Sterling—even if

Patrick knew the answers, he wouldn't tell me. What was it that Sterling said? Scott had let Sterling's last name slip, and he'd been dealt with. What the hell did that even mean?

I didn't know, but I bet Patrick knew—I bet he knew much more than he was letting on.

No, Patrick wouldn't be the source of my information.

When the car stopped, I looked up and through the darkened windows at the front entrance to the small airport where I'd flown in less than a week earlier. As Patrick got out of the car and opened my door, warm afternoon air replaced the cool. I turned to see the driver going back toward the rear of the car to retrieve my bags. "I thought we had airline tickets?" I asked more than said.

"You had airline tickets. You still do."

I shook my head. "That doesn't make any sense."

"It does, ma'am. The world thinks you're flying commercial."

I spoke in a low whisper, matching Patrick's responses. "Why would the world care?"

"Your bags," the woman whose name I couldn't remember said.

"Thank you...?"

"Shelly, ma'am. If or when you're back in Boulder, I'm at your service." Her smile grew as she looked to Patrick. "Anything for Mr. Sparrow."

"He'll be pleased."

My eyes narrowed as I took in their conversation. Had she been the one who took Louisa and Jason's picture? Was she the one who stole the scarf to turn around and have it delivered?

I didn't ask, knowing I wouldn't learn anything.

A young man joined us on the sidewalk. "May I help with the luggage?"

Through the small office and out to the tarmac, Patrick, the young man, and I walked. "Looks like a long trip," he said, commenting on my bags.

"Packing light has never been my thing," I replied as my feet stopped and mouth opened at the sight of the large plane before us. A bird was painted along the side. Unlike its real-life equivalent, the caricature made the creature artistically fierce. With the gray head, white cheeks, and a black bib, it appeared more predator than prey. The open beak covered the very front while its piercing dark eye surrounded the window to the cockpit.

This wasn't a for-hire charter. This aircraft belonged to Sparrow.

What the hell had I gotten myself into?

ARANEAE

*P*atrick stopped at the bottom of the stairs, motioning me upward. Each step was harder than the one before. As my stomach twisted, I decided finding a restroom was my first priority before we took off. What little breakfast I'd eaten many hours ago was moving precariously upward as the taste of bile bubbled in my throat.

"Welcome, Ms. Hawkins," a woman in uniform said as I stepped inside away from the sunshine. "I'm your pilot today, Marianne McGee." She lifted her hand to the right, away from the cockpit. "This is Jana and Keaton, your attendants for today's flight."

"Hello," the two said in unison.

I barely heard them as I took in the opulence of the aircraft.

It was nothing like the one I'd flown on before. There was a shiny round table, large by any standard, with six seats as well as two along the side facing one another. Beyond the table was a wall with openings on either side.

As I gazed the direction she'd pointed, Jana spoke, "May I show you around?"

Swallowing the bad taste, I nodded, afraid to open my lips.

Walking a step behind, I followed her as we passed through the opening that led to what appeared to be a living room or perhaps a theater room. I turned, seeing the large screened television on the wall we'd passed.

"The first area is where Mr. Sparrow conducts work and conferences when flying with his employees or clients. In this area..." She waved her hand. "...he relaxes or teleconferences. Beyond is a bedroom, bathrooms, and a small kitchen."

"It's..." I shook my head. "I don't seem to have words."

Jana smiled. "Mr. Sparrow travels frequently and prefers to do it in comfort. I'll say he works more than he sleeps, but the bedroom is there if you'd like to rest."

"I think I'd like to find one of the restrooms."

She nodded. "Follow me. And after you're settled, let me know what we can bring you." She pointed to a keypad and screen on the wall. "You can reach us there."

I turned a circle. "Where will you be?"

"Out of sight. There's an area off the kitchen."

"Ms. Hawkins."

I turned to the sound of Patrick's voice. "Yes?"

"Would you like any of your luggage in the main cabin?"

"I-I...my carry-on, please."

He nodded and turned away.

Jana's hand landed on my arm and her smile grew. "I believe the gift on the bed is for you as well."

My stomach knotted as I feigned a smile.

I wasn't up for another empty box or veiled threat. I was here. What more did he want?

My first stop was the bathroom. While not large—I'm in a damn airplane—it was regal, complete with a golden faucet in the sink and lever on the commode.

I leaned on the edge of the sink and stared into the lit mirror. My brown eyes gazed back at me as the color drained from my cheeks. "This isn't good," I said softly yet audibly. "Normal people don't own a plane like this. Fuck that. Normal people don't own planes. There's more to this man than you know. You may have been named after a spider, but never forget, birds eat spiders."

That thought was the last straw as my head grew heavy, the small room blurred, and my legs turned to jelly. Falling to my knees, I managed to get my head over the commode as the bile I'd been fighting won the battle. I should have eaten lunch. My empty stomach contracted as I spat the nasty-tasting liquid, emptying the contents of my mouth. Closing my eyes, my body shivered as I laid my head down, my arms resting upon the toilet seat—my pillow.

Time passed, but I wasn't sure how much or how long until a knock on the door caused me to open my eyes.

"Ms. Hawkins, Marianne has completed her checklist. She's ready to take off if you are?"

On shaky legs, I stood. Surprisingly, my reflection looked better. Though my makeup was smudged and hair tousled, there was once again natural color in my cheeks.

Was I ready?

Could I say I wasn't? Could I get off this plane?

Cupping some water into my hand, I rinsed my mouth. Another splash on my cheeks and I wiped the dark mascara smudges from beneath my eyes. After smoothing my skirt, I took a deep breath and opened the door to Jana's smiling face. I peered over her shoulder toward the front of the plane. From the angle and distance, it was difficult to see into the table room. Nevertheless, I could see that the door to the outside was already closed. My escape route was gone.

I inhaled and exhaled in submission. "Where should I sit?"

"That's up to you. Your carry-on is in the bedroom. However, for takeoff and landing, you must be seat-belted."

I made my way to one of the theater-like chairs facing the large television and sat.

"May I bring you a drink?"

I thought how wonderful it would be to have wine or perhaps a martini. Would she have whatever I ordered? By my surroundings, I was certain she would. Patrick could deliver me to Sterling Sparrow passed-out drunk. That would show him.

Then again, the thought left me with a sinking feeling. It would be better to have my faculties about me when we met again. I looked up at Jana's expectant expression. Oh, that's right; she wanted me to answer her question. "Water would be nice."

"As soon as Marianne clears me to walk around, I'll bring you some. Ice?"

"Just a bottle is fine."

"Have a nice flight, Ms. Hawkins. And don't forget your gift."

My gift.

Another empty box or a threat?

Who was left for him to threaten?

My *gift* could wait.

Whether it was Marianne's skills or the plane itself, I barely noticed the smooth takeoff as we left the ground and glided through the air. Soft white clouds appeared out the window as we flew through them and above. Blue sky shone with the evening sun's rays. A few moments later, Jana appeared with my water as well as a plate of cheese and fruit. Though I didn't want to accept, my empty stomach churned and grumbled, telling me that food was welcomed.

"Would you like to watch a movie or listen to music?"

"Music would be nice." My voice was barely my own as I obediently answered, returning her kindness. Was it kindness? Did she know she was transporting someone against her will?

Yet it wasn't.

Sterling Sparrow had orchestrated the whole thing. He wasn't kidnapping me—not technically. I had willingly packed my belongings. I'd walked to the car and been driven without complaint. I'd climbed the stairway entering this gilded cage and played the agreeable participant.

If Jana or even Patrick would ever be questioned, they could honestly say I'd traveled willingly.

Soft music filled the air. At first, I was surprised by the selection; it was one from my work playlist. And then so was the second. I reached for my phone. It was still with me. How did he continue to know so much about me?

My nerves pulled tighter with each mile. Alone in the cabin, I had time to allow my mind to wander. I tried to concentrate on the music, yet with each note, all I could do was contemplate my questions and worries. I looked about, wondering where Jana, Keaton, and Patrick were. Shouldn't I at least be able to hear them? It wasn't like they could go far.

With my water gone and most of the food consumed, I

settled back and continued listening to the familiar songs. Though I knew them all by heart, my mind didn't register the lyrics. More questions came, each one more imperative than the one before.

What would happen when we landed? Would I have my own room? Why had he even mentioned that? What did he expect? My gut told me I knew the answer to that question. He had been very direct about what he expected—sex.

What did that make me? Was I his whore, girlfriend, or fiancée?

I'd been promised to him.

For what?

To be his wife?

The cheese and fruit stewed and churned with each question. And then I recalled what Jana had said: *Don't forget your gift.*

My head said not to go in the bedroom, to stay where I was. "Don't go," I said softly in the lonely cabin. Yes, I could talk to myself. There was no one else to talk to, making even my own voice comforting. I could use the box on the wall and call Jana. Maybe she'd tell me more about Mr. Sparrow.

I realized she'd been the first person to willingly give me information: he traveled frequently. He spent more time working than resting. He transported clients and employees. Maybe she could tell me who he really was.

My fingers found their way to the buckle, undoing my seat belt as I stood.

I eyed the panel on the wall, but that wasn't where my feet were taking me.

How in the hell did Sterling expect me to follow his directions when I couldn't even follow my own?

Steely determination mixed with unhealthy curiosity pushed me toward the aft of the plane. To the left was the hallway that contained the bathroom where I'd vomited. Farther down was another door, but something told me that wasn't where I wanted to go. The length of the wall to the right of the hallway made me think there was the bedroom. Slowly, I turned the handle on the doorway to whatever was beyond the wall.

I was right.

As the door pushed inward, I took in the room complete with a king-sized bed. A fucking giant king-sized bed on an airplane. Ignoring the large gift box on the bed, I opened a sliding door to a mostly empty closet. There was a suit hanging inside along with a white shirt. I lifted an arm to my nose, inhaling the spicy cologne. Quickly I dropped the material and closed the sliding door. There was one more door. I opened it to a second bathroom, complete with a shower.

Of course. Every airplane needs a private en suite bathroom.

For some reason I recalled a television show called Pimp My Ride or was it Truck? The point was that truckers made the personal area of their semi-trucks amazing. Most had bedrooms, but I remembered one with a pinball machine. In a truck.

That was how I felt in this plane. It was as if Sterling had instructed someone to pimp his plane with the best and most outlandish accessories. I half giggled, wondering if I searched long enough, I'd find a pinball machine.

Taking a deep breath, I went to the bed and sat on the edge. The mattress was unusually high. The cover was plush beneath my touch as I stared at the gift. This box was black and the bow was white and black. I recognized the Saks Fifth Avenue packaging. They were one of Sinful Threads' distributors.

Untying the bow, I lifted the lid and pushed back the tissue paper.

A gasp came from my lips.

This box wasn't empty.

The small card atop the contents had *Araneae* on the outside of the envelope.

Before opening the note, I reached into the depths and removed a spectacular dress. It was a deep ruby red, and judging by the designer label, it cost more than anything Sinful Threads sold, and we priced our merchandise high.

Sheer, silky thigh-high stockings were held together by another black and white bow. And at the end of the long box were two smaller boxes. Inside the larger one was a stunning pair of Saint Laurent red patent-leather sandals. I didn't need to read the sole to know the brand. The sandals had the signature logo heel that was at least four inches high. I opened the smallest box to a long platinum necklace and dangling diamond earrings.

Lifting one of the earrings from the velvet box, I inspected the quality.

Surely these weren't real?

Right, Kennedy. Saint Laurent shoes and cubic zirconia earrings. Damn, if they were, he'd dropped some serious money on this outfit. But from the looks of the plane, serious money wasn't an issue.

He must sell a lot of real estate.

My hands shook as I reached for and opened the envelope.

Araneae,

In this box you'll find the wrapping for my delivery. The bathroom has been supplied with everything you'll need to prepare yourself.

As with any gift, I am counting the minutes until I can tear the wrapping away and reveal what is mine.

Sterling

Was I going to do this?

As panic and uncertainty flooded my circulation, I pulled my phone from the pocket of my skirt. We'd been in the air for over an hour and a half. How much time did I have? Why hadn't I opened this sooner?

I rushed into the bathroom and began opening drawers. They were filled with cosmetics—all high-end. In the shower were shampoos and conditioner as well as perfumed soaps and lotions. I opened more drawers to other items: brushes, combs, hairdryer, curling wand, straightener, and even a razor.

Was that for my legs or somewhere else?

Oh hell no.

I'm a real blonde, and I had no intention of erasing the evidence.

I stared at the supplies. There was no way I had enough time to do whatever he wanted me to do.

Did I even want to?

I didn't.

Then again, if my goal was to obtain information from Mr.

Sparrow, was it smart to begin this deal by disobeying his instructions?

What had he said about my library research? *While technically not a direct violation of what you'd been told, should warrant reprimand.* Again, reprimand? What did that mean?

As my heart pounded, I went back to the bedroom. On the wall was another panel like the one in the main cabin. I pushed the intercom.

"Yes, this is Keaton. May I help you?"

"Um, this is Kennedy...Ms. Hawkins." *No shit. He knew who I was.*

"Yes, Ms. Hawkins. May I help you with something?"

"I was wondering how much time I have until we land."

"You will need to be seated in fifty-seven minutes. We will land in sixty-eight."

Well, that seemed rather precise.

"Is there any bad weather expected?" I didn't want to be in a shower with a razor and hit an air pocket or some terrible turbulence.

"No, ma'am. The captain plans on a continued smooth flight."

Less than forty minutes later, freshly showered, teeth brushed, made-up, and wrapped in a sinfully plush towel, I approached the bed where I'd left the contents of the box. Suspiciously missing from the collection were underclothes. I wouldn't need a bra or even be able to wear one with the dress's plunging neckline, but panties seemed like a good plan.

It was then that I recalled my carry-on bag. I looked around. Jana had said it was in the bedroom. I hadn't noticed it before on a stand against the wall. I said a silent thank-you for my traveling routines. Whenever I traveled overnight, especially if my baggage was checked, which is what I'd expected, I also packed a small nylon bag within my carry-on that contained essentials—a toothbrush, underwear, and pajamas. I'd never needed them until now.

The dress fit like a glove, the bodice tight around my breasts and ribs as the skirt flared at my hips. The coolness of the platinum necklace chilled my skin as it fell between the swell of my breasts and I secured the earrings in place. One by one, I slipped my feet into the heeled sandals.

I stood motionless in front of a full-length mirror. My reflection was different than it had been when I arrived, and while I didn't like the reason for what I'd done—it felt too much like submission—I nevertheless looked good. The person in the mirror was the woman Louisa always said I could be.

No, I was the person who would take Mr. Sterling Sparrow to his knees.

"Okay, Mr. Sparrow. I complied. Now it's your turn." I don't think I said it aloud, but I may have.

I reached out to the wall, my first step in the tall heels a bit wobbly. "Come on, Kenni. You're not going to seduce him if you fall on your face." I took another step and then another. By the time I made it back out into the cabin area and to my seat, I was as steady as the luxurious airplane.

"Ms. Hawkins," Jana said, coming from behind. As soon as she saw me, she smiled. "You look lovely."

That should have made me feel good—that's how normal people react to a compliment. Yet it didn't. I'd done as he said —cleaned myself, brushed my teeth, shaved my legs, styled, and basically prepared myself as a sacrifice for slaughter. I couldn't think about that. I had to stay strong.

"Thank you, Jana," I managed.

"I was asked to inform you that after we land, Patrick will pull the car onto the tarmac. After your luggage is loaded into the car, you will be ready to go. Before we land, may I get you anything?"

"Do you have whiskey?" I wasn't sure where the question came from. Perhaps it was my subconscious knowing I needed some liquid confidence to carry on, to be "ready to go."

Her cheeks rose. "On the rocks?"

"Straight."

"Yes, ma'am."

As she started to walk away, an image of Sparrow's dark eyes materialized in my mind. "Make it a double," I called as I secured my seat belt.

The amber liquid burned for only a second before numbing my throat as its potent effect slowed my rapid pulse and warmed my circulation.

"You can do this," I said aloud, getting quite used to talking audibly to myself.

I wasn't certain what made me do it—a sense, a feeling, a presence...

I looked up to the doorway beside the television and sucked in a breath. The previously open space was now filled with his broad shoulders and height. Like the image I'd had, he'd materialized. Yet he wasn't an apparition. The mountain of a man was real.

In stunned silence, I scanned him up and down. His clothes were casual compared to the outfit he'd prepared for me. He wore blue jeans, worn in all the right places, hanging low from his hips, and showcasing his long legs and thick, powerful thighs. His collarless shirt fit well, highlighting a broad neck, a defined torso, and broad biceps.

Though I could gaze upon his body for hours, that wasn't what stilled my pulse to the point of feeling faint. It was his eyes, the way they looked, not at me but into me. No longer was I imagining his dark stare. It was trained on me.

How was he here?

We hadn't landed.

"Sterling?"

The tips of his lips moved upward as his penetrating stare scorched my skin. From the tips of my toes in the ridiculously high shoes, all the way to the chain lying between my breasts, and up to my recently styled hair, he took in every inch. Each second his eyes roamed was the strike of a match, igniting tiny fuses and detonating each of my nerves, until my skin peppered with goose bumps and my nipples hardened.

That wasn't the only effect of his stare. Thank God I'd brought underwear.

I gripped the armrest as the airplane lurched, descending quicker than before. As if physics played no role in Sterling Sparrow's existence, other than his eyes and lips, he didn't move. He didn't speak.

I squeezed my thighs tighter as I released the armrests and my fingers balled into fists at my sides.

The silence turned deafening, alerting me that the music was no longer playing.

And then, he moved. Step by step, he came closer. Even his movement made no sound, until he gracefully folded his massive body, sitting in the chair to my left. Warmth filled me as he reached for my hand.

I didn't fight his effort, yet my fingers remained fisted.

With an upturn of his grin, he gently pried open my fingers, one by one, until all five were extended in the palm of his large hand. He then leaned forward.

My pulse quickened as his warm lips brushed my knuckles. The connection set off more detonations as parts of my body that had remained untouched heated.

With my hand still in his, Sterling continued his stare. It was as if in that gaze, there was concern that if he looked away, I would disappear. His brown eyes grew darker, swirling with emotion and saying what his lips were not.

Finally, I couldn't take it any longer. "What the hell?" My tone was a meek whisper in contrast to my words. "You've been here the entire—"

His finger came to my lips as his deep voice filled the silent cabin. "No, Araneae. Not yet. Let me enjoy my gift and the beautiful wrapping. For soon I will enjoy something even more gorgeous...what's underneath."

ARANEAE

The way he was looking at me may be doing something to my body, twisting it in ways I'd only read about in books, but my mind was no longer meek. Alarm and energy surged through me. I was trapped by not only the seat belt but also his stare. With fight or flight my only options, I couldn't take the confinement any longer. Pulling my hand free of his, I scrambled for the buckle of the seat belt, and reared my head away from his silencing touch.

My head shook from side to side. "No, this isn't happening." My tone grew stronger with each word. The buckle opened as I pushed away. I wasn't his prey nor was he my captor. As I stood and stepped, the high heels and plane's descent did little to assist in my escape.

Physics may not affect Sterling Sparrow, but apparently the same didn't apply for me. According to Newton's law of motion, every object will remain at rest or in uniform motion in a straight line unless compelled to change its state by the action of an external force.

As my mind jumbled and feet shifted, I was surrounded by outside forces, coming at me from every direction.

The lurching of the plane as it continued its descent and the propulsion of my body as I leaped forward worked in tandem to send me hurling toward the wall and television. My hands went out in hopes of saving myself before my face collided with the giant screen.

And yet...the world stopped. The impact never came.

All at once, I was heaved back. A grasp of my wrist pulled me backward moments before strong arms surrounded me, and I was thrust back to the seats. No longer sitting in my own chair, my escape attempt had landed me squarely on Sterling's lap.

Struggling was fruitless. Sterling Sparrow's hold exceeded a plane seat belt, even in one as plush and luxurious as his.

The emotions from before and those building over the past week came out, not as anger or rage but as tears that could no longer be contained.

The salty moisture burning my eyes was an insult to me and my strength. I turned away, not wanting him to see the way my body had again defied me.

He didn't speak, nor did I as the plane continued its course. His lips brushed the top of my head as his hold loosened and he shifted, helping me stand and then sit again where I'd been.

His movement brought more than his loosening grasp to my attention. As I repositioned myself in my own seat and he stood, my gaze unconsciously went to the front of his jeans.

He may not have acknowledged my tears, but just as mine had done, his body betrayed his words and actions.

When our gazes met, his dared me to acknowledge what we both knew had happened. Looking away, I decided it wasn't a challenge I was currently prepared to fight. With something that sounded a bit like a growl, Sterling turned away and walked to the panel upon the wall. Pushing a button, Marianne's voice came from the speaker. "Captain McGee."

"Marianne, change of course."

"Sir? We've filed our flight plan, our landing is anticipated, and we're approaching—"

"Do we have enough fuel to reach the cabin?" Sparrow asked, not allowing her to finish.

"Um, yes, sir, we do. The airport—"

Again he interrupted, "Contact the civil aviation authorities for both countries and alert them to our change. Also alert the proper channels that we're crossing the border. Make them aware of our manifest. If my calculations are correct, we should have another two and a half hours of flight."

"Yes, sir, roughly. I'll let you know when I have the exact information."

My eyes grew wide as he came back toward me. "Crossing the border? What border?"

Sterling sat beside me and stretched his long legs out in front of him as he exhaled. "It appears you're not ready for the plans I had set. I'll have Patrick get word to those who need to know that we will be unreachable for a few days."

The bubbling concoction of emotions boiled over as I sat straighter in the seat. "Unreachable? No. I told you that I would have daily contact with Louisa. You promised."

His dark eyes turned my way as his tone dripped with insincere affection. "My sweet Araneae, I made no such promise." His long fingers upon the armrest clenched and unclenched as he weighed his words. "Something you should know about me is that I keep my promises. A man's word is his most valuable tool or most respected weapon. I said that you'd get back to Boulder and have time to settle whatever you needed to settle before being delivered to me. You were given that time. You've been delivered. My word has been kept."

I shook my head. "No. On the phone... you said..." I tried to remember exactly what he'd said. I'd given him my demands, yet had he promised? "...that you'd consider my demands."

He didn't respond. Instead, he answered my question from before. "The American border. My cabin is in Ontario."

"No. This is insanity. I have a company to run. I told you that I will not step away from Sinful Threads."

"And you won't...not for long. Every CEO deserves a vacation."

"A vacation? A vacation?" My volume grew with each phrase. "Being kidnapped over the border is not a vacation."

You are not kidnapped. You willingly entered this plane. The cameras at the airport will show that. Along with the excessive amount of luggage and you telling others you were going away, there is plenty of evidence of your willing participation."

The plane's trajectory changed, more noticeable at first, until we were soon cruising steady and level as we had before.

I didn't have words as I sat in stunned silence and he typed out a text, or maybe it was more than one. Whatever he was communicating and to whomever, it was meant to be done without my overhearing. I had no doubt he could have texted Marianne too. The verbal command wasn't only for her but, meant for me also. He was changing our plans and neither Marianne nor I were able to alter that change.

Perhaps the only external force aboard this plane was Sterling Sparrow.

With each minute, my mind searched for answers. Thank goodness I'd left Louisa that note. It was my only hope that she would begin a search.

"Ms. Hawkins?"

I looked up to Jana's smiling expression as she handed me my phone. I'd left it in the bedroom and had been too lost in my thoughts to hear her approach. My gaze went from her to Sterling, wondering why she'd bring me my phone in his presence.

He didn't speak, yet a quick nod of his head told me that she was doing his bidding.

"Thank you."

As I reached for it, she asked, "May I get either of you anything?"

My fingers surrounded my phone as I contemplated how to send a message without Sterling knowing. I could contact Louisa or Winnie; either would be able to help.

"That will be all, Jana," Sterling said. "We are not to be disturbed unless you're called."

She nodded and took a step back. "Yes, sir."

As she walked away, I looked down at the phone in my hand.

Before I could speak, Sterling did. "I would assume that in that beautiful head of yours you're thinking about the SOS message you plan to send. Perhaps more than one?"

My eyes widened as I lifted my gaze to his. Though I expected the dark stare, I was caught off guard by the sense of amusement in his expression. "Do you think this is funny?"

A deep chuckle filled the air. "I do. And a bit disappointing."

"Disappointing?"

"Araneae, your predictability is disappointing. Your fiery spirit is more than amusing—it's electrifying." He nodded toward my phone. "Contact your assistant and your business partner. Tell them whatever you want to say, as long as you make it clear that you'll be unreachable through the weekend."

I sucked in a breath. "Weekend? That's four days."

"And that you'll be in touch with them when you return from this much-needed getaway."

"I won't do that. I need to be accessible."

"No."

With the level flight, I once again had steadfast footing as I stood. I took a few steps, turned, and took a few more. With each pass I collected my thoughts and my words. Taking a deep breath, I began, "I get that you're in control of this plane. I get that you think you're somehow in control of my decisions, but you're not. I have a company. I have a friend who is weeks from giving birth." I stopped my pacing and looked him in the eye. "Tell me you won't hurt them."

Sterling's gaze widened. "As it has always been, it's in your hands. You see, Araneae, you have control, too."

I let out an exasperated breath. "I'm going with you." I lifted my hands and gestured toward the windows filling with red hues from the setting sun. "You see, I forgot to pack my parachute so my escape opportunities are limited."

His lips curled upward. "And yet once again failing to obey, you packed quite a bit."

Deciding not to take that bait, I went on, "As I was saying, many things can happen in four days. I need to be accessible."

"Tell them they may *only* contact you in the case of an emergency. Patrick will keep your phone. If an emergency occurs, you'll be notified."

My head shook as I contemplated his offer. "I want my phone with me."

"First, we have some rules to discuss."

"Rules?"

Sterling stood, his height, despite the heels on my shoes, dwarfing me as it had the first night in the office. "I've waited longer than you know for this."

He stepped closer, reached for my hands, and removed the phone from my grip. While domineering, there was no anger or wrath in his touch. Without argument, I released the phone as he tossed it in one of the chairs.

Before he continued speaking, he once again secured my fingers, enveloping them in his warm grasp. "I've always known it would happen, that one day you would be mine. It's too easy for me to forget that you haven't had the same knowledge. In my anticipation, I wrongly assumed that you'd be ready to learn about yourself, your future, and your past. It seems that by your little display earlier, you're not."

"I am ready. I want to know."

"Then behave."

"You act like I'm a child."

He squeezed my hands as his eyes darkened and head tilted. "Araneae, if you think there's any part of me that sees you as a child, you're mistaken." He took a step back and scanned me from my toes to my eyes. By the time our gazes met, there was no doubt how exactly Sterling Sparrow saw me. Though we were flying nearly a mile over the earth, the heat in his stare could ignite the forests below, decimating the pristine land to ashes.

"I don't know you," I said, repeating something I'd told him before.

"You will. That's why we're going to the cabin. It will give us uninterrupted time to become acquainted."

I wanted to ask how acquainted. Instead, I acquiesced. "Fine."

He chuckled. "You're agreeing to go where you're already going?"

"No," I said, straightening my shoulders and lengthening my neck. "I'm agreeing to sending the messages you mentioned and to allowing Patrick to monitor my phone. However," I said, removing my hands from his and taking a step back, "I want a promise—your word—that if a message comes through, at any hour, I will be notified."

I watched as his Adam's apple bobbed.

"Sterling, I mean it. I need to know what's happening. Louisa and Sinful Threads are...well, they're my family."

"You have my word. You also have my word that they aren't."

The relief in his first statement was quickly washed away. "What do you mean? Do I have family? Real family? What do you know?" *And how do you know it?* I didn't ask the last part.

He reached again for my hands. "I've already told you that I know all about anyone or anything that belongs to me. Soon you'll acknowledge that that includes you."

ARANEAE

"You may change into something more comfortable if you would like," Sterling said after my messages were sent.

I may.

Fuck him.

Leaning back, I crossed my legs at my knees, bobbed my high-heel sandal, and settled against the soft seat. With my hands gripping the arms of the large plush seat, I found my most defiant voice. "Thank you for your permission. It's not necessary. I'll wear whatever the fuck I want, when I want."

His grin curled upward as one brow lifted.

With a *humph* I rebelliously folded my arms over my chest like the child he told me not to be. I was well aware that sitting here in the outfit he'd told me to wear, freshly showered, and *fucking prepared,* my words held less substance than a boat filled with holes, sinking to the depths of Lake Michigan.

After a few minutes, he spoke, "I wasn't expecting you to do it."

"Do what? Get on the plane?" *Because more than once I'd regretted the decision.*

His expression of power from before was replaced with something different—perhaps an attempt at understanding? Maybe I was reading too much into it.

"No," he said. "I knew you'd do that. I told you. I know your weakness."

"Yes, so you said. I care. I give a shit about other people. How horrendous of me."

"That isn't your only weakness, but it's the only one I'll currently admit to exploiting."

I sat taller and purposely turned toward the row of windows on the other side of the plane from Mr. Sparrow. The view from before of light blue sky was gone, replaced with darkness. I wondered about the time of day or night. I was at a complete loss. Like many other things, the only answer I would get would be from the arrogant man seated across the room. After my brief exchange with both Winnie and Louisa, my phone had been safely stowed with Patrick, or so I'd been told. Since I didn't think it went with the red dress and most likely expensive jewelry, my watch was also tucked away of my own doing in my carry-on. That meant my only gauge of passing time was the length of the flight. I'd lost all sense of most everything since Sterling materialized and changed our destination.

"I didn't think," he went on, pulling my attention back to him, "that you'd wear what was in the gift box."

I tilted my head. "Perhaps I'm learning your weaknesses as well."

His grin transformed into a smirk. "Be careful, Araneae. I have none. There were powerful men who have thought otherwise. They're no longer alive to test their theories."

"I'll keep that in mind."

He stood from where he'd been seated and walked my direction. Although every voice in my head said to look away, I couldn't. Despite his height, within the confines of an airplane, he displayed no awkwardness. I presumed his location was irrelevant. In all situations, Sterling Sparrow moved like a lion: majestic, strong, proud, and above all, powerful. He was the king of the beasts and everyone within his realm was either a peasant, present to do his bidding, or prey, waiting to be devoured.

As he came to a stop in front of me, the twisting in my core told me that I didn't qualify as a peasant. No, I was his prey. I craned my neck upward, attempting to remain expressionless as I strived to maintain eye contact.

I'm not prey, asshole. If I'm yours, as you've said, I'm the lioness.

"It would be good if you did," he suggested.

It was my turn to smirk. "I didn't realize that real estate was such a cutthroat business. Besides, it seems to me that if my death was your goal, and as you yourself have said, you've been watching me for some time, my demise would have already occurred."

"If that had been my goal, it would have. It wasn't." He crouched to his haunches before me as his large hand grazed my exposed ankle, sparking heat as it moved up to under the hem of the dress, uncovering my knee. His eyes met mine. "My goal has been achieved. It always is. I don't fail." His broad shoulder shrugged as his grin turned either sly or sinister—I was yet to have him completely figured out.

"However, it's also wise to keep in mind that goals can change."

His grip of my knee tightened. "I also prefer to know that when I give instructions, they're carried out—completely. The entire time we've been together in this cabin, I couldn't help but wonder if you'd done that."

"Done what?"

"Tell me if you did as I said."

"Stop talking in riddles. You've said a lot. What are you asking?"

"Are you wearing everything in the box?" Standing, he offered his hand, encouraging me to also stand.

Heat flowed from our connection, flooding my core as I made it to my feet. My heels wobbled as I remembered what I'd added to the outfit.

Like velvet moving the wrong way, his deep voice rubbed my nerves as he slowly shook his head, stood back, and assessed everything about me. "I recommend you avoid poker," he said with a hint of amusement.

"I'll have you know I excel at poker. Five-card draw is my game."

His chuckle filled the cabin. "Then your opponents were amateurs. Though your life is one, you're not good at keeping secrets. That is why until now you've been spared the truth. In this case, your body is giving you away."

I tried not to think about what he knew about my life.

When it came to here and now, he was right. My damn body was a traitor. It and I were no longer on speaking terms. As infuriating and arrogant as this man could be, in his presence my body was a flush of energy—most of it now settled between my legs.

"Your cheeks are growing pinker," he said. "Your feet are shuffling, and your breathing has changed. I could continue on about your ice-hard nipples and wet pussy, but for now I plan to learn what you did or didn't do that has you reacting this way."

I tilted my head from side to side, giving him a view of each ear. "The cubic zirconia earrings are in place."

"Three and a half carats per earring. Common cut with near-perfect clarity. I never settle for imitations."

Holy shit.

I looked down and lifted the platinum chain. "The necklace is in place. You can see the sandals and the dress."

His arm snaked around my waist, pulling me closer until my breasts collided with his broad chest. "You know what I'm asking. Don't make me spell it out."

With my chin lifted, I stared through veiled lashes, and leaned my hips inward. I was this man's kryptonite. I had no idea why, but it wouldn't stop mc from using it.

A shallow breath escaped me as he roughly pulled me even closer.

Earlier, I'd covered my skin in the rose-scented lotion from the bathroom, yet at this moment, it was his scent that filled my senses. Masculine, clean, and spicy, the aroma surrounded us like a cloud as not only our chests connected, but also once again, his body declared his desire.

"Do you think it's wise to push me?" he asked, his voice growing deeper. The gravelly tone had the same effect as his cologne and erection, twisting my insides.

My response was breathy. "You've said more than once what you want."

"If I lift that pretty red dress, will I find what was in the box for you to wear?"

"There was nothing in the box for me to wear beneath this dress."

The vein in his neck pulsated as his hand lowered from the small of my back to my behind. His fingers splayed, grabbing my ass, yet thankfully, the material was too thick for him to feel the underwear. "Answer my damn question, or I'll find out for myself."

"Your instructions didn't say I couldn't add another item."

Something resembling a growl came from his chest, the vibration coursing through me in a way that made me wish I hadn't added the panties. He lowered his face to my neck as his warm breath skirted my skin. "I, on the other hand..." The breath of each word sent shivers through me. "...am an excellent gambler. I take sure bets, and Araneae, I'd bet you added panties. I'd double down that they're soaked."

"Sterling..."

"Tell me I'm wrong."

I was beyond verbally answering, yet I couldn't lie. My forehead shook against his cheek, the abrasiveness of his beard growth scratching my skin.

Pinching my chin between his finger and thumb, he pulled my eyes to his. "Speak. Don't ever be afraid to speak the truth to me. Lies and half-truths..." His jaw clenched. "...those should be avoided at all costs. The payment will be higher than you can imagine."

I nodded, as best as I could within his hold, curious to ask exactly what he meant, but not confident enough to question.

When his eyes widened, I admitted what I'd done. "The note didn't specifically say not to..." I swallowed. This wasn't speaking the truth. My breasts heaved as I exhaled. "I had panties in my carry-on."

"And?"

"I'm wearing them."

"And?"

I wasn't sure what he wanted.

"My bet," he said. "I doubled down."

"Yes, they're wet."

He hummed, acknowledging my truth, just before his lips found my neck. A moan left my throat, filling the cabin as he peppered kisses upon my sensitive skin. My mind told me to step back and create space. My body disagreed. From the first time we spoke, Sterling had made it clear that sex was going to happen. I knew it would. I'd entered the plane knowing what the future held. Hell, I'd changed my clothes knowing what it meant.

It was going to happen.

Wasn't it better to get it over with?

His grip of my ass brought our bodies even closer as his hard and fierce erection pushed against my tummy. The pressure built as the zipper of his jeans undoubtedly strained. His face bowed as he leaned forward to continue his attack.

Lower and lower along my body his lips explored. They were like a torch to my skin, moving past my collarbone and down to the neckline of the dress. Another gasp escaped when he pulled the material of the dress aside, exposing one breast and then the other. The coolness of the air combined with the warmth of his mouth did things to more than harden my nipples.

"Fuck, they're as perfect as I imagined." He teased one and then the other. "Better than I imagined."

His praise and attention turned my insides from twisted to molten as heat and desire combusted within me. Shamelessly, I ground my hips toward his erection as I pulled his face to my skin. The abrasion of his beard was my undoing as I ground against him.

Surprisingly, there was no embarrassment in baring myself to this man.

After all, I was his, no matter how much my mind protested.

A tweak of his fingers, a lick of his tongue, no matter the weapon, his skill was unmatched in my lifetime. My breasts were unprepared for battle as blood engorged each one and my nipples grew painfully taut. The life-giving liquid was no longer circulating my body, my knees weakened and wobbled until I questioned if they could stand with my unsure footing on the skinny heels. It was as his teeth joined the battle that my knees and legs finally gave out. I found myself fully supported by his arms.

Saving me from falling, Sterling gently lay me back and just as quickly followed me onto the soft carpet of the plane. His dark eyes shone as he devoured me with his gaze. It gave me strength to lift my arms and surrender to desire.

"Reach under your dress and give me what I didn't tell you to wear."

The heat from my core exploded as my entire body filled with need. I didn't know this man. Yet I was considering...

"Araneae." His voice rumbled like low thunder as his thumb trailed my exposed nipples, around and around. "I'm not going to fuck you—you have my word—until you want it. Give me those panties so I can show you how much you want it."

He was right. My body wanted what only he could offer. Somewhere during the kisses and nips my mind had ceased to argue. Or maybe the arguments were drowned out by the sounds of my moans and whimpers. Either way, it was my body that now had the microphone.

"Don't make me repeat myself."

Repeat himself?

My mind was too clouded with his presence to remember his words.

I swallowed my question as I tried to remember. And then I did. He'd told me to remove my panties—what he didn't tell me to wear. Keeping my eyes on his, I did as he said. Slowly I moved my hands under the skirt of the dress until my fingers were latched over the waistband. Lifting my ass, I began to pull them along my legs.

His gaze continued to darken as he slowly shook his head. He seemed to be fighting two thoughts—either amazed that I'd defied him or surprised that I was now obeying.

Once my panties reached my knees, Sterling placed his large hands over mine and directed their movement. By the time they reached my ankles I stopped, lying back and allowing him to take them the rest of the way over the tall heels.

"Fuck," he growled, more than spoke.

I peered upward as he lifted the red lace thong. It wasn't my usual undergarment. It had been a gift that Louisa bought as a joke a while ago. I rarely wore it or its matching bra, so it made sense to have it as my emergency backup.

"This weekend is to learn the rules," Sterling said. "One to remember is to do as you're told the first time. It's a good way to avoid punishment." He lifted them to his nose and inhaled. "Though I do enjoy your sexy scent."

"I-I..." I said, lifting up to my elbows and considering what he'd just said. "You didn't say—"

"And now I'll have it with me." He stood, pushing the panties into the pocket of his jeans and offering me his hand. "Come with me, Araneae."

Pulling my legs back, I held tightly to his hand as he lifted me from the floor. Once I stood, I reached for the material of the dress to cover my breasts.

Sterling shook his head. "No."

"What?"

Instead of answering, he led me from the main cabin toward the bedroom. My steps stuttered with each attempt until they were no longer moving but secured in place. Sterling turned back my direction. "Keep walking, Araneae. I gave you my word, and based on how wet the lace in my pocket is, I'd say you want it."

"I didn't say..."

"I can fuck you out here and everyone will hear it, or you can keep walking."

"But you said—"

He didn't let me finish. "No one is that fucking soaked who doesn't want it."

I straightened my neck. "I will walk, but I haven't said yes." As we passed the threshold to the bedroom, Sterling stopped and tilted his head toward the bed.

"Bend over the bed."

I looked from him to the bed.

Bend over? What the fuck was he going to do?

It was as he reached for the buckle of his belt that panic

replaced my curiosity. "Sterling, you never said *only*. The note didn't say anything about adding clothes."

In the silence of the room, he again tilted his head toward the bed.

He wasn't going to fuck me. He was going to punish me.

ARANEAE

The tightness in my core moved. No longer sure of my wiles—no longer sure of anything—I debated my options. I was alone in this flying mansion with a man nearly twice my size. I'd dressed in the outfit he'd prepared. I'd removed my panties when he'd demanded.

What could I do now? Scream? Would Patrick come to my rescue?

In another situation, most likely. Involving Sterling, never.

Reaching for my hand, Sterling tugged me forward. Then, with his hands on my shoulders, he spun me toward the bed.

I craned my neck his direction, refusing to let him off without a fight—at least a verbal one. "You're an asshole if you think this is acceptable. I'm not a child to be disciplined. Grown-ups talk."

The vein in his forehead became visible as he leaned closer. "Grown-ups also fuck. Which one will it be?"

"Fuck you," I replied as I leaned forward, my exposed breasts flattening against the soft cover of the mattress.

Without speaking, he splayed his large hand on the small of my back, causing it to arch and raise my ass higher as my toes stretched.

I'd wondered earlier why his bed was so high. Now I had my answer.

"Put your hands behind your back."

"Fuck yourself."

His hand pressed harder into the small of my back as his other one grabbed my hair, turning my face toward his. Each word was separate and distinct as his features contorted. "Keep up your demands, Ms. McCrie. You will regret every fucking one." Releasing my hair, he lifted the skirt to the dress and exposed my ass. Cool air found my core. "Do. You. Believe. Me. Now?"

The rage within him should make him ugly. Maybe the rage did. However, it was his obvious restraint that didn't. This chiseled mountain of a man was on the verge of losing control. Like barbed wire, the reality poked from all directions. I should be terrified.

Yet I wasn't.

He wasn't over the edge, and he wouldn't go there. Somehow, I knew that.

His internal tug of war was real, yet restraint was winning. That observation kept me grounded.

There was no doubt that I was attracted to Sterling's power from the first time I saw him. That dominance radiated about him like a shimmering force of energy. For most of my adult life I'd fantasized about a man like him, one willing to push me to explore my boundaries and submit. I'd never found that in a man—until now. And now that I had, reality was different.

For me to give up control, I had to trust the person to whom I was giving it. As my cheek lay against the soft cover, I wasn't sure if I trusted him.

Did I have a choice?

"Araneae."

My name came as both a reminder and warning. My mind searched for what he wanted. And then I remembered. My hands.

"Asshole," I muttered as I did as he requested. As soon as I did, the strong leather of his belt wound around my wrists and forearms, securing my hands until my shoulders bowed. "Sterling, please..."

His large hand ran over the skin of my ass, each time moving lower.

"Sterling," I called, my voice regaining its own strength, "do it. Punish me. I added the panties."

He leaned down, our eyes meeting. "What did you say?"

"I said punish me. You said your word is true. You gave me your word that my choice was that or fucking. I'll take the punishment."

Without a word, he stood and the next thing I knew the belt around my lower arms disappeared. However, as I started to move, his hand came down again on my back. "I didn't tell you to move."

There was finality in his voice that quelled my growing sense of rebellion. With my hands now free, I balled the soft cover as I closed my eyes and waited. It wasn't his belt, but his hand that came down upon my exposed ass.

Pain exploded through me, starting on my ass and setting off a chain reaction.

I buried my face in the cover as tears pricked my eyes.

Another spank and then another as I swallowed my tears.

His large hand ran over my sore skin in a comforting way that while intensifying the pain, did something else. Each pass moved lower and lower until he was alternating pain with pleasure.

Holy fuck!

I wanted to hate everything there was about this man. I had every reason, yet with each dip of his fingers my body lit up, not a candle flickering in the wind, but like fireworks on the Fourth of July. It wasn't until his touch finally penetrated my entrance that I called out his name. "Sterling!"

His rhythm was contagious as the rest of the world disappeared. The only thing that mattered was his next move. A slap to my ass and then his touch, sometimes to my tender skin, other times more intimate. I couldn't predict no matter how hard I tried.

Mini detonations exploded like sparks in a forest awaiting a raging fire. The world around us disappeared as my entire body reacted. I wasn't thinking about what was right or what was wrong. The reason I was with him no longer registered. I was consumed as Sterling stirred my senses, lifting me higher and higher toward the greatest orgasm of my life.

The sound of his zipper was barely noticed as my body hummed. Part of my mind reminded me that I'd made my decision—I'd chosen the punishment. Yet I knew I'd done that for one reason. I'd chosen punishment as a way to deny him sex. As I strained on my toes and held tightly to the cover, I no longer wanted to deny him. The desire within me was too strong. Having him inside me would certainly send me over the edge. Though I could protest, say that I'd chosen the punishment, at that moment, I wanted him more than I wanted to be right. I wanted him inside me. I wanted to explode.

I waited as the anticipation built.

No longer fearful, I was on the brink of a devastating explosion, and the expectation was as erotic as what the future held.

The cabin filled with Sterling's breathing, labored and heavy. It took my endorphin-filled brain a moment or two to process. It was as his breathing came with a rumbling moan that I realized what was happening.

Letting go of the covers, I did what he'd told me not to do. I moved and rolled to my back.

Anger and jealousy washed away my desire, anger that he was finding pleasure and jealousy that it wasn't with me. Looking at me with the darkest stare was the man I'd have willingly accepted inside me. Yet that wasn't what was happening.

I pulled my gaze away from his and moved it lower. His shirt had ridden up, exposing defined abs. It was lower yet where I couldn't look away. Below his open jeans revealing his trim waist where a trail of dark hair led to...his large hand moving rhythmically along his hardened shaft. Big and thick, the head glistened with the beginning of what was to come.

My tongue darted to my lips as I gaped, mesmerized by the sight. I'd never before watched a man pleasure himself. It was beautiful in more ways than I could have imagined.

I wanted to reach out, to help him, but the vision was too perfect, and yet my body cried out to come. I'd been so close. All at once, it happened. Stream after stream spurted toward me. The flames of desire that had been burning within me were doused. Now rage rose from the ashes of desire.

His cum coated my exposed breasts and onto the front of my dress.

The scent of musk filled the room as I jumped from the bed, my high heels landing on the floor as I sent lasers from my own dark eyes. "What the actual fuck?"

His posture straightened as he finished and casually worked to confine his still-large cock back into his jeans.

His sneer was directed at me. "Good girls get to come. You asked for a punishment, there it was. You got it."

"What about the damn dress?" I asked, reaching for the blanket and wiping the silky liquid from my skin. I could clean my breasts and chest. I could move the dress into place and cover my breasts, but that wouldn't hide the deep red stain as the luxurious fabric absorbed his seed.

He shrugged. "As I recall, you decide what you wear and when. Wasn't that what you said? It's up to you, but once again, you might consider changing into something more comfortable." He tilted his head and scrunched his nose. "Something...cleaner."

Slapping my hands against my hips I looked from the dress to him. "You're a fucking asshole, you know that? If this weekend is about getting to know you, I think I've learned enough already."

The tips of his lips curled upward. "Araneae, you were the one who told me to fuck myself. You also told me you chose punishment over fucking. The person it seems you should be angry with is the one who gave those orders. Maybe next time you'll let me be the one to decide. You see, my plan had been to watch you come."

As I began to respond, loud recurring pounding upon the bedroom door diverted our attention.

"I said we weren't to be disturbed," Sterling called.

"Sir, unless there's an emergency."

The response got the attention of both of us.

Patrick continued, "Mr. Sparrow, you haven't answered our text messages." His voice held more than a hint of urgency. "There's a situation. It needs your immediate attention."

Sterling reached for his phone. As soon as the screen came to life, his countenance changed. From the beautiful man I'd watched come or even the smug asshole who'd demonstrated just how far he'd go to prove his point, he morphed into someone different. The man before me now was a granite statue like the man in the parking lot, one who currently radiated both power and rage.

"Sterling, what is it?"

He didn't answer, taking two long strides toward the door. Just before opening it, he turned my way, his stone expression still sculpted and unmoving. "Grab that blanket and cover your dress. I'll have Patrick bring you more clothes."

I momentarily looked down. I'd moved the dress to cover my breasts. The only thing about my appearance that was unacceptable was his doing. *Fuck him.* I wasn't going to pretend that we were in here playing poker.

When I didn't move, he shook his head and reached for the doorknob.

Patrick's eyes opened wide, going from Sterling to me. Ignoring the ten-ton elephant in the room, he asked, "Sir, did you see the messages?"

"I need more details."

As they started to walk away, I called out, "Patrick."

Turning, his eyes stayed steadfast on mine, not on the dress. "Ma'am."

"I need my suitcases in here as soon as possible."

Patrick's gaze moved from me to Sterling.

"Whatever she says," Sterling said, "listen to her."

My hands went to my hips. "Then after you get my suitcases, tell Marianne to turn this plane around. I want to go home to Boulder."

"Anything except that," Sterling replied to Patrick, before turning my way and adding, "One day you'll learn to refrain from making uninformed demands. Obviously, today's lesson wasn't enough." With that he turned, and with his long strides, disappeared from view.

With a quick nod, Patrick followed one pace behind his boss.

Fuck them both!

STERLING

"*S*ir, I apologize you didn't know sooner. We tried numerous times to reach you," Patrick said.

"I was...occupied."

Was that an acceptable excuse?

No.

Araneae McCrie had been in my presence for only a few hours and already she was diverting my attention and messing with my head. The last few hours flashed before my eyes in less than a second. Everything about her set my soul ablaze, from her apprehension when she boarded the plane to the defiance burning in her eyes when she refused to cover the dress.

Apprehension was expected, but what woman would refuse to cover a cum-stained dress?

The answer ignited my skin and brought my half-mast cock back to life.

The kind of woman who was stubborn, outspoken, and

proud. A kick-ass woman who refused to be anything less than the person she'd been born to be, even if she didn't know what that meant. Araneae's regal attitude radiated about her as if she'd been raised to understand her place in this world, which she hadn't. Whether working at Sinful Threads, protecting her friends, or standing in a stained dress, she fascinated and intrigued me like no other woman.

My head shook as I recalled her making demands —of *me*.

No one did that. No one told me what to do. My father had tried.

The thought of him prompted me to glance down at the ring on my right hand, the one with the family crest. The difference was that with my father I strived to possess what he flaunted. With Araneae, my desire was for her to share it.

Nevertheless, I needed to stay focused—and not on her.

My goal—her—was accomplished.

I had her. It was time to think about business. I hadn't gotten to my status in this world by letting anyone or anything distract me. I needed to push her out of my brain, if only until the current emergency was handled.

Out of my brain was difficult—out of my re-hardening dick was impossible. Just the thought of her bent over that bed...the light-blonde trimmed hair near her core. I was glad she wasn't bare. Some men liked that, but not me. It was like fucking a child. No, Araneae was not a child. She was all woman, an intelligent, determined, beautiful one at that.

It took every ounce of self-discipline for me not to take her when she was there, bared to me. I wanted her more than I'd wanted any woman—ever. Her pussy was wet, so damn tight, and quivering. She was on the edge. We both knew it.

Araneae wasn't the only one. I was there, too, hard as steel and ready to blow.

One pinch of her swollen clit and she would have begged to have me inside her.

I would have rather come in her tight pussy than over her tits and dress. A small smile tugged at my lips. I'd marked her —made her mine. It may be animalistic. That didn't mean it wasn't true. She could use whatever she wanted: shower, lotions, or perfume. None of it mattered because the moment I showered her in my cum, I'd secured what had been promised to me almost two decades before. I'd claimed what was mine.

As that slide show of memories replayed, I knew she was going to be a handful. Fuck yes. Each tit fit perfectly in my hand. Her ass was made to cup and hold. With each step it was clear; I was up for the challenge.

Gritting my teeth, I stormed through the cabin of the plane. Everything that happened in that bedroom was her doing. She wanted it. Araneae made her decision to avoid fucking. No matter how much punishment it was on both of us, she'd gotten what she'd requested. Eventually she would learn to be definite and certain before making demands—of me or anyone else.

Regaining her name as well as being my wife will give her more power than she'd ever dreamt of having. That kind of authority required self-discipline.

While the emergency was serious and required my input, I was thankful that Patrick interrupted us when he did. As accurate as my thoughts were in trying to teach Araneae a lesson, my restraint when it came to her was about gone.

Her scent lingered as I ran my hand through my hair, a

million questions coming to mind. My feet continued determinedly until I reached the round table near the cockpit of
the plane. I hit the button on the table as a computer screen
rose before me, and a small panel opened to a keyboard
and mouse.

My fingers began typing as my lips simultaneously
demanded answers. "This wasn't the flight we had originally
booked?"

"No, sir. It's the one that Ms. Hawkins was changed to
this evening."

"Tell me that Reid is on this." Reid was still in Chicago, on
one floor of my apartment that was devoted to the Sparrow
outfit. He had every resource at his disposal.

"He is," Patrick said, taking the seat to my right and acti-
vating his computer.

"How many people on the flight?"

"One hundred and thirty-seven seats plus crew. The mani-
fest hasn't been released to know if the plane was full." Before
I could comment, Patrick continued, "Reid is looking into it.
You know he'll get it."

I did. He was the best. "What happened?"

"The official statement is that the crash is still under
investigation. Some sources are speculating birds. The aircraft
was flying lower than normal to avoid a building weather
system. However, at that stage of the flight, their altitude
should have been too high for a bird encounter. Those usually
occur at takeoff or landing. The airline isn't willing to claim
aircraft or technical malfunction or even pilot error without a
thorough investigation."

My chest tightened at the thought of the emergency

landing that jeopardized over a hundred lives. "The pilot saved them."

"Like the miracle on the Hudson. He and his copilot landed in a cornfield in north-central Iowa. Thankfully the area was unpopulated and open. The closest town has a population of less than a thousand people at last census.

"The crew evacuated the plane immediately. Moments after the captain disembarked, the plane exploded. The wreckage is still burning and too hot to get near. It will take the NTSB years to sift through the debris."

"I want a complete list of passengers, the ones who were scheduled and missed their flight, those on the flight, and whose luggage was on board. I want to know if the flight was transporting anything else—packages, mail, commerce. Anything." A thought punched me in the gut. "No casualties?"

"Not yet. There were a few injuries with the landing and evacuation. They're being transported to hospitals. Des Moines is a thirty-minute drive. It's taken some time to get enough ambulances to the crash site."

"I want the names of every passenger who is injured and a detailed description of the injuries. What about...our decoy?"

"She's safe. I received a coded message as soon as she was released. She made a statement to the authorities and refused medical attention. I hadn't gone to the trouble of assuring similar blood type, just that she visually appeared to be Ms. Hawkins."

"Whatever she earned, double it. Be sure she keeps quiet."

"She's a professional and would like to work for you again. She won't say a word. Her decision to refuse treatment was the best option and demonstrated her ability to think on her feet. Their likeness is truly remarkable. It's my opinion that she could be useful in the future."

The screen before me came to life with live reports from outside Maxwell, Iowa. The chaotic scene flashed with a multitude of lights from the sirens of police and ambulance vehicles as, in the background, the wreckage of the 737 continued to burn. The reporter was speaking about the topography of the land. While known for its open fields, this area of Iowa also had a large portion of uninterrupted forest.

While most reports were hailing the pilot a hero, some speculated about human error. I leaned back against the large leather seat and listened. Finally, I said, "I think we both know that the pilot isn't responsible. We need to confirm who is."

"Unless the pilot works for McFadden or is connected in some way."

My gut twisted at Patrick's words. I was off my game, not thinking about every possibility. He was right. It was too early to make assumptions. "Learn everything you can about this man and his copilot, too. I want to know about every invest-ment, every cent they have, their properties, their debts, and their fucking children's debts. I want to know if their spouses like to shop, play the ponies, or go to casinos. I want to know if there's any connection to anything that sends up red flags: dark web, porn sites...anything. I want to know the last time each of them took a drink and when they last took a shit. I want everything."

Patrick didn't answer verbally; however, the way his fingers flew over his keyboard told me that my orders were being communicated through our secure network to Reid and his team. I'd have answers soon.

Both Patrick's and my screen dinged with the announcement of an incoming message.

My eyes grew wide at the new newscast Reid had sent our way. It was the crawl at the bottom of the screen: *Two confirmed dead in four-apartment blaze, Boulder, Colorado.*

The table creaked as my fist landed hard upon its surface. "That's her building, where she lived up until today. This is war. Full-out fucking war."

Patrick's expression was one I'd seen before, one I'd seen as bullets flew and IEDs detonated around us, as men and women we knew were sacrificed for a cause we were told to believe in. The Sparrow name wasn't a cause we had to be told to believe in. Sparrow and all it meant was how we were here, flying in this plane, communicating on networks that exceeded the technology used by our own government.

Word had gotten out that McCrie was found. The implications were widely speculated, and it appeared that there were powers willing to do anything to stop her.

"Do you think you should tell her?" Patrick asked.

"She's not ready to know it all."

He shook his head. "About the fire. The two people were her neighbors. I'll find out their names. Our research showed that she was friendly with an elderly woman who lived below her." His fingers continued to type. "Powell...Jeanne Powell."

"Is she one of the casualties?"

"Reid is looking into it. There's that whole not releasing information until next of kin are notified. That won't stop him, though. He'll find out."

I let out a long sigh. "She may think she does, but Araneae McCrie doesn't have any friends. Kennedy Hawkins may have, but that life is over. She isn't ready to know that either."

"One thing at a time," Patrick said. "Should you tell her about the apartment?"

I hated the idea of telling Araneae that her home for the last few years was gone. I hadn't wanted her to pack the things she had. I'd wanted her to rely solely on me. Fuck, I could buy her anything her heart desired.

The ring on my hand grew heavy as I stared for a moment at the crest. It was the same ring that bruised my cheek as a child, the one that glistened as my father conducted back-room meetings and ordered unimaginable atrocities. It was the same one that was visible from the podium as Allister Sparrow announced his candidacy for mayor.

It was the one I was wearing when the police informed me that my father was dead.

My neck straightened.

No. I was glad Araneae disobeyed me and packed anything and everything that meant something to her. Mementos gave us roots. Hers had been severed by the cutting edge of more secrets than she was ready to face. She deserved to keep what she could of a time when her life seemed...normal.

Because that time was gone forever.

"Find out everything," I said. "I'd suspect that soon her phone will receive a message from someone telling her what happened, not about the plane—there's no way they'll know that was connected to her—but about her apartment building. When that happens, I want to be able to fill in the blanks."

Patrick's gaze met mine. "Do you still plan to make her public?"

"He needs to know I have her and she's under Sparrow protection."

"It's a risk."

"No. My men and women won't let me down. Call your informant in Boulder—the woman. Find out what happened at the apartment. We both know that fire is used as a cover-up. Find out who was on the premises prior and how the fire started. My guess is that someone was looking for her or for something else." Another thought occurred to me. "And double the protection on Jason, Louisa, Winifred, and the Nelsons."

"Even the girl in Boston, the sister?"

"All of them. They're not dying on our watch unless we learn they need to."

ARANEAE

*C*lean and showered for the third time in twenty-four hours, wearing ripped jeans and a light sweater from my suitcase as well as a comfortable pair of ankle boots, I was ready to get out of the flying mansion. I hadn't rewashed my hair, but the style from before was gone, transformed to a low braid and my makeup was minimal. Mr. Sparrow's diamonds and necklace were back in their box.

A knock came on the bedroom door. "Ms. Hawkins?"

When I opened the door, I found Jana. We were about to land, and I needed to take a seat with a seat belt. As I entered the cabin area, voices seeped from the round-table area; however, with the partitions shut, the meaning of their words was muffled and undistinguishable. Though the content was out of my reach, the tone wasn't. Whatever caused Patrick to interrupt Sterling and me earlier was resulting in heated discussion.

"Will Ster—Mr. Sparrow be joining me?" I asked Jana.

"I believe he and Patrick will complete the flight where they are. They've asked not to be disturbed."

I recalled Sterling making the same request earlier regarding the two of us.

The idea that I wanted him with me as we landed was preposterous. After what had happened and what he'd done, my thoughts were all over the place.

I hated him but was attracted to him. I loathed his arrogant attitude and superior declarations yet yearned for his powerful and dominant ways. My feelings and misgivings weren't restricted to him; I also despised myself. I was angry for allowing the intimacy we'd shared, yet my body craved more of his touch.

I didn't know him, and yet I'd allowed it—and more than that, I'd wanted more.

The image of him stroking himself replayed constantly in my mind. It was playing behind my eyes as I held tightly to the bar in the shower with one hand, while using my other to take matters he'd left unfinished to completion. I was certain it wasn't as earthshaking as Sterling could make it; nevertheless, by the time I stepped under the hot water and the vision of him finding satisfaction came to mind, I was without options.

Each replay of that scene made it more difficult to despise the man or even the action. After all, I'd drawn the line in the sand by declaring punishment over sex.

Was it fair to be angry that he'd listened?

Was it even possible to harbor rage when he was so fucking beautiful, his handsome face so full of emotion as his large hand moved over the tight skin, and his cock glistened as angry veins came to life?

Stop it, Kennedy, I said to myself—most likely inaudibly. I couldn't be sure of anything.

This man was danger personified. There was obviously more than real estate to his wealth and power. What had he said? Only the information he wanted to be found was visible on the internet.

His claims to own me—or have me—were ridiculous. He'd threatened everything and everyone whom I loved. It wasn't unacceptable to find him attractive. There wasn't a woman alive who wouldn't. Nevertheless, finding him attractive and willfully submitting to him were two different things. First and foremost, I couldn't submit to his arousing control without trust, and so far, he'd given me no reason to believe that he can be trusted.

Or had he?

Was what happened in the bedroom more accurately a reason to trust him?

He did as I demanded.

The questions and answers and internal dialogues hadn't stopped since I stepped into the shower. As much as my feelings were scattered, it all came back to one thing: Sparrow was the name my mom had warned me about.

The plane pitched and stilled, giving that uneasy sensation of an aircraft slowing in midair. Whether flying in this crazy pimped-out private plane or commercial, it always felt as if the engines were stopping when in descent. Gripping the arms of the seat, I hoped that wasn't the case.

Like each time before, the plane didn't fall. It continued its descent.

Beyond the windows, blue lights illuminated the otherwise

vast blackness. Wherever we were landing was remote. Other than the runway lights, no other light pollution existed.

Once we were on the ground and stilled, Jana again joined me, minus her customary smile. "The helicopter is ready for you, Mr. Sparrow, and Patrick. Keaton, Marianne, and I will follow with the luggage."

I swallowed as I looked at her, expecting her to say she was punking me, this was a joke, a bad dream, or perhaps fill the cabin with laughter. I wanted her to say that she was mistaken; I wasn't really getting into a helicopter in the middle of a pitch-black night. When she didn't respond, I did. "A helicopter? Are all of you going to the cabin too?"

"Yes, ma'am."

Many questions came to mind, such as why? Don't you have a life? Can one man really change the plans of six on a whim?

Just as quickly, the answers came to mind.

Jana's lackluster expression meant that she did have a life and plans, as did possibly others on this flight. None of that mattered. The most crucial answer was to my final question: yes, one man could change everything, especially if that man were Sterling Sparrow.

"Are you flying in a helicopter?" I asked.

"No, there will be a vehicle. Your trip will be quicker. The drive is at least another hour. The cabin staff has been notified of our arrival and scrambled to prepare, but we're needed to bring a few more supplies."

"I can ride with you," I said excitedly.

She shook her head. "No, ma'am, Mr. Sparrow's directions aren't negotiable."

"I've never been in a helicopter," I admitted, my anxiety audible.

Her customary smile returned as she tilted her head sympathetically. "Mr. Sparrow would never risk his or Patrick's safety. I have every reason to believe that sentiment extends to you also. I assure you, the helicopter is the quickest and safest mode of transportation. Perhaps we'll return to the plane in the daylight and you'll see the beautiful yet dangerous terrain. The roads are...interesting."

"Would you rather fly?" I asked, sensing her unease.

"Ma'am, that isn't for me to say."

"Can the helicopter accommodate one more passenger?"

"It depends on the one they sent."

Holy crap, he has multiple helicopters, too.

"But," she went on, "I would presume that it could."

Sterling's words came back to me from when I'd asked Patrick for my suitcases. *Whatever she says, listen to her.* I reached out and took ahold of Jana's hand. "I'd like you to come with me. You've been so reassuring. I think it would be nice to have another woman along."

"Ma'am, as I said—"

"Kenni—Araneae." I corrected, using the uncommon name. "Please call me Araneae." I pronounced it as Sterling had many, many times—*uh-rain-ā*. "And I'll inform Mr. Sparrow."

"I-I don't want to seem insubordinate..."

Her words trailed away.

"On the contrary, you'll be helping me out. Since the luggage is coming to the cabin later, let's go throw some things in my carry-on for the rest of the night, and then

Keaton can deal with the rest." I turned to Jana. "Do you have a bag...personal things to stay?"

"Yes, ma'am..." She smiled. "I mean Araneae. It's customary. We're never certain of Mr. Sparrow's plans."

I narrowed my gaze. "Why do you do it? Why put up with him?"

She didn't hesitate. "Because I could never thank him enough for what he's done. A day or two of unexpected travel is a small price."

I wanted to ask what he'd done, what warranted that type of loyalty, but time was of the essence. The door was opening, and soon I'd be expected in a helicopter—in a fucking helicopter.

"Are you sure about my traveling with you?" she asked.

Unbuckling my seat belt, I stood. "I am."

Okay, Mr. Sterling Sparrow, let's see if you meant what you said.

When Jana and I arrived at the bottom of the stairs onto the tarmac—or what was supposed to be a tarmac—Patrick was waiting. Beyond our bubble, the degrees of darkness varied. In the starlit sky, I made out tall trees and looming hills or were they mountains?

It seemed obvious that Marianne was experienced with the remote location. It still begged the question, where in Canada were we?

"Ma'am," Patrick said, "I'll take your bag. Jana, thank you. We will see you and the rest of the crew later at the cabin."

"She's coming with us," I declared.

"Mr. Sparrow said—"

I laid my hand on his arm and smiled. "To listen to me. I said she's coming with us."

The obvious rebuttal was on his lips, yet instead of voicing it, he simply said, "Yes, ma'am." And turned to her. "Jana, you'll sit in the second row with Ms. Hawkins. I'll take the third."

"Mr. Sparrow?" I asked, my voice raised as we walked closer to the helicopter and the roar of the spinning blades and rudders grew louder.

"He'll be next to the pilot," Patrick replied louder than before.

Of course, he would.

That was probably where he was during the beginning of the flight, copiloting the plane. What could Mr. Sterling Sparrow not do?

Control me was the answer that immediately brought a small smile to my nervous lips.

If I'd thought I could speak to Sterling at any point during this transition, I'd been mistaken. Though he delivered a pointed look to Patrick about the inclusion of Jana, not another word was spoken as his granite features remained in place and we boarded the vessel.

The only change in the plans I'd been given came with our seating assignment. Per what I assumed were Sterling's instructions, Patrick took the copilot's position, Jana sat in the third row and Sterling sat seat-belted beside me. Up until that moment it was his only acknowledgment of my presence.

In his defense, it wasn't as if I could question him or him me. Our ears were covered by large earphones connected to microphones that broadcast our conversation to everyone in the helicopter.

Prior to liftoff, there was an ongoing discussion between the pilot, Sterling, and Patrick about longitude, latitude, and wind shear. I didn't understand what they were saying, and as the conversation became more specific, I was certain I didn't want to. Instead, my instinct was to turn to Jana and ask again if she was certain this was safer than the roads.

If her answer was yes, I wanted to know where the hell we were.

The only illumination within the helicopter came from the control panel, giving everyone an eerie green cast. As the pilot began to lift the giant machine off the ground, my circulation rushed to my feet. For the second time in a day, my stomach lurched, threatening to rebel. Quickly, I closed my eyes and fighting the seat belt, lowered my head to my lap, certain that this aircraft wasn't equipped with a luxurious bathroom.

One deep breath in. One deep breath out.

I concentrated on repeating the process until a large hand came to my leg, searching for my hand tucked defensively on my lap.

Finding it, Sterling gave my hand a gentle squeeze. "I never thought to ask." His voice came through the earphones. "Have you ridden in a helicopter before?"

I turned my face toward him. Even in the green cast, I saw that his expression was different than when he'd been dealing with others. There was something resembling concern or dare I say, compassion. Swallowing the acid bubbling from my stomach, I shook my head.

"I actually prefer it to airplanes," he said, his tone casual, like we weren't leaving the earth in a tin can with propellers. "Once you get used to it, there's less turbulence. And in the daylight, the view is beyond compare."

I turned back to the floor, my chest still against my thighs and repeated the breathing.

Letting go of my hand, he gently stroked my hair as the helicopter rose higher and higher. With each passing minute, I calmed. He was right. Maybe it was the smaller size that gave the illusion of floating or the white noise of the whirling blades. I wasn't sure, but finally I sat up.

The sky was alive with stars as beautiful as in the mountains of Colorado. The moon was barely a sliver of light, its near absence part of the reason for the intense darkness.

"Are you feeling better?" he asked.

"I think I'll make it without getting sick."

His deep chuckle came through the wireless earphones as he again reached for my hand.

This time I reached back, allowing our fingers to intertwine. The connection was reassuring, giving me warmth throughout and calming my earlier rapid pulse as we floated through the night air.

"How much longer?" I asked, to no one in particular.

"About twenty minutes," Sterling answered.

I'd heard the pilot's voice before we'd lifted off and I knew Patrick's, yet none of that mattered. In the short time I'd known him, I was becoming accustomed to Sterling's deep tenor. I would recognize it anywhere.

"How can he tell where we're going?" I asked.

Again Sterling chuckled as Patrick turned my way and smiled.

"Matt," Sterling said, presumptuously speaking to the pilot, "why don't you distract my fiancée with the particulars of VFR? I'm certain she'll find it fascinating."

As the pilot began speaking about visual flight rules, lighting conditions, and infrared sensors, all I heard was Sterling's qualifier when identifying me.

Fiancée.

Before I could submit to the overwhelming rush of uncertainty and lower my head again, he squeezed my hand. When I looked his way, he ever so slightly shook his head no.

My eyes widened, searching for understanding in this silent conversation we were now having.

His lips moved, yet he wasn't speaking. There was no sound besides the pilot's voice coming through the earphones. Whatever Sterling was saying, this message was just for me.

"Follow my lead."

I mouthed the words back to him, replacing *my* with *your,* and he nodded. It wasn't simply the nod, but the way that even in the green hue, the usual darkness dimmed in his gaze as his lips curled ever slightly upward. I was beginning to realize that this change of expression was a rarity, a peek into a man who others rarely saw. I wasn't sure why he would share it with me, but that belief that he was gave me the strength to do as he'd asked...and follow his lead.

"...the cloud ceiling is more dangerous than darkness. Flying in dense clouds should be avoided at all costs. Darkness is simply the absence of..." the pilot continued speaking, dominating everyone else's attention and keeping what was happening between Sterling and me private.

I looked up again as Sterling gave my hand another squeeze.

"We need to talk."

I didn't need to repeat what his lips mouthed. He was right. We needed to talk—about so many things.

I nodded.

ARANEAE

I didn't know what to expect or even exactly where we were. With a man who had a flying mansion and apparently his choice of helicopters, what could one possibly expect when he said he was taking you to his cabin?

At the first mention, my mind's eye saw a one-room log-house structure, similar to Ma and Pa's from the children's books about growing up on a prairie. However, with the evidence I'd experienced thus far, I doubted it was that simplistic. Upon learning that not only Patrick, but Jana, Marianne, and Keaton would join us and the staff had been notified, it made sense that the cabin was bigger than one room.

Just before the helicopter began to lower, a conversation began between Sterling and Patrick. Though I wasn't paying attention, I became acutely aware when my earphones went silent. I glanced back at Jana with my hands over my ears. As our eyes met, she shrugged. Perhaps she was accustomed to being left out of things. I wasn't.

It wasn't as if I could complain. With the sound went the ability to give audible feedback.

The helicopter continued downward in the black sky, hovering above an open expanse of ground. In the distance on one side appeared tall trees while in the other direction was darkness that seemingly went on forever. Only the glistening of stars differentiated the earth from the sky. As the helicopter's spotlight highlighted our destination, the area surrounding our landing pad was briefly illuminated. A yellow glow spilled from the windows of the cabin, as Sterling had called it. Though it had the rustic log exterior walls, it wasn't a single room or even a single story. If his plane were a flying mansion, his cabin was a wooden castle.

From the air, the building appeared to expand a great distance in each direction in what could best be described as U-shaped. The helicopter pilot set us down within and yet outside of the top of the U.

As the blades beneath the helicopter settled upon the earth, Sterling turned my direction. With a click of a switch, I once again had sound. "Always wait for the propellers to stop completely. They're high when they're spinning, as when we boarded, but as they slow, they sag under their own weight."

It didn't seem like advice that needed to be questioned.

During the time it took for the blades to stop, three people I didn't recognize came into view in the distance near the *cabin*.

No longer did I need to question the time of day. When I'd redressed in the jeans and light sweater, I'd added my fitness watch that now told me that it was after midnight—at least in Chicago. I'd changed it to central time when I put it on. Now, I wasn't certain of the time zone. Nevertheless, these people were awaiting Sterling's arrival. I couldn't decide if I were impressed or disgusted.

The night air chilled through my sweater as the doors of the helicopter opened, reminding me that we weren't in Chicago as I'd been promised. After helping me from the helicopter, Sterling held tight to my hand as we walked down the dew-covered grassy slope from the landing pad to what I'd decided, based on the outdoor furniture and fireplace, was the back of the cabin.

I wanted to ask about our talk. I wanted to do a lot of things, but as everyone from the helicopter congregated around us, there was something about his expression that didn't invite conversation. Whatever he wanted to discuss—and honestly, what I wanted to discuss—would be better done in private.

"Mr. Sterling," the spokesperson of the three-person welcoming committee said. "Welcome back."

"Rita, it's late. Could you show Ms. McCrie to her room?"

"Of course."

It was my first indication that my room and his weren't the same. The knowledge came as more of a blow than I anticipated. "Sterling?" I said softly, looking back to him.

His expression remained stoic, yet his dark stare lightened a bit. "We'll talk later."

"Ms. McCrie, if you'll follow me?" Rita said.

There was something about being surrounded by strangers, all of whom knew him, worked for him, and were loyal to him, that stopped me from questioning further.

Before I left the group, I turned to Jana. "Where are you staying?"

She tilted her head to the far wing. "There are plenty of rooms down there." She reached for my hand. "Thank you for letting me fly."

Sterling and Patrick had walked away, yet we had an audience. I returned her smile. "Thank you for flying with me. It wasn't as scary as I anticipated."

Jana scoffed. "It was better than the drive."

"Ms. McCrie."

It took the words a moment to register.

Oh, she meant me.

I followed the older woman across the slate patio to the glass doors surrounded by more windows. The glass panes went all the way up to a tall peak another story high. Warm yellow light that I'd seen upon our landing flooded the interior in a welcoming glow. Once inside, I stood motionless for a moment, in awe of what I assumed was a living room, complete with pine wood paneling and a giant antler chandelier. Rustic chic would probably be the best way to describe the furnishings. Dark leather sofas and heavy wood tables surrounded a huge stone fireplace that like the ceiling was at least two stories high. In front of us and on the next level was a banister walkway connecting the different wings.

"This way," Rita said.

"Oh, my carry-on. It's still in the helicopter." I'd been too overwhelmed to remember.

"It will be brought to your room."

I sighed. This was not the way I was used to living. Even when traveling, I was completely content to wheel my own luggage.

As we progressed, she pointed out the important areas like a professional tour guide. I wondered how many women Sterling had brought here. How many times had she done this same speech?

Was I jealous?

Of course not. Simple curiosity was all.

"The kitchen is stocked with most things you'd want. You're welcome to help yourself, but know we're here to help also."

She went on pointing out the kitchen as I took in the particulars—a stainless steel and hard-surface beauty accented with copper. We continued the tour to a dining area too large for one man, a library that took my breath away—complete tall shelves filled with books and over-stuffed chairs and lounges perfect for reading, and finally Sterling's office. We didn't go inside as the door was shut, and Sterling and Patrick were already within. All of these destinations were located in the wing with the room where I would apparently be staying. Up the stairs we went until I was looking down on the room we'd entered. With the reflection of the interior lights, I questioned what was beyond the windows, farther than I could see in the darkness as we landed.

"I wish I could see the view," I said, stilling at the banister.

"You'll see it after the sun rises. Even after all the years of living here, it takes my breath away. From this elevation, the lake is spectacular where the mountains come together." She resumed walking. "Legend has it that the valley was dry until early pioneers rerouted the rivers. Today the lake has a surface area of over one hundred miles."

"Where are we?"

"Ontario," she replied with a purse of her lips. "Surely you knew that?"

I was reminded of the flight attendant on my trip from Wichita to Boulder. "I did. Sterling...Mr. Sparrow said that. I was hoping for a more specific location."

"We're in northwestern Ontario. I suppose it would be easiest to say north of Minnesota."

I shook my head as I continued to follow her along the hallway, the walls covered with more of the knotty pine, a shade lighter than that on the floor. We passed multiple closed doors as we walked upon long rugs, red in background filled with black bears.

Finally, she came to a stop and opened a door. The spacious bedroom was complete with a four-poster king-sized bed, one that I was pleased to see was a normal height. The decor fit the cabin, rustic with warm shades of red, gold, and brown. Windows lined one wall covered by wooden blinds.

"There is a bathroom right over there," she said, pointing the opposite direction of the windows. "And if you need anything, there is a phone on the bedside stand. It rings to the kitchen or our rooms. We can help you out no matter the time."

"Maybe some water. Other than that, I believe I'm ready to get some sleep."

Rita nodded. "I'll bring you a bottle of water. In the morning let us know when you wake. We'll bring you coffee or tea or whatever you want. You may eat in here or in the dining room. Mr. Sparrow said to let you know that you're free to roam wherever you would like."

"Tell me, Rita, where is there for me to go?"

Her stoic expression cracked as her cheeks rose and eyes

shone. "Ms. McCrie, the cabin is rather isolated, but there are plenty of places to go especially this time of year. If you decide to hike, please let us know. We have bear repellent and a tracker. It's too easy to get lost."

Bear repellent.

I shook my head as my eyes opened wide. "That will be a definite *no* for hiking."

Again she smiled. "Come see me tomorrow. I'll give you a better tour."

"Thank you, Rita."

As soon as she left, I turned a complete circle, taking in my surroundings. Sterling had said I wasn't kidnapped, yet wasn't I?

Stepping to the windows, I peered out into the darkness. I couldn't even point to a map and place my current location. My phone came to mind. Could Google Maps find me? From what I'd been told and could decipher, an additional two and a half hours of flight and a helicopter ride had me on the edge of some legendary lake created by Paul Bunyan.

In the morning I'd learn more. Currently, I was too tired to care.

I made my way to the bathroom. Sterling's wealth was difficult to ignore. The attached bath was bigger than the one in my apartment, complete with a claw-foot soaking tub and glass-block shower that could easily fit me and four of my closest friends. If I hadn't taken two showers in the last five hours—three since I woke—I would have given that tub some serious consideration.

The day had been long and the evening longer. My tired muscles and mind told me that I was ready to go to sleep and take a reprieve from whatever life and Sterling Sparrow could throw at me. However, my carry-on with my nightgown was still missing. It was then that I noticed a thick white chenille robe hanging from an ornate hook in the bathroom.

No matter how many questions I had going through my head or how difficult it was to make sense of what was happening, exhaustion was winning.

Five minutes later, my face washed and teeth brushed— yes, of course the bathroom was well stocked—wearing only my bra and panties under the robe, I stepped back into the bedroom.

"Shit!" I exclaimed as the man in the shadows became visible. "Don't you ever sleep?"

In an armchair in the corner of the room, my carry-on by his side and a bottle of water in his hand, was the king of the house. Complete with his smug expression, he sat in a plush chair, leaning back with his ankle over his knee.

He didn't answer, remaining silent as his dark eyes searched me up and down. Suddenly, the robe no longer felt as though it were soft and thick. From the way his gaze sizzled, I had to look down to be sure it hadn't magically become transparent.

Finally, the silence shattered as his deep tenor asked, "Are you ready to talk?"

ARANEAE

Wrapping the robe tighter, I walked toward him, took the water bottle from his hand, and made my way across the room. After placing the water on the bedside stand, I sat near the end of the bed facing him. "I'm exhausted. Don't you sleep?"

"Occasionally."

"Will you tell me what the fiancée remark was about?"

He lowered his leg and leaned forward, placing his elbows on his knees. "I'll tell you more than that." When I didn't respond, he went on, "Like everything else, it was for your protection."

I tried to ignore how even in the middle of the night, Sterling Sparrow was strikingly handsome. His dark hair was more mussed than usual, reminding me of the times I'd watched him run his fingers through the now-wavy mane. His cheeks had more beard growth than when he'd first appeared on the plane or even the first time I saw him in the parking lot. And with the way he was seated, the defined muscles in his biceps bulged as his large hands balled in fists under his square chin.

It was nearly impossible to not think about what those hands had done to me. Though we'd been together in the plane hours ago, it now seemed like a lifetime. That was how it felt to be near Sterling Sparrow, as if we'd known each other for a lifetime, not simply a week. Yet that wasn't the case. It had been only a week since Patrick tricked me into going to the distribution center. A week since my breath was first stolen at the sight of his dark stare.

Seven days later I was sitting on a bed in his remote cabin, wearing only a robe and underwear; that reality was difficult for my tired brain to fathom.

"Protection from whom?" I asked, attempting to focus on our conversation.

Sterling stood.

I smiled as his fingers again raked his hair. Maybe I was beginning to figure out at least a small bit of this complicated man.

Walking to the windows and back, he began, "I wanted this conversation to wait."

My pulse kicked up a notch at the possibility of what he had to say. I too stood. Now in my bare feet, I was easily eight to ten inches shorter than the man before me. Yet despite his size and power, unlike the first time I met him, I held no fear of him, only of what he could tell me. Tentatively, I moved closer. Laying my hand on his forearm, I repeated my question. "From whom do I need protection?" When he didn't answer, I questioned, "From you?"

His lips quirked. "Most definitely."

I pulled my hand back, shocked at his honesty. "What?"

"Oh, Araneae, it should be obvious by now that not all of my intentions are honorable." He teased the opening of the robe. "With everything in me, I want to open this wrapping." With just one finger he traced from behind my ear to my collarbone and to the valley between my breasts. My skin burned in the wake of his touch, the heat flooding my core as he pushed back the soft chenille robe and exposed the lace of my bra.

My tongue darted to my lips as my breathing deepened. His dark stare wasn't looking at my eyes. Its laser precision was focused on my breasts, almost as if he could see through the material.

"Sterling," I said, bringing his gaze back to mine. "You said talk."

He took one step and another as my feet moved backward in sync, and our stare stayed locked upon the other. My retreat was short-lived as my shoulders collided with the wall. The faintest remnants of cologne mixed with the scent of night air and helicopter fuel lingered around him, creating a masculine concoction. Leaning forward, his arms came to rest on either side of my face. With each second, his gaze darkened. With every ticking of the metaphoric clock, I reconsidered my earlier thought about fearing this man. Sterling had just admitted I needed protection from him. Maybe I did.

"If you had any idea of how long I've waited for you..." His deep voice resonated, echoing off the walls. "Sunshine, you've always belonged to me."

Sunshine?

His lips brushed my forehead. "Your mind is fighting it, but your body knows it's true."

I had to turn this around or there was no going back. My

battle wasn't with the man who had me caged but with myself. I detested his forwardness and proprietorship, and at the same time, those were only two of the qualities that made me want Sterling Sparrow. The list was growing by the minute, and the fog of his presence wasn't helping.

I lifted my hand to his hard chest. "I don't know how long you've waited. That's what you were going to tell me."

His eyes blinked as his Adam's apple bobbed. "You're right. You need to know...about more than that." He stood taller, moving his arms and releasing me from his hold.

"Will you tell me?" I asked.

He took a step back, removing the masculine scent and clearing the space between us. "You tell me first."

"Tell you what?"

"Tell me what you know about your past. It will help if I understand what you've been told."

Walking to the center of the room, I let out a breath and spun. "Fuck, Sterling. You've told me more in the last week then I've known my entire life. I only heard the name Araneae once before you. Once. I'd never heard the name McCrie..." I shrugged. "...I mean, I guess I'd heard it, but not in relation to me. And tonight, Rita is calling me Ms. McCrie." My hands slapped the sides of my robe-covered thighs. "Really...how totally fucked up is that?"

His head bobbed as the cords in his neck pulled tight and jaw clenched. "I'm trying to see this from your perspective, but I'm failing."

"Tell me who besides you I need protection from."

For the first time, I saw the fatigue in his expression that I was feeling.

"My team has been working on learning more, but at this

SECRETS 197

time I'm not prepared to give you a definite answer. All I can tell you is that you have been targeted."

I shook my head. "Targeted for what? Why?"

"You really don't know? Tell me what you do know."

Did I trust Sterling Sparrow with what little I knew?

I'd been willing to trust him with my body—I supposed I had—and seconds ago, I was on the verge of doing it again. Were my secrets more precious?

I'd trusted other men with my body, yet I'd never shared the truth of my childhood with them. Was Sterling different?

"Araneae." His dark stare was as penetrating as it had been in the parking lot.

Sterling Sparrow was different. He knew more than I did. That was why I'd agreed to come with him to Chicago—and for my loved ones. My heart told me that I could have found another way to protect those I held dear. However, in twenty-six years, I'd never been given another opportunity to unlock my secrets.

Swallowing, I sat back at the end of the bed. "Fine. All I remember of my childhood were my parents."

His eyes grew wide. "You remember your parents?"

"My adoptive parents, not biological."

He nodded.

"I can't remember anything or anyone before them. They never lied to me. I don't remember when they told me that I wasn't biologically theirs, but I always accepted it." A memory curled my lips. "They used to say that not everyone could create a baby, but they were blessed to have been given theirs. They called me their gift." Sniffing, I wiped a renegade tear. "They were the only family I ever had.

"When I was sixteen years old, my dad—my adoptive

father—died in an automobile accident. The next few days were a blur until one afternoon my mother told me we were going to go for a drive. I had nothing prepared. I didn't know where we were going—I thought maybe to Dad's grave. We hadn't had a funeral, and I was having a hard time understanding what was happening."

Sterling was back in the chair where I'd found him. The distance gave me strength to keep talking, telling a story that I'd never before spoken aloud. Ever. Not even to Louisa. She, like everyone else, had been told the story of Phillip and Debbie Hawkins. Over the years those fictional parents had taken on Byron and Josey's traits and characteristics. It was easier to tell stories and only change the names. At some point the Hawkinses and the Marshes had become synonymous for my parents.

Ironic, especially when in reality, neither biologically were.

"Where did she take you?" he asked.

"To the airport. I recall that she was driving like a bat out of hell." The decade-old scene replayed in my mind. I crossed my arms over my midsection to ward off the chill that accompanied it. "I was scared. Her behavior was odd—out of character. My mom was one of the most sensible and determined women I'd ever known, and she was swerving in front of semi-trucks, and acting like..." The idea of what I was about to say had never really mattered before. Now it seemed important.

"Like what? I need to know."

"Like we were being followed."

Small lines grew deeper around his dark brown eyes as again he gripped the arms of the chair.

Shaking my head to clear the memory, I moved my hands to my lap and went on. "She handed me my new identity. Just likc that. On a cold afternoon, I suddenly had a new name with all the supporting documentation."

"Until that time you were Araneae?"

I looked down at my hands and back to his gaze. "No. I told you that I only heard that name once before you. I grew up believing my name was Renee, Renee Marsh."

"And when did you hear your real name, other than from me?"

I half laughed because this reality was as they say, stranger than fiction. "I suppose if I hadn't heard it that afternoon from my mom, I wouldn't have believed you when you said it."

"She told you?" he asked. "Your adoptive mother knew who you really were?"

I nodded.

"Did she tell you anything else?"

I looked back at my hands as I wrung one and then the other. Though I didn't look up, nor did I hear him, I knew Sterling had stood. As strange as it sounded, I felt it—a shift in the force surrounding me as he moved closer.

His hand reached out, lifting my chin, changing my view from my lap and hands to him. "Tell me."

"I asked her why I had to go, and she said there were dangerous people after me. It had something to do with my biological father. I never understood exactly, and..." More tears fell from my eyes as I swallowed. "...I never spoke to her again to learn."

"Dangerous people?" His thumb gently wiped the tears from my cheek.

"I asked for a name." The air around us quivered with expectant energy as Sterling waited for me to finish my thoughts, my limited knowledge of what life had dealt me. I met his gaze. "She said Sparrow."

A micro-expression of shock flitted across his features at my confession. Perhaps not shock, but pain. It was as if I'd physically struck him with my words instead of my hand. This time I reached for the large hands before me as I stood. "She said a man named Allister was in charge, but one day it would be his son, Sterling."

"Allister is no longer a concern."

Dropping his hands, I tilted my head. "He's your father, isn't he?"

"He was."

I reached my palm to his abrasive cheek. "Oh, Sterling, I'm sorry. I forgot. I remember reading that now."

"Don't be sorry that he's gone. The world's a better place."

"Still... I know what it's like to lose a parent." I shrugged. "More than one." A question came to mind. "What about your mother?"

"She's in Chicago. Didn't she come up in your research?"

The question sent a tingling sensation to my ass, remembering that he had told me not to do research on the last name he wrote on the envelope. "I didn't research the name McCrie. That was what you said."

There was a glint within his dark eyes, as if his mind and mine had taken the same path. He took a step back. "Fuck, Araneae, there are so many things I need to tell you, and with one sentence you have my cock wanting something altogether different."

I did have an effect on this man. There was something powerful in that knowledge.

"I think I may want the same thing."

His brows moved upward as my cheeks warmed under his gaze. "You're saying yes?"

"I'm saying there's a greater possibility now than before."

Sterling took a deep breath and reached into the back pocket of his jeans. I don't know what I was expecting, maybe a condom. What I wasn't expecting was my phone.

"You said you wanted to see this, no matter the time of day or night."

Suddenly nothing else mattered.

Oh God. Louisa!

My stomach dropped and panic coursed through my blood as I reached for the phone. Sitting back on the bed, I fumbled with the screen. "Shit, you've had this all along, and you didn't tell me? Sterling, you promised. Is it Louisa?"

"The message is from her."

I stared up in disbelief. "You read it? You read my message? How? My screen is locked."

He didn't reply, yet the answer was obvious. Nothing, not even a pass code, stopped Sterling Sparrow. Instead of responding, he waited as I read the string of texts.

"CALL ME, I HAVE TO TELL YOU SOMETHING."

"KENNI, I'M GETTING WORRIED. TELL ME YOU MADE IT TO YOUR GETAWAY."

"BABE, I HATE TO DO THIS IN A TEXT, BUT MAYBE YOU'RE STILL TRAVELING AND I NEED TO GO TO SLEEP. I SAW IT ON THE NEWS, AND THEN JASON AND I DROVE OVER THERE. HONEY, YOUR APARTMENT— IT'S GONE. THERE WAS A FIRE. I'M SO GLAD YOU WEREN'T THERE. THE NEWS IS SAYING TWO CASUAL-

TIES. THEY AREN'T RELEASING NAMES. CALL ME IN THE MORNING, AND HOPEFULLY I'LL KNOW MORE. I'M SO SORRY."

By the time I finished, my hands were shaking. "I-I need to go back."

"Think about it. Think about what I said earlier."

"Fuck, Sterling. You've said a lot of things, and at this moment, I don't give a shit what you say. I need to get back to Boulder. Have Marianne get the plane ready, and I'll leave now."

The eyes before me darkened as his expression hardened, returning to the statuesque air.

I jumped from the bed and retraced the path he'd paced earlier, my steps giving me the added determination. "I want to call Louisa. I need to know. I have this neighbor—"

"Mrs. Powell," he said, interrupting my thoughts.

I turned to him, my voice growing louder with each statement. "How the fuck do you know that?" Before he could answer, I went on. "Oh, that's right because you know everything about those things that belong to you. Well, I have a news flash for you. I am not a thing to be possessed. And I don't belong to you."

Sterling took one long stride, maybe two.

I let out a gasp as he seized my shoulders. The look in his dark eyes sent a chill through me as if ice water had been added to my veins. There was no question: I'd misjudged my safety in this man's presence. The steely determination staring at me left no room for debate.

"You do belong to me, and your mother was wrong. I'm

the one man who you don't need to fear, not when your safety is in question. However, if you don't stop making uninformed demands, I'm not above taking you over my knee and reminding you again about the lesson we had earlier."

"Fuck you."

"No, Araneae, we've already discussed that. You're the one who I'll fuck, and I will. Right now, you need to think about what happened. Someone set your apartment on fire, most likely after ransacking it. Patrick has Shelly looking into it. We don't have proof, but we believe someone set the fire to cover a break-in."

My head shook. "Why? My apartment has never been broken into before."

"Are you sure?"

"What do you mean? Of course, I'm sure."

"You never went for something and it wasn't where you remembered putting it? You never thought the pillows on your couch were arranged differently or things were moved inside a drawer? Maybe the jewelry you left on the dresser was put away in your jewelry box or the towel you remembered leaving on the bathroom floor was hung up?"

With each statement my stomach twisted. I had. Every one of the things he'd said, I'd done and experienced. "I-I always chalked it up to—"

"But now?"

My heart thumped in my chest. "Why burn it?"

"To cover up whatever was done. More importantly, they're sending a message to me. That was why in the helicopter I referred to you as my fiancée. The people on the plane, I trust. Matt is a new addition to my transport company. The regular pilot was unavailable on short notice.

We're watching Matt closely but can't be confident he isn't a plant. That's why I had Patrick sit copilot. Patrick is armed and a hell of a great chopper pilot. If anything had gone awry during the flight, Patrick would have taken care of it. Right now, I want the world to know that you're mine, and you're under my protection."

"I don't understand." The fight I'd been feeling a moment earlier washed away, leaving me limp as Sterling asked about things moving and being out of place. The instances he mentioned hadn't only happened at home but also at the office. I'd go to open a file drawer that I was certain I'd locked, and it would be unlocked. The chaos room, not that I should have been able to tell, would be changed. I'd always assumed that any rearranging was Louisa, but what if it wasn't?

"When we know more, you will too," he said reassuringly.

I wasn't certain I believed him. "Sterling, I'm exhausted. May we continue this in the morning?"

"I believe the current time of day qualifies."

He was right by the clock. "You may not need sleep, but I do."

"There's one more thing."

I shook my head. "I don't think I can take *one more thing*. Please let it wait." And then my eyes opened wide. "Unless...is it about my friends? Did something happen?"

"Your friends are safe, and so is Mrs. Powell."

Relief flooded my veins as I sank back to the bed. "Thank you."

"She's hospitalized for smoke inhalation, but the reports are positive."

"Hospitalized? What about her cats?"

"Jesus, Araneae, stop thinking of others for a second. This fire was about you."

"If it was about me, then I want to be sure her cats are safe."

He shook his head, but something in his expression told me that as ridiculous as he thought my request was, he'd do as I asked. I couldn't explain it, but the feeling was there. "Thank you, Sterling. Please don't tell me anything else tonight. Let me sleep knowing they're safe."

When he came closer, my skin warmed. I expected him to do something—kiss me good night or tell me it would be all right. Instead, he reached for the phone on the bed beside me.

"Seriously? You're taking my phone again?"

"You need your sleep."

"Tomorrow—when I wake," I corrected, "I'm calling Louisa."

He walked toward the door. "When you wake, we're going to have lesson number two on making uninformed demands."

As the door opened, he flipped the light switch and disappeared into the hallway. The click of the shutting door echoed through the dark room as I remained sitting on the edge of the bed.

Fuck you, Mr. Sparrow, and your lessons.

ARANEAE

*a*ccording to my watch it was after ten in the morning when I finally woke. As my eyes opened, I had that strange sensation of disorientation: that feeling of not knowing where I was, as if my dream world and reality had come together, crashing in an unknown dimension. It didn't help that I was only wearing my underwear, and the damn underwires were reminding me why I don't usually sleep in my bra.

I'd been too tired physically and especially mentally after Sterling left the room to worry about finding my sleeping clothes in my carry-on. Though I imagined lying awake worrying about my apartment, I didn't. Knowing that Jeanne was safe and the things that meant the most to me had been packed, my last thought before falling asleep was about my neighbor's cats.

Opening the blinds, the room flooded with sunlight.

I'd never been in Canada before, not even to the Canadian

side of Niagara Falls right over the US border. From the view from my windows, the land surrounding Sterling's cabin was pristine. The window looked out toward the tall trees I'd seen last night.

While in college, I'd gone on a Northern Pacific vacation with the Nelsons, Louisa's family. I remembered how the pine trees seemed straighter and taller than those in Colorado or those I could recall from Illinois. The trees currently outside the window reminded me of those, while the growling of my stomach reminded me that it had been forever since I'd eaten. The cheese and fruit on the plane had been it.

Warm water washed over me as I showered, waiting for the food I'd called and asked to be delivered to my room. Though I hadn't eaten much since getting on Sterling's plane, I was definitely clean. Shower number four since I'd awakened yesterday morning.

A covered tray met me as I wrapped the warm robe around myself and made my way back into the bedroom. More importantly, there was a decanter of coffee. My mouth watered as I poured the rich dark liquid and added cream.

As I ate and sipped the delicious brew, I let last night's late conversation replay in my head. It was as I recalled Louisa's texts that I decided I needed to find Sterling or Patrick soon—whoever had my phone. I had at least one call I needed to make. Probably more.

Less than thirty minutes later, I was fully dressed with my long hair dried and secured in a side ponytail. Taking one more look in the mirror, I was ready to find my phone and whatever else Sterling Sparrow had in store. My jeans were the same as last night but the sweater was different, a soft shade of pink. The low-heeled ankle boots I'd worn on the helicopter were currently my only choice, besides the ridiculously high sandals from Sterling's gift.

I was still waiting on the delivery of the rest of my luggage.

For a split second, fear prickled my skin as I reached for the doorknob, wondering if it would open. And then without resistance, it did.

Rita had said that Sterling mentioned I could roam.

That still begged the question, to where could I roam? Despite my choice of footwear, not anywhere that required bear repellent. Of that I was certain.

As they had last night, my steps stilled when I reached the walkway above the massive living room. The windows extended higher than the second floor, bathing the room below in shimmering sunlight. Beyond the glass and the yard where we'd landed last night, was a glistening lake extending to the horizon as the sun's rays reflected off the blue water sparkling like diamonds.

I had visions of Lake Tahoe, another place I'd visited with Louisa before she was married. At first, we had a condo in Big Bear, a drive from the lake. We'd stayed there until we returned one night to find the door to our condo ajar.

I gripped the edge of the railing. Nothing had been missing and the resort claimed that the most likely explanation was that the maid had forgotten to latch the door. Needless to say, we weren't comfortable staying there any longer and moved to a hotel closer to the lake. I couldn't remember the name, but it had a casino.

Sterling's words from last night came back...*are you certain you've never been broken into before?*

Certainly, what happened in Big Bear wasn't related.

That's what I told myself as I stared out at the untouched wilderness. His words were making me paranoid. That was all it was. As I gave it all more thought, radiating warmth covered my back as the unique spice of Sterling's cologne filled my senses. Like last night, I didn't need to turn to know who was behind me.

"Good morning."

The deep tenor reverberated from my ear to my toes and everywhere in between. Slowly, I spun as his hands landed on the railing and strong arms once again caged me. The sunshine from the windows glistened in his gaze as I lifted my chin to see him better. I had to stop myself from reaching up and placing my palm on his cheek. Now cleanly shaven, I yearned to feel the smoothness under my touch.

What was wrong with me?

So far, this man had done little to give me anything other than paranoia. He claimed I was his, threatened my loved ones, and took me not to Chicago as planned but to a remote location that I couldn't even pinpoint. He held the name my mother had warned me about, and yet in his presence under his burning gaze, every reason I had to despise him was reduced to ash.

"Good morning," I managed.

"Do you always sleep this late?" His cheeks rose as his lips curled upward.

"Only when a man keeps me awake into the early hours of the morning."

One side of his grin quirked higher as his eyebrows rose. "I believe my goal will be to keep you awake every night, only I plan to use a different technique."

My insides twisted at his meaning while at the same time I

cursed my non-padded bra and the lightweight yarn of my sweater. He'd said last night that he always accomplished his goals. Would sex be one of them? I didn't ask.

Clearing my throat, I said, "I was on my way to find you."

"To finish our conversation or explore my new technique?"

It was my turn to grin.

As I'd dressed, I gave myself a pep talk, telling myself to stay strong and concentrate on learning more of my past. And yet despite the lecture, as my blood warmed in his presence and my insides turned to molten goo, there was no doubt that I was failing miserably. I couldn't remember ever being as attracted to any man as I was to Sterling Sparrow. No matter how many times my mind protested, when he was near, my body was kindling and he was the match.

I leaned back to give myself more space. As I did, half of my body suspended over the railing. "I was thinking you might have my phone."

"This is a do-not-disturb getaway, remember?"

"It's a little hard to forget."

His hand landed in the small of my back, pulling me toward him. "I didn't bring you here to lose you over a railing." His motion stopped millimeters before our chests collided.

I imagined inhaling deeply. Would my nipples brush against his t-shirt? Would he know how hard they were?

It was then I noticed his casual attire. In hiking boots more rugged than mine, he was wearing a darker pair of jeans than yesterday and a soft gray t-shirt that covered the defined abs I'd seen yesterday when he was...

Stop it, Kennedy.

I took a step to the side. "Thank you for saving me. Now, about that phone."

His nostrils flared as he took a deep breath. Just as I was about to argue, he pulled my phone from the back pocket of his jeans. "Also, you should call your apartment complex and let them know you're out of town and have been since late yesterday afternoon. If we're right and the fire originated in your unit, you'll be under suspicion."

"What? No. Why would they think that?"

"It's better to be proactive."

With his hand on the small of my back, we walked down the large wooden staircase to the living room below. Once there, I waited for him to move on. When he didn't, I finally asked, "Do you mind? I'd like some privacy as I talk to Louisa."

"I do mind. It's very important to keep any information about you to a minimum right now. From what I've seen and heard, being discreet isn't one of your strengths."

"You know what?" I asked, my free hand moving to my hip. "You really can be an asshole."

Scrunching his lips as if stopping himself from smiling, he nodded. "Most people are wise enough not to tell me that to my face, but yes, I've been made aware of that virtue."

"Virtue? It's not a virtue. I'm going to make my calls in private."

Before I realized what he'd done, Sterling snatched the phone, stealing it from my grasp. "The choice is yours: make the calls here and now or forget the calls and Patrick will respond to Louisa's texts by text message and your apartment complex by email."

"You are fucking unbelievable."

"Make up your mind because we have plans."

"Give me my damn phone, and tell me why I would agree to any plans with you."

Amusement now overpowered his expression. "Does that mean you'll make the calls here and now?"

"It means that apparently I don't have a choice, but I'm pissed."

"Good," he said handing me the phone. "A little fire in your blood will make our plans all that much better."

"Bastard," I muttered as I scrolled to Louisa's number. Before I hit *Call* my chin was lifted until my gaze met his dark stare.

"I wish that were the case. Unfortunately, I had a father."

"Sterling, that isn't what I meant."

"I rest my case. You're too quick to speak without thinking. Now, hurry your calls to Louisa and the apartment complex."

"Next you're going to tell me to put it on speaker."

He nodded.

"Fuck you." Securing the grip on my phone, I walked to one of the large sofas, one facing the windows, and turned my back on my new telephone monitor. As I hit *Call*, I lifted the phone to my ear. There was no way I was putting it on speaker. I also wondered if it mattered. Sterling had told me a week ago that all my devices were monitored. Most likely, not only was he hearing what I said, but Patrick or someone in his network was hearing both sides.

Though Sterling had the decency to stay out of my view, that didn't mean I couldn't feel his presence in every nerve in my body. Each nerve and each small hair were like tiny lightning rods, buzzing with the energy Sterling Sparrow emanated.

Louisa answered on the first ring. "Kenni, thank God."

The sound of that name brought a smile to my lips.

It wasn't until she asked where I was that I turned toward Sterling. I wanted to trust my best friend—I did. However, if Patrick could monitor my phone so could the people who set my apartment on fire. "Where am I?" I said aloud, repeating her question.

"Canada," Sterling said softly from across the room. "Nothing specific."

Was this safe to not tell her? I remembered the note I'd hidden in my freezer. If the apartment was gone, that included the refrigerator and the note. What if Sterling was the person I needed to fear? What if his people had started the fire?

I didn't want to believe that.

"Canada," I said with as much excitement as I could muster.

"I-I'm shocked," Louisa replied.

"It's absolutely beautiful. The perfect spot to unwind a bit before things get crazy in Chicago."

"Jeez, Kenni. I thought you'd be more upset about the apartment. And this trip...it's not like you."

"I am upset," I retorted. "I can't believe what happened. At least Mrs. Powell is safe."

"I don't know how you know that, but nevertheless, two people are dead."

Her words were a punch to my gut. I'd been so relieved that it wasn't Jeanne that I hadn't given the proper attention to the fact that people were dead, most likely because of me. "Have they released the names?"

"No, but from the looks of your building, I'd venture to guess it was the people who lived across the hall from you. The top level is totally gone. I can't imagine if you were home...

"Oh, a man from your insurance company called the office. Winnie took the message. She told him you were out of town but would contact them as soon as you could."

"Wow, that was fast." I tried to remember the couple living across the hall, thinking how sad it was that people went on with their lives without reaching out to those around them. "I never talked to those neighbors, really. I saw her a few times in the hallway. We usually just nodded."

"Franco called," Louisa said, changing the subject. "I know you can't get there until you get back from Ca-n-a-da." She elongated the word. "But I told him you were going to be spending more time in Chicago and you'd stop by. He said inventory is balancing now, but there is a new concern regarding a driver. There was something about a blip on the security tape."

"A blip? What do you mean?" I didn't like the way that sounded.

"A time stamp issue. When I told him you'd come see him, he said he'd explain it to you."

"Okay." I changed my tone. "How are you feeling?"

"Fat and awkward," she said with a laugh. "I'm ready to hold little Kennedy in my arms and not inside my body. I swear, if my skin stretches any more, it's going to pop."

Hearing her joke and talk about the baby filled me with both joy and concern. "You're radiant."

"That's what people say. I'm convinced it's code for you look like a blimp."

Laughing, I shook my head. "Give Jason my love. If I don't answer when you call or text, it's probably the reception here. Leave me a message, and I'll get back to you as soon as I can." I turned back to Sterling for the last part.

After we disconnected the call, I called my apartment complex, explaining as Sterling had advised that I was out of town and devastated by the loss.

"Ms. Hawkins," the lady from the apartment's office said, "there was an insurance adjuster here first thing this morning asking for a detailed log of everything in your apartment. I told him to send you an email."

"My insurance company or the complex's?" I asked, remembering what Louisa had said.

"Not ours, so I assumed yours. He asked for your email address and the best way to reach you."

My pulse increased as I stood and walked closer to Sterling.

Hitting the speaker button, I said, "Can you please repeat that?"

"The insurance guy asked how he could reach you." Her voice dropped a decibel. "I thought it seemed strange that your insurance company wouldn't have your contact information. I should have taken his picture. He was blond. I remember that."

"And you're sure it wasn't someone from your insurance company?"

"I'm positive. I didn't give him your number or email. I said I'd relay the message."

"Did he leave a number?" Sterling asked, too softly to be overheard.

I repeated his question. As she replied, Sterling typed the number into a text message. "Thank you," I replied. "Contact me if you need to. I may not answer right away..." I wouldn't. "...but you can leave me a message."

Upon disconnecting the second call, Sterling extended his hand. I thought about my emails and other places I could access from my phone and just as quickly decided it wasn't worth the argument. As I gave him back my phone, I said, "You really do need to work on that asshole thing. I repeat, it's not a virtue." Before he could respond, I asked, "You don't think that insurance guy is connected to this mess you were talking about, do you?"

"We're going to find out."

"Louisa said someone called the office too. Winnie told him I was out of town."

Sterling shook his head.

"Now that I have his number, I could call him?" It was meant as a statement but came out more like asking permission.

"Not now and sure as fuck, not from your phone." He tilted his head toward the windows. "It's beautiful out there and unlike the summer heat in Chicago, it's in the low sixties. That's why I built this cabin up here. Those plans we have... we're going down to the lake."

"Down. How far down and what about up? Wait? Rita said something about bears."

Sterling had begun to walk down the hallway toward his office, yet he turned back with a grin. "Only black bears, the grizzlies are mostly farther north. And as long as we don't get between a mother and her cubs, we'll be fine."

"But what if we end up between a mother and her cubs?"

Sterling shook his head. "Araneae, I wish you'd get your priorities straight. Someone set your apartment on fire. An unknown man is trying to reach you, the plane you were supposed to be on crashed, and you're worried about bears." He turned away. "As for all of it, as I said, you belong to me. I protect what's mine."

I watched his fading outline, wide shoulders, and long legs as he disappeared into the dimly lit hallway. Once he was gone, my knees gave out, landing me back on the soft leather sofa. I wasn't prepared to again fight his declared proprietorship. My mind was on something else he'd said.

A plane crashed?

A plane crashed—were there casualties? Two people were dead from the fire, and who was the man trying to reach me?

Somehow bears didn't seem as important.

ARANEAE

My ears buzzed with the silence of the cabin and the aftershock of the bomb Sterling had just dropped. Finding my way to my feet, step after step, I followed the path Sterling had just taken until I was standing outside a mostly-closed door to his office. Rita had pointed out the room last night. Even if she hadn't, I would have known its purpose from the fury of voices coming from within.

I recognized Sterling's and Patrick's. It was the third voice I didn't know.

"The number goes to a burner phone," the unknown voice said.

"Find out where it was purchased. See if there's a money trail."

"Boss, it was purchased with cash in Schaumburg. That's where the trail ends. I'm looking into security cameras. Once I find him, I'll do face recognition."

There was a beat of silence before Sterling replied. "So this man in Boulder has a phone from outside Chicago. What a fucking coincidence."

"There's something else," the unknown voice said.

"Wait," Sterling said, "The lady from the apartment complex said he was blond."

"Shit," Patrick said. "I know that's not much of a description, but Andrew Walsh has gone MIA since Kansas."

I knew that name. How did I know it? I took another step toward the door.

"Sparrow," the unknown voice said, "you should know, the pilot of the 737 died last night."

I sucked in a deep breath as Sterling yelled, "Died or was killed?"

"Freak accident. He's from New York. He'd just gotten back to Manhattan when he slipped from the platform in the subway. The train was moving fast..."

I groaned as my stomach lurched at the image playing in my head. The Sinful Thread New York market was mine. I rode the subways there. I'd been on those platforms. They were usually filthy dirty, and I'd seen my share of rats, but they weren't slippery.

"What have you learned about his financials?" Patrick's voice asked as the door was abruptly opened inward, and I was met by Sterling's dark expression.

"Get out," Sterling barked to Patrick. "The call is done for now."

Neither Patrick nor the other person on the speaker phone responded.

My heart beat wildly as I watched Patrick close the laptop

that had been in front of him on a long table filled with papers. Lifting the computer, he stood to leave. Though he didn't speak, his blue eyes flashed my direction screaming what I already knew. *I was in trouble.*

I took a step back as Sterling reached for my arm, changing my direction and pulling me inside the room.

The silence grew as Sterling closed the door and spun my direction. The man from earlier at the banister and even the asshole with my phone was gone. Rage seeped from his every pore as his jaw clenched. If I knew him better I might assume he was weighing his words or perhaps his future actions. Contemplation was in his expression, and the sensible part of me feared what he would decide.

"Don't be upset with me," I said, breaking the silence. "You're the one keeping information from me. You're the one who dropped the bomb out there..." I pointed toward the door. "...about a plane crash."

"I tried to tell you last night, and you said you didn't want to know."

"That a plane crashed! In the future, if it's something that big, tell me. Besides, you can't just say something like that and not expect there to be—"

His lips crashed with mine as simultaneously his fingers reached for my ponytail and entwined in my long hair. His kiss sizzled and bruised my lips. He was stealing not only my words but also my breath. Gasping, I moaned as a strong arm pulled me against him, smashing my breasts against his wide chest and uniting our hips. There was no mercy or tenderness as his tongue filled my taste buds with coffee and mint.

He was a starving man and I was his meal.

This was more than lust. It was a power struggle, and I'd be damned if I would back down. My hands moved up to his chest, my fingers fisting his shirt, as I lifted myself up on my toes and my tongue continued the battle of wills.

Beneath my grasp, his heart beat in time with mine, fast and furious. Moving from my waist, his large hand found its way under my sweater, his fingers splaying on the skin of my back as heat radiated from his touch and the tugging of my hair intensified. Every nerve in my body was on fire. Like gasoline to a flame, from my rock-hard nipples to my now-drenched core, I was ablaze.

Abruptly, he released me, turning to the table where Patrick had been seated and sweeping the papers off the edge, the neat piles now fluttering haphazardly to the floor. Before I could comment or even form words, Sterling reached for my waist and lifted me as if I weighed nothing, placing me at the table's edge. With another tug of my hair he brought my eyes to his.

"I'm either going to fuck you or spank your ass for eaves-dropping. Either way, those jeans are coming off."

"I-I..." My tongue grew thick as he reached for my boots, yanking the small zippers at my ankle and dropping each one to the floor, followed by my socks. "Sterling..." With the exactitude of an aficionado, he undid the button of my jeans and lowered the zipper.

I was too twisted and tied up with emotions to argue as I lifted my ass from the table's surface, allowing my jeans to be pulled down my legs. As my white lace panties came into view, a long, deep hiss filled the air.

His stare seemed to go on forever as I willingly lifted my

arms, and with one quick motion he added my sweater to the papers and clothes on the floor.

"Which is it going to be?" he asked, eyeing me up and down, taking in my attire or lack thereof.

Good girls get to come. I recalled his declaration from the plane.

I lifted my chin and with all the dignity I could muster, I asked the question I never imagined uttering—to anyone. "Are you going to let me come?"

He didn't answer. Pushing my legs farther apart, he stepped between my knees, his hand going to the crotch of my panties. "You're fucking soaked."

Instinctively my thighs tried to close, yet his body wouldn't allow it. "Sterling."

"One more second and I'm making the decision for you, and the result will be a fire-red ass *and* my cock buried deep inside your dripping pussy."

I shouldn't like the way he was speaking to me. My mind knew that, but again I wasn't listening to my mind. No. All I could hear was the deep tenor that even without his dark stare or the way his fingers rubbed over the crotch of my panties had my nipples rock-hard and me on the verge of a spontaneous orgasm.

"Fuck me." The words were barely out of my mouth when his large hand came to my chest, his fingers splayed, and he pushed me back until my spine was flat against the cool, hard table. The rip of lace and sound of his zipper were barely heard over the pounding of my heart. I tried to sit upward to see the cock I'd watched explode a day before, but each of my movements came up against the pressure from his hand. The ceiling above glistened as sunlight danced over the knotty pine when all at once it happened.

I screamed out as he filled me completely with one thrust. Like his kiss from before, there was no warning shot, no preparation. Not that it mattered. I was so wet his length and girth met little resistance as he stretched me to where pain and pleasure intersected.

"So fucking tight."

Clawing at the shiny wood, I found the edge of the table. My fingers curled, trying to hold on as he pounded, hard and fast. Sterling was a man consumed. Each thrust filled me as never before as the pressure within me began to build.

The second his hand left my chest, I sprang upward, no longer satisfied with this being a one-man show, and reached for the hem of his t-shirt, pulling it upward. It too joined our growing pile of clothes. My hands roamed his tight abs as his continued motion rubbed over my bundle of nerves, relieving the building ache in my clit and sending shock waves in every direction.

I couldn't repeat anything I said. Though my own voice was recognizable, the sounds were not. I wasn't alone. We were a chorus of words and primitive noises, like none I'd ever heard.

My nails dug at his broad shoulders as I leaned forward. No longer supported by the table, it was Sterling's grasp of my ass that kept me from falling. The new position was everything as my toes curled. My lips covered the tight cord of his neck as I tried to stifle my scream.

I didn't succeed.

Every nerve within me detonated as my entire body convulsed. From my toes to my scalp, I was a mass of explosions. The sensation flooded my circulation like nothing I'd ever experienced. My fingers blanched as I held tightly to his shoulders, the muscles within me contracting, and stars appearing behind my now-closed eyes.

Secure in his grasp, I floated, falling from the highest high when my pants, whimpers, and gasps for breath were lost to the deep roar coming from Sterling. I opened my eyes in time to watch his beautiful expression as his cock buried deep within me throbbed. It was better than watching him pleasure himself, as for a moment he basked in the sheer bliss of our union.

I couldn't register what we'd done until he set me again on the table's edge and eased out. As I gazed down at his glorious cock, shiny from our connection, it hit me.

"You didn't use a condom?"

"And I won't."

"What?"

"We're both clean and you have the birth control insert. I've never had skin-to-skin sex with anyone else."

How could I believe him?

"But..." I could have asked how he knew my medical status, but the question would be pointless. Sterling Sparrow knew everything.

"Araneae, you're mine in every way." He ran his finger over my core and brought the glistening digit to his lips and sucked. "I plan to take you in every way. The sooner you get used to that idea, the easier it will be to accept what's happening."

Jumping from the edge of the table, muscles I didn't know existed announced their presence. Nevertheless, I refused to show Sterling the effect he had on me.

Okay, I supposed I showed him when I screamed out his name or was coming hard on his cock. That didn't matter. Now was different.

Lifting my sweater, I turned and met his stare. Wearing only my bra, I lifted my chin. "This changes nothing. I will repeat it until you get it straight. I belong to no one. I decide what I do and when. Yes, I chose sex, but only because you looked...angry and I didn't trust you with my ass."

His dark eyes smoldered as the asshole had the audacity to smile. It took all my self-control not to slap the smirk from his arrogant and too-fucking-handsome face.

Sterling took a step closer, his beautiful cock still free and bobbing heavily with each step, and reached for my ass. "Sunshine, I was angry. I still am. And as for your ass, you will trust me with it." He ran his thumb over my lips. "And this mouth too."

A long breath exited my nose as the fever within me burned. It wasn't the lust and desire of minutes ago. No, this was pure, unadulterated irritation, like a small pebble in the bottom of your shoe that you couldn't dislodge. Sterling Sparrow was like that to me—no matter my concessions, he still continued to rub me the wrong way. "You don't get it. I'm here for one reason."

"To protect your friends."

"Two reasons," I corrected. "There's that, but you promised me information and so far, it seems that you're falling short."

In reality there was nothing short about Sterling Sparrow. And even though I'd just had the absolute best sex of my life, I wasn't giving in.

"You still aren't seeing what's right in front of you."

I refused the temptation to look down at what had just been inside me. "Then tell me. Tell me everything." When he started to respond, I lifted a finger to his lips. "No, Mr. Sparrow. It's your turn. I'm going back upstairs and cleaning up. I suggest you do the same. When I come back, you owe me."

He stepped back from my touch as he tucked himself back into his jeans. Licking my lips, I tried not to notice that he wasn't wearing underwear or that his shirt was still gone and his six-pack abs were really eight.

Obviously, I noticed.

He eyed me up and down. "Don't leave this office until you put your clothes back on." His gaze narrowed. "No one gets to see that pussy but me."

He had no idea how close I was to opening the door just as God had made me and walking naked up to my room. Hell, I was almost ready to take off the bra. And I would, except pissing Sterling Sparrow off more than he currently was wasn't my goal. I pulled the sweater over my head. "Fine."

"Tell me, Ms. McCrie, what do you think I owe you?" He lifted his brow. "After all, I just gave you the best orgasm of your life."

The words to argue were on the tip of my tongue. I could tell him that it wasn't even close, that I could give myself a better orgasm even without a vibrator, but it would all be a lie. My knees were still weak from what we'd just done.

Peering down at the floor, I reached for my jeans. To the side of them was what used to be my panties. They were now rendered useless; one leg having been ripped before he pulled them from my body. I stepped into my jeans, closed the button and zipper, and picked up my socks and boots.

Sterling eyed the destroyed lace still on the floor. "It appears my collection is growing."

"Fuck you." I stood straighter. "You owe me my secrets. You owe me the truth of who I am and why you are now a part of my upside-down life. And today you're going to give me answers."

STERLING

*T*he smile I'd been fighting bloomed, covering my face as Araneae turned her regal jeans-covered little ass to me, and after making her demands, walked away, slamming the door in her wake.

My siren, my temptress, my sunshine—I wasn't sure exactly what she was, other than mine. I'd known that when I had her, it would be better than any other sex of my life, and I'd been right about that. What I hadn't expected as I watched her walk away was my uncertainty. I wasn't one hundred percent certain if I'd been the one to take her or if she'd taken me.

Lifting her ruined panties from the floor, I reached the edge of the table and cleaned the shiny surface with the lace, wiping the remnants of our connection. With each swipe, I heard her melody of a voice as she made her choice: *fuck me*. I saw her nearly naked body lying back, her legs wide as she opened herself to me.

I saw her pouty lips and shimmering coffee-colored eyes as I drilled into her. My God, she was so snug that my balls grew tight, and I worried I'd blow as soon as her taut walls contracted around me. And then after all of that, after letting her—making her—come undone, Araneae had the audacity to question me about the condom, to make demands of me.

My cock stirred at the sight of her standing in only a white lace bra, her silky hair disheveled, and her fair skin reddened by my grasp, telling me what I would and wouldn't do. She was infuriating in a way I'd never known.

I couldn't remember any other woman to walk out on me after sex, to tell me to clean up. That was my modus operandi. I made demands. I gave orders and they were carried out.

Araneae wanted answers, and I'd give them to her, just not all at once. She might think she was ready to learn all her secrets, but she wasn't.

I'd screwed up when I mentioned the plane crash. That was what she did to me. So fucking defiant, turning her back to me and talking on the phone without the speaker, I was hard in the living room just watching her.

From my angle all I could see was that long yellow hair lying over her slender sensual shoulder. As she spoke, my mind was elsewhere, with her on her knees, my cock buried in her throat as I fisted that ponytail. It was why I couldn't resist twisting my fingers in her silky locks the moment I took her lips with mine.

Damn, she tasted so sweet.

I shook my head. Araneae wasn't all sweet. Yes, her lips, tongue, and essence were, but the woman herself was a fucking hellion. The way she came at me, ripping off my shirt, was like nothing I expected. Her fire pushed me in ways I wasn't used to being pushed, and all it did was make me want her more.

I'd been upfront with her about my desires. And I would have her, in every way possible. Of that she could be certain. After this morning, I was more eager than ever. Her little display showed me that despite her hesitation, she wanted it as much as I did. The fire when we touched was a mere candle compared to the roaring inferno when we were joined together.

Together we could decimate the forests surrounding this cabin for miles and miles.

Tucking her panties into the pocket of my jeans, I reached for my phone and sent a quick text to Patrick. I wanted more information on the pilot's sudden demise. I didn't care that the office reeked of sex or that the papers he had organized were now on the floor. Patrick could deal with that later when Araneae and I went for the walk I promised.

My hope was that being surrounded by crisp clean air and the beauty of this place would ease a bit of the heartache my words—her secrets—would inflict.

A knock on the door refocused my attention. Slipping my shirt back over my head, I pushed it into the waist of my jeans and answered, "Patrick, come in."

ARANEAE

This time when I reached Sterling's office, in fresh jeans, underwear, and a t-shirt covered with a light jacket, I didn't hesitate. I also didn't knock. I'm not sure if that was what Sterling expected; however, from the stares I received from both him and Patrick, walking in and declaring it was time for us to talk was also not what was expected.

Whether it was or not, it did the trick. A few minutes later, we were out of the cabin.

The fresh, warm breeze blew my hair as we stood at the crest of the hill and peered down toward the lake. Was his cabin built upon a hill or a small mountain? I couldn't be sure. Either way, with our eyes covered by sunglasses, we took in the spectacular view. Greens and blues dominated the scene as wildlife flew and scampered about.

"We could walk," Sterling said, "but you were right about the hike up. It takes almost three times as long as the hike down."

"Unless we're being chased by that mother bear," I said with a grin. "I'm pretty sure I could find some speed." I turned to Sterling. "I ran track in high school...well, back in Chicago." Looking off to the distance, I added, "You probably already knew that."

Sterling reached for my chin, bringing me back to his gaze. "I didn't. Thanks for sharing."

"I wasn't that good, but I believe a bear would be the proper motivation."

"I have a better idea," Sterling said as he took my hand and led me away from the crest, back toward the cabin.

I peered back over my shoulder. "I thought we were going to the lake. We're headed the wrong direction."

A deep chuckle filled the air. "And here I thought you weren't perceptive. We're going to the garages. How are you at driving an ATV?"

"Kick-ass, actually."

Sterling stopped and turned my way, his lips agape. "Seriously?"

"Wow, two things about me that you didn't know. Hell yes. I love to go with friends up into the mountains and ride. It's especially great above the tree line. No obstacles."

He shook his head. "I believe you. I do. The thing is that there are a lot of obstacles here. How about we ride together?"

"Okay."

He led me around the other side of the cabin. The cobblestone driveway created a circle with a sidewalk that led to an entry, complete with two grand extra-tall doors.

The garages were a series of outbuildings off to the side of the driveway, connected by a gravel service road. We came to a stop outside of one building as Sterling entered a code into a security pad. The garage-style door opened to a large concrete space, and as my eyes adjusted to its contents, I sucked in a breath. There was an assortment of all-terrain vehicles as well as minibikes and other recreational vehicles. As my eyes adjusted, I zeroed in on one model, silver with air control suspension, Fox air assist shocks, heavy-duty bumpers, and 14-inch tires. "Oh my God. You have a Can-Am Outlander MAX 1000 Limited," I practically squealed as I hurried toward the limited-edition ATV.

When I looked up, Sterling was staring at me like I'd grown an additional head.

"What? Didn't you believe me?"

Shaking his head, he walked away toward a cabinet near the back of the garage before returning with two helmets.

"Here, Evel Knievel, no stunts on today's drive."

"You're no fun."

His grin quirked as he ran a finger over my cheek. "I believe I could argue that you weren't saying that an hour ago."

No, I could barely talk an hour ago. Shrugging, I didn't say that. I wasn't going to give him that satisfaction.

As I secured my helmet over my head, he flipped a switch on the side that just as in the helicopter, gave us an audible connection.

After tugging at my chin strap, he stepped forward and swung his leg over the wide seat of the model I'd just ogled and with his hands on the handlebars gestured behind him. "Jump on, sunshine. We'll take this one."

Placing my fists on my hips, I tried to ignore how hot he looked straddling the king of the beast machine, wearing sunglasses, jeans, boots, and the same gray t-shirt that earlier I'd ripped from his toned torso. "When you said ride together, I thought you meant I'd be driving."

Sterling's laugh was the most genuine I'd heard since I met him as he shook his head. "No way. Get on and hold on tight."

A sexy, quick move with his feet, kick-starting what I knew could be done with a button, and he revved the engine.

After the roar of the motor filled the space, I climbed onto the rear seat. A large hand landed on my knee as his raspy tenor came through my helmet. "Squeeze those legs tight. I like having your legs around me."

The ATV bucked as Sterling hit the gas, causing me to scream as I wrapped my arms around his torso. "You did that on purpose."

My comment was met with another laugh.

Leaning forward with my face against his back and my arms around his waist, I closed my eyes and inhaled his masculine scent: spicy cologne as well as the faint aroma of fresh air and musk.

After taking a quick lap of the property high on the hill, Sterling pulled to the front of his cabin. Waiting on the porch in front of the giant doors was Rita with a basket in her hand. Before I could ask what it was, Sterling had the Can-Am Outlander in neutral, was off the seat, and securing the basket behind me. "Thank you, Rita," I heard through the helmet. As he got back on, he gave me a wink. "Lunch. I know that after my morning activities I could use some sustenance."

"Asshole," I muttered.

Once again the ATV bucked and I held on tight.

My seat had a back, and once Sterling stopped bucking the ATV and maneuvered us to a partially overgrown path, taking us between giant conifers, I was able to sit back and enjoy the ride. The way to the lake was mostly quiet, minus the roar and vibration of the machine between our legs. Occasionally, the path would lead to open fields. When that happened, he'd increase the speed as wind and sunshine bathed our faces. Along the way, occasionally Sterling slowed to point out different species of birds and other wildlife. There were deer, moose, and a variety of smaller mammals—wolverines, pika, rabbits, and squirrels. Luckily, at no point did he show me a bear.

As we got closer to the shore, the breeze picked up and the scent of fresh water overpowered the pine from within the trails in the forest. Once we stopped, I waited as Sterling pulled out a blanket from the basket and covered a soft area of long grass, smashing it down and creating a more comfortable place to sit.

"How long are you going to make me wait?" I asked as he handed me a bottle of water.

"Araneae, if I could, my answer would be forever."

"Why?"

"Because I like you the way you are right now. I don't want that to change. I thought I did, but now that you're here…" His large hand reached out to cover mine, the connection sparking as it had since the first time. "Now that you're mine completely, I don't want to ruin it."

A lump formed in my throat as I took him in, really looked at him. "Sterling, what are you going to tell me?"

"I've been debating."

I sprang to my feet. "What the hell are you debating? My life is covered in a veil of secrets, and you have the ability to rip it off, to shed light on what I've never known."

"What if it isn't light? People are determined to silence you. The plane crash I didn't tell you about..."

I nodded as I sat again.

"There were a few more serious injuries. A few broken bones from the landing and evacuation, but overall, it could have been much worse."

"I heard someone say that the pilot died? He was hit in a subway tunnel." I didn't want to remind Sterling of my eavesdropping, but at this point it was water under the bridge.

"The day of the crash, his wife filed for divorce. She also received a large financial infusion into an offshore account. She has a small business and without going into a lot of detail, that business is connected to a shell company. The thing I can't understand is that you didn't fly on the flight we'd booked a week earlier."

"No, I flew on your plane."

"Not officially. Officially, you're still in the United States. The ticket for that particular flight wasn't purchased until Wednesday morning."

"How can you do that, make it appear that I wasn't here?" Queasiness tugged at my stomach, as anxiety brought my small hairs to life. "Why would you do that?" I scooted away from the man in front of me. "No one knows I'm here." Panic grew as my fingers came to my lips. "Oh God, are you...? Was my mom right?"

Sterling reached out and took my hand, stopping my retreat. "That's a lot of questions."

"Sterling Sparrow, look me in the fucking eye." I ripped off my sunglasses as moisture overflowed my lids and waited for him to do the same. Once he did, I went on, "Are you the one targeting me? Are you going to... am I ever going home?"

His dark eyes fluttered closed as he took a deep breath, his nostrils flared, and the cords of his neck pulled tight.

"Am I targeting you? I have been for a long time." He reached for my knee. "Not to kill you. That's not me. And for your second question, I suppose it depends on your definition of home."

"Boulder."

"Then, no."

"The United States?" I asked, my voice less steady.

He nodded. "The first time I ever saw you I was about thirteen. You said it was fucked up that Rita was calling you McCrie. Imagine what it's like to be called into your father's office. I don't mean the one at the firm, the one with the fucking windows with the view of Lake Shore Drive and Lake Michigan. I mean the one in our house, the one where he met with the real people who made the Sparrow name mean power as well as wealth."

STERLING

Nineteen years ago~

"*G*et over here, boy. Pick one."

The office reeked of smoke and stale whiskey as if every old book on each regal shelf had taken those scents and infused them within their pages. The windows were covered with heavy drapes as the main source of light came from my father's computer screen. He was putting on a show to the room full of men who worked the Sparrow outfit.

I didn't like being around my father, much less the men who worked for him. There was something about them that made my skin crawl. The way they looked at me in a way I knew they shouldn't. I was too young to realize that I was a threat. The thought hadn't even occurred to me. My mother didn't like me to be around them either, but even she couldn't stop a direct summons from Allister Sparrow.

At thirteen years of age I was beginning to develop, to mature. My shoulders were growing wider. I was six inches taller than at the beginning of school the previous year. Lifting weights in football helped with the muscles as well as my strength. I could bench-press double my weight, one of the few accomplishments my father ever praised.

I was pretty sure I would need to start shaving soon, but my mother only laughed when I mentioned it. My face wasn't the only place that hair was growing.

None of that made me feel grown up in this den of wolves. No, I was keenly aware that I was a pup compared to each one of them as their beady eyes watched, and they took amusement at my plight.

My mind scrambled with what this summons was all about. The large monitor on his desk hummed. Swallowing my fear and showing none—because even at thirteen, I knew animals like the ones within his office had the ability to sense fear as easily as blood—I walked proudly around my father's desk to view the screen of his computer. My back may have been straight and my expression cool, but with each step, my gut somersaulted.

"It's about time, Allister," a man I knew as Rudy said. "Kid's a teenager now. Time to wet his dick."

"Question is... what does he want?" another man asked as the room roared with laughter.

"Doesn't matter when money's no object."

"Hey, Allister, you could get him one of each."

I'd lost track of who was speaking, trying to ignore the comments as I swallowed the bile and looked up to my father's stare bearing down on me.

His large hand landed squarely on my shoulder. "Boy is a Sparrow," he said to the room, "he'll choose wisely."

My father then slid the computer mouse my direction, his

crest ring reflecting the light from the small desk lamp that created a circle of illumination on his ink pad and the folder lying there.

Though I'd never done any of the things they were talking about, I wasn't naïve. I was street-smart enough to understand what their snide comments and laughing in the smoke-filled room was all about. I'd watched a video or more on websites that I could find. I'd seen my friend's dad's magazines. I'd jacked off in the shower.

I'd done it in bed once, but the maid told my mother, and I was determined not to repeat that conversation.

When I clicked the mouse, the screensaver disappeared, and my father's screen came to life.

The first picture was a naked woman. Not a rarity, as I'd soon learn they were all naked. This one, though, was a woman, probably in her twenties, much older than me, with huge breasts, her legs spread, and one hand teasing the bare place between her legs. The lady had long, wild red hair and she looked as if she were in pain—I'd later learn it was an expression of pleasure. The picture was like the ones in my friend's dad's magazines but different because I was viewing it in front of my father and his friends.

That didn't mean she wasn't alluring. Even at thirteen, my dick moved. Not thinking, I reached down to hide my reaction, only to be met with more laughter.

"Boy, you're not ready for the likes of her," my father said with a laugh. "Besides, she's all mine and a handful at that."

"Two handfuls," someone chimed in.

The glint in my father's eye told me he wasn't joking. This woman, who wasn't my mother, was his, and from that moment on, it would be a secret I was meant to bear.

Wanting to make that woman disappear from the screen, I clicked the mouse.

The next picture wasn't erotic. It turned my stomach. The picture on the screen was of a much younger girl. She didn't have the same look on her face as the older woman. This girl was naked, her breasts barely developed and her pussy bare. I wasn't noticing any of that as much as the utter terror in her eyes. Quickly, I clicked. I clicked again and again, but the pictures were all similar. Young girls, posed to be attractive, perhaps even alluring. In some of their stares there was fear, in others, nothing—like black eyes on older dolls I'd seen at the museum. They were lifeless, dead. Each photo filled me with more and more disgust.

And then the young girls were gone. The next screen filled with a young boy. I turned to my father.

"Don't tell me, boy, that you want one of them."

"Told you, Allister, one of each," a deep voice boasted. "That's what my old man gave me. Made me fuck them both the same night. Great lesson too..."

I tried to block out the voice as more laughter filled the room, and the food I'd eaten stewed in my twisting gut. "No, sir," I replied truthfully.

My answer didn't affect the sequence of photos. The next ten or so were of young boys. Based on the kids I'd helped coach in Y10 football camp, if I had to guess, these boys were seven or eight years old. They hadn't grown any hair down there, and the ones who forced a smile had the giant front teeth with smaller ones behind. Each one was posed as the girls had been, their private parts visible, and their eyes equally as filled with terror, or dark and dead.

Even at thirteen, I knew my answer couldn't be 'no, thank

you, I want none of them.' I couldn't reject my father's gift in front of these men and walk away without consequences.

In this room, if I were ever to be a part, a *live* part, of my father's world and not a scared kid on the computer screen, I had to make a decision. It was then I noticed the manila folder lying on the ink pad on his desk. There was the corner of a glossy photo sticking out.

Next, I did the unthinkable—the unimaginable. I touched something on my father's desk without his permission. That action had previously resulted in a crack against my cheek or against the side of my head. Even my mother wasn't allowed in his office without him. I can't say why I did it, but I did. I reached out and threw open the folder.

A glossy photo floated across the desk. It was a girl— young, maybe less than ten. I didn't know. She had yellow blonde hair and pink cheeks and was wearing clothes. The lack of nakedness wasn't what registered. What mattered to me, even at thirteen, were her eyes. They were the softest brown, as if they were made of the material from my mother's suede coat. It wasn't only their color. It was their expression: smiling. There was no fear or terror, no death or defeat. The girl in the picture was smiling at the camera, the way a young girl should.

I straightened my neck and turned to my father. "Her."

The gregarious laughter from earlier faded to coughs and throat-clearing as my father sat forward. "She wasn't one of your choices."

"Think about it, Allister," a voice from the room said. "If the rumors are true, she could—"

"Shut the fuck up," Allister yelled as his hand pounded the desk. "How the fuck can the rumors be true? She's a kid."

"Where else did it go?"

"Fuck, it's more than the missing money. Some believe that she has the evidence to back up her daddy's claims."

"Enough!" my father roared, silencing the room. He turned to me. "You're going to have to prove yourself, boy, before you get the likes of her."

I turned to the room. "I will."

"If you do, you can have her. Her dad owes me."

"Fuck," Rudy said, "he owes more than you."

"I'll be the one to collect," my dad said matter-of-factly.

"I'll do it. She's mine," I said and turned to the room. With more determination than I possessed, I stared into the eyes of every yellow-toothed jackass in the room. And then with a nod to my father, I walked out.

When the door shut behind me, I hurried to the closest bathroom and threw up the contents of my stomach and then some. I'd made it out of that room. I wasn't sure how I'd done it. The only other thing I knew was that despite not knowing her name, I would prove my worth because as of that day, she belonged to me.

ARANEAE

Present~

I stared in disbelief as Sterling finished his story. This wasn't even close to something I could have imagined. How could I?

Each word turned my stomach. "What about the other children?"

Sterling didn't speak at first, his dark eyes warning me that there were some secrets best left buried. Instead of answering, he asked me a question. "Who have I repeatedly told you to worry about?"

"Myself," I replied as I pulled the jacket sleeves down over my hands to ward off the chill. "It was me, wasn't it? My picture was on your father's desk?"

Sterling nodded as he took a long swig of the water bottle. "I didn't know your name at first. I didn't know anything about you or anything that those assholes were talking about.

I just knew that those men could cause the life to go out of your eyes. I knew they had that power—I'd seen it.

"I vowed it wouldn't happen."

I stood and stepped from the blanket, my boots crunching the pebbles beneath my steps. Stopping at the shore, I stared out over the water as wave after soft wave came onto the mixture of sand and pebbles, only to disappear again into the depths of the lake.

Was that how it was with secrets? One would be revealed only to be swallowed up by the whole.

My mind couldn't process.

Sterling didn't touch me, but I could feel his presence behind me. I turned to face him. "How old are you?"

His head shook. "Of all the questions—"

"How old are you?" I asked louder.

His hands came to my shoulders. "Thirty-two, -three soon."

My mind scattered. *Thirty-two minus thirteen equaled nineteen. Twenty-six minus nineteen.* "Seven," I said.

"I know that now."

The reality nauseated my empty stomach. "And you don't think that's fucked up? Really fucked up, like worse than Rita calling me by a name I don't know."

"I think it's totally fucked," Sterling said. "I was determined to find you. There's something else I should probably confess."

"What?" I took a breath. "Do I want to know?"

"I spent many years between obsessing over you and hating you."

"Hating me? You didn't know me. You still don't."

A half smile came to his lips as he squeezed my shoulders. "I know you were shitty at running track but are kick-ass on all-terrain vehicles."

"I wasn't shitty," I argued with a shrug. "I wasn't good. That doesn't mean I was shitty."

"I know you're a true blonde."

Though I didn't want it to, blood rushed to my cheeks. "There was a razor on the plane. I thought it might be for...but I couldn't."

"Good. Don't." Sterling took a step back. "You think that the one story I just told you was fucked up?" he asked.

My eyes widened. "Yes."

"Sunshine, if my life were an iceberg, I just showed you the very tip. Over time I realized that I didn't really hate you. There were times that I hated what attracted me to you in the first place."

I blinked, recalling the story of my picture. "My eyes."

"Your vibrancy. Like the fucking sun. That's why I call you sunshine. That's what you've been, before you even knew my name. In every picture I'd receive, every video, or report, you were shining. I didn't know exactly what took you from the Marshes—I was away at the University of Michigan when that went down—but even that... you didn't let it ruin you. In college you were thrown curves. Sinful Threads started slow, and through it all you wouldn't give up." Letting go of my shoulders, he cupped my cheeks. "Even with me, you don't cave. You don't back down. Men who have known me for most of their lives wouldn't dare talk to me the way you have. In you, there's no fear, no fucking doll eyes." His tone slowed. "Maybe I didn't hate you. I envied you."

I lifted myself to my toes and brushed a kiss over his lips. I wasn't sure what made me do it, but once I did, I didn't regret the impulsive decision. "I need more," I said.

"Can you handle more?"

"You said you didn't know what took me from the Marshes. Does that mean you do know now?"

His jaw clenched as his Adam's apple bobbed.

"Okay, who has targeted me and why?" There were a million other questions popping into my head. I only gave voice to the ones I longed to know.

When he didn't answer, I reached for his hand and led him back to the blanket. Opening the basket, I found sandwiches and a container of fruit that Rita had packed. Handing Sterling one of the sandwiches, I opened the fruit container and placed it between us.

"If you're counting on the old saying that a way to a man's heart..." He looked down at the sandwich he was unwrapping. "...and think that food will make me tell you anything any faster, you underestimate me."

My cheeks rose as I grinned. "If you think I don't have other tricks up my sleeve, you underestimate me."

His dark eyes shone as he took a bite of the sandwich.

As I ate, I thought about his story, the dark, dead doll eyes. Sterling's eyes were the darkest brown I'd ever seen. I wasn't sure I would ever want to know the things he'd seen in his life. Yet describing them as dead or lifeless couldn't be further from their real description. In every encounter, his eyes were alive and animated. Calculating, contemplating, and searing with desire. There was no reason for this man to envy my vibrancy. Everything about him emitted dynamic energy, strength, power, and control. The air around him sizzled with the force of his presence.

Once we were done eating, I laid my head down in his lap and looked upward. The view from this angle was equally as handsome, the cut of his jaw and girth of his chest as he leaned against his back-stretched arms.

Slowly, he sat forward as his fingers came to my hair and began to gently twist and stroke. "You know, when I imagined your face near my cock, you were positioned a little differently."

"You're really incorrigible."

"I believe the word is insatiable."

"Please tell me more. What about my birth parents?"

That broad chest expanded and contracted as he weighed his words. "You may have guessed that Sparrows are not only involved in real estate. There is a world that isn't mentioned in polite conversation. It exists. It's powerful and dangerous, yet it does its best to stay under the radar."

"I'm not sure I want to know more about that."

"I'm certain you don't. And you won't."

I reached for his hand that was now resting on my stomach and intertwined my fingers. "Go on."

"What I can tell you is that it's a dirty business, all of it. We're hardly the only family involved, but I've worked very hard to make Sparrow mean much more than it did when my father was alive. I'm not proud of all I do and have done, but I can justify it when I lay my head down at night. Usually."

I thought of him saying he sleeps *occasionally*. I didn't want to know what he couldn't justify, what kept him awake at night.

"I brought you here to the cabin because things will be different in Chicago."

"How?"

He tilted his head down and kissed my forehead. "The man you're with right now doesn't exist there."

I recalled the aching in my groin from the way he'd taken me earlier in the day, and a smile tugged at my lips. "If you're a figment of my imagination, I have a great one."

"Here is safe. Nothing about Chicago is."

I sat up. "Then let's not go back. Come with me. We can go to Boulder." My enthusiasm to continue whatever this was between us surprised even me.

His smile was sad as his head shook. "I can't. I never can. And neither can you. Like you are mine—belonging to me—so is Chicago. I've worked hard to get where I am, to where Sparrow is—Sparrow Enterprises as well as the Sparrow world that isn't discussed. It's me. I'm it. I took it from others, made it mine, and rule it." He squeezed my hand. "The only thing missing from my empire is a queen, and you were born for the job. I can't walk away from it—we can't. Don't you see?"

My head shook from side to side as his words weighed inside me.

Queen.

Fiancée.

His sunshine.

I was only ready to commit to one of those titles.

"My team and I have discovered that these recent attempts on your life and the targeting of you are for one reason. Up until recently, to many in the underworld you were a rumor, a myth, like a ghost who lurked just outside the third dimension. My father found you. There's another family...I can't say too much." His hand raked his hair. "I can't explain it all in one day or probably even a lifetime, but over time there've been reported sightings. Once I had power, my people made sure that those reports went unsubstantiated. Even those who should have known, who have the power to do what has been done..." A vein in his forehead popped to life. "...had you in their grasp, but didn't realize who you were."

My brows lowered. "What do you mean?"

"Patrick was there. You were safe." Before I could give that more thought, he went on. "It's different now. The rumored Araneae McCrie has come out of the shadows of fabled lore to reality. You'd been discovered as Renee Marsh, and from what I could learn, when it was no longer safe, your life changed. Except to a privileged few who knew the truth, you were secured and hidden as Kennedy Hawkins.

"I take responsibility for bringing you into the light, but it would have happened anyway. Having you in Chicago was too risky. You, sunshine, are many things, and not the least of which is my perceived weakness."

"Yours?" I recalled his story. "Those men...?" I said. "The ones in your father's office?"

Sterling nodded. "Some remember, some are dead, and some have forgotten. Some couldn't handle the reality of my leadership. Some didn't live to question it further. Others, a very few, had made contingency plans, attempting my demise while seeking protection with another family. The reality of their lives—what the public sees—allowed them to live. It's a decision I regret."

"Why take me back to Chicago if it isn't safe?"

His gaze was penetrating as his hand grasped mine. "Because as fucked up as it sounds, it's the only way to make you safe. We're going to show you to those who think they matter, those who will do anything to get to me. And we will make fucking sure they know you're mine."

"Maybe I can go back to being Kennedy?" Did I want that? Did I want to leave Sterling? This man I hardly knew had marked me as his own in more ways than sex. There was a connection I wasn't sure I wanted to sever—or even sure I could.

"No." He didn't mince words. "You're mine. Many years ago, I made that declaration, and now the word on the street is that it's come true. Daniel McCrie's daughter isn't dead. And with you, they expect to discover the secrets that disappeared from your family when your father decided to double-cross the wrong people."

"What secrets?" My eyes opened wide. "His name is Daniel?" I couldn't believe my own lips. I was finally saying my birth father's name. "Is he still alive?"

"That's where the stories must be wrong, where lore has overtaken reality. Otherwise you would know the secrets, right?"

My mind scrambled. "I guess that makes sense. What am I supposed to know?"

His head slowly shook. "I should have known that you didn't."

"How without asking?"

"Because your father was deep in the dark world I now control. He was also an esteemed attorney. Today they call people like him fixers. Those people learn secrets that no one should know. It's their job to make problems go away—any problem. If I told you what he supposedly knew, if you knew..." He ran his finger over my cheek. "...I would be responsible for taking the light out of your eyes. I've done enough. I won't do that, too."

ARANEAE

o matter what trick I tried—and I admittedly shamelessly tried most contained within my limited arsenal—Sterling refused to share more of my past. He promised he would but not until I was ready. The reality was that I knew more about myself than I had a day ago, much more than a week ago. He didn't answer if my biological father was alive, and yet he discussed him in the past tense. While I wanted to rip the Band-Aid from my past, I had to concede that maybe Sterling was right: too much would be overwhelming.

Not that Sterling Sparrow wasn't overwhelming in and of himself.

I decided that if once we arrived in Chicago, the man I was with at the cabin was going to disappear, while we had the chance, I wanted as much of him as I could get. So while he didn't share more secrets regarding my past, he did share secrets to my body that even I hadn't known.

The bedroom Rita had assigned to me no longer was on my radar. One nearly twice the size with two walls of windows, including a balcony that looked out over Paul Bunyan's lake, was where my things were moved. We had two nights with a day in between before we were destined to return to Sterling's realm. While not all of the time was spent in bed, admittedly a majority was.

There was also a wall or two, a sofa that if I was positioned right, lifted my ass much like the bed on the plane had done, and also an amazing gigantic shower.

Sterling was serious when he said he only occasionally slept. There were many times I'd wake to an empty bed, only to be reawakened to his hard, warm body not only rousing me but also my desires. The abrupt connection in his office was replaced with hours of unimaginable and sometimes infuriating skillful foreplay.

He didn't lie or make excuses. When he was away from me I knew he was working, doing whatever it was that Sterling Sparrow did. There were times his phone would ding, and by his mumbling I knew it was a summons from Patrick or others who worked for him. I found it difficult to believe Sterling answered any summons. It was more likely, as on the plane, that there was a continuous cycle of metaphoric fires that required his attention.

I hoped they weren't more real flames.

I'd corresponded with both Winnie and Louisa daily via calls or texts, but my emails were left unattended. The only unexpected call I received was on Saturday afternoon. Patrick brought me my phone and indicated there was someone waiting. I didn't recognize the number. Yet I reasoned, he wouldn't give it to me if it were unsafe.

"Hello?" I answered tentatively.

"Who was that deep-voiced gentleman?"

I sprang from the sofa where I'd been sitting on the back patio. "Jeanne!"

"I wanted to let you know I'm all right. I'm sorry I didn't look after your apartment better."

Tears prickled my eyes. "You're okay. That's all that matters. I'm scared to ask, but what about Polly and Fred?"

"Oh my goodness. There was this nice lady who visited me in the hospital. Her name was Shelly. She told me that she found them and would take care of them until I was released."

A lump formed in my throat. "That's amazing."

"A miracle. That's all."

"Where are you going to live," I asked.

"Well, you know how you've been telling me to look into one of those senior communities?"

"Yes." I nodded along with my answer despite the fact she couldn't see me.

"I got a call. Something with the doctors. They're worried about me living alone. You know Rossetti's, that nice one outside of Boulder?" She didn't let me answer, but I did know. I'd even looked into it for her, but the cost was astronomical. "They have a program and because I no longer have a place to stay and they have an open apartment...the price is less than my rent and it includes meals and onsite medical care."

My chest filled with emotion, knowing that no such program existed. Not officially anyway.

"Well, dear," she went on, "it's just another miracle. This could have been a tragedy; instead, it's a godsend."

Tears came to my eyes with the accelerated beating of my heart. "Jeanne, I'm so happy for you."

"What about you? Where will you live?"

I scoffed. "I'm pretty sure the same one who got you set up has plans for me."

"The Lord is truly amazing."

He was, but I was one hundred percent certain that a heavenly being wasn't responsible for this round of miraculous events. "Please call me with your new address," I said. As soon as I did, I realized I could probably get the information from Patrick.

After we hung up, I found Patrick waiting just inside. At least he had the decency to give me privacy. "Thank you," I said, handing him the phone. "For everything."

"It's just a phone, ma'am."

"Right."

I couldn't describe what happened on this getaway. It was as if a new person came to life inside me. Maybe I wasn't a spider but a butterfly emerging from a cocoon. How could someone who'd lived two different lives already be granted a third?

I didn't know.

Sunday morning—our final day—I woke to the streaming of sunlight and a soft, cool breeze from the opened windows as a strong hand pulled my naked body closer to his warmth. It seemed impossible that I could want more of what he gave or that my body could even handle it. I was deliciously sore in all the right ways, and yet the prod of his erection against my lower back was all it took to turn my nipples to rocks and flood my core.

A moan escaped from my lips as his hands wandered. My breasts grew heavy as he skillfully manipulated my hardening nipples. With his other hand he found the evidence of my arousal as his long fingers roamed.

When I wasn't certain I could take it any longer, large hands came to my waist and I was lifted until I straddled his toned torso. My fingers splayed over his hard chest before my kisses followed the indentations. I smiled peering toward his dark stare. "How do you stay so buff if you don't work out?"

"Who said I don't work out?" His voice vibrated through me, starting at my core.

"Me. I haven't seen you work out."

Before I knew what happened, I was flipped to my back and our positions were reversed. The room filled with my laughter as Sterling slid down my body and my legs opened for him. I squealed as his tongue teased.

Lifting his head, he peered my direction with his shining dark stare. "Sunshine, if you don't think what we've been doing is a workout, I've been doing it wrong."

My cheeks rose higher. "I'm pretty sure you haven't been doing it wrong. I mean working out like weights or running. I found a workout room yesterday when I was searching for Jana."

His smile evaporated as he climbed higher up my body. "Why were you searching for Jana?"

I shrugged. "I hadn't seen her. I mean, I haven't seen anyone but you, Rita, and Patrick for the most part. There is that other lady who cooks, but she doesn't say much, and I don't even know her name."

"Did you find Jana?"

He seemed more concerned than I expected. "I did."

"And?"

"Sterling, what? She thinks you're the greatest person since sliced bread."

"Bread isn't a person. I don't want you talking to anyone."

I shook my head. "You're being silly. Seriously, she would do anything for you. There's no reason to be concerned."

He lifted himself on his elbows, his face inches from mine. "Araneae, you don't get it."

I wiggled my hips. "I haven't yet, but I was pretty sure it was coming."

Sterling growled as he seized my lips. "No."

"What?"

I shivered as the blankets that had been covering us flipped back and Sterling moved from me and the bed to the floor. Unashamedly naked and looking like a Greek god—one chiseled out of granite—he walked the length of the room and back. "Don't you understand that no one can be trusted?"

I sat up against the headboard and pulled the sheet over my breasts, a little shocked and disappointed by the turn of events. "No, but I suppose you're going to tell me."

"Fuck..." His hand went through his bed-messed hair. "...you act like this is a game. Shit gets real tonight. It's been real, but this is life and death." He turned my way. "I've tried to tell you that the world you're used to living in and the life you had is gone. I can't make it come back." His arms flexed as his hands balled and un-balled in fists at his side. "Hell, I didn't think I'd want to...to lose you once I had you, but now..."

A lump formed in my throat as I looked down at the blanket over me. Taking a deep breath, I moved my gaze back to him and blinked away the tears his confession instilled.

"Tell me what you mean. Are you saying that now that you've had me, you wish you could return me?"

He spun my direction. "Are you fucking kidding me?"

I slapped the bed at my side. "That's what you just said."

"The hell it is." His answer boomed through the room and open windows. "The answer to that ridiculous question is no. I will never give you up. You can count on that. Araneae, you're mine. I just wish I could give you this." His hand went out and about the room, the windows, and open blue sky beyond. "I'll try as often as I can, but even here, everywhere, you need to remember that there are only three people you can trust with your life: me, Patrick, and Reid."

"I don't know Reid."

"You will once we get to Chicago. No one else is one hundred percent trustworthy. No one."

"Jesus, Sterling. If this is about Jana, you're overreacting. She isn't a threat."

Sitting on the edge of the bed, he reached for my hand. "That's the problem right there. We don't know."

"Then how do you know about Patrick and this Reid guy?"

His back straightened. "We've been to war together."

"Metaphorically?" I asked with a tilt of my head.

"No, sunshine. Two tours in the desert and nearly a lifetime in Chicago's underground. I trust them with my life and because of that, yours. No one else has shown that kind of loyalty. I repeat, no one. Period."

"I have a job to do and a business to run, remember?" I said, crossing my arms over my chest. "I'm not being held up in some tower of your castle for my safety."

"I remember. And we've been working on that, securing

you office space because you sure as hell aren't working from your warehouse or distribution center."

I wanted to protest, saying it wasn't in Sinful Threads' budget, but he didn't take a breath.

"Patrick will be your new shadow. And the same rules apply. Talk Sinful Threads all you want, but nothing personal. Nothing. Don't mention me or us."

"Sterling, you're being—"

His finger landed on my lips. "Keep arguing and I'll find something better for those lips to do."

A smile crept under his touch. When he lifted his finger, I said, "Oh, Mr. Sparrow, you're going to have to do better than that. If you think having me suck your cock is a punishment..." I let the sheet drop. "...please, punish me all day long."

Okay, I hadn't done that yet, but it didn't sound all that bad to me.

The stern expression that had been staring at me a second earlier shattered as he moved from sitting on the edge of the bed and rolled, moving the sheet and lifting me back over his stomach. I really wasn't sure how he did it or what happened. Maybe it was some maneuver he'd learned in the army, maybe he was really quicker than the speed of light—a superhero or maybe a supervillain. I wasn't sure. All I knew was that by the way he was staring at me, I was certain that in a few seconds I'd be riding the most glorious rock-hard cock I'd ever known.

With his hands on my hips, he lifted me over him. My hands fell to his shoulders as he purposely lowered me just enough so the head of his penis brushed repeatedly over my entrance.

My struggle was futile. Finally, I slapped his shoulder.

"Stop it."

"Stop?" His brows quirked.

"Let me..." I wiggled.

"Tell me that you'll do as I said."

"You're an asshole."

He lowered me enough to let his cock slide in.

"Oh." The relief of my growing wanton need was instant, and then just as quickly he lifted me off him.

When I only glared, Sterling smirked. "Sunshine, I can come up with all kinds of punishments."

"Fuck you."

"I think that's what you want. What do I want?"

I was beyond wanton. That's what he did to me. My desire was almost painful as my empty core throbbed, and his hands held tighter to my hips. I'd probably have his handprints bruised into my sides, but at this moment it wasn't my concern. "Fine. I'll do as you say."

My eyes closed as he lowered my body, filling me completely. As the pressure built and he started to lift me again, I opened my eyes and gripped his shoulder. "Don't do that."

His lips quirked. "I want more. Tell me what you will do."

"Only trust you, Patrick, and some guy I don't even know."

"And?"

"And I won't talk about personal things. Or even to other people that I can't trust." For a split second, Louisa came to mind, but honestly the shaft below me was my bigger concern. I'd argue Louisa and Winnie later.

"Yes." My relief was immediate as I slid down, his cock completely filling me.

"Ride me."

It was the first time I'd been on top, ever. The power was intoxicating as I varied my movements, up and down, backward and forward. My long hair fluttered over his face. The sensation was overwhelming as I moved faster, only to slow as the cords in his neck became visible. I tried to stay slow, but the pressure became too much as my toes curled. It wasn't just that I was close to another fantastic orgasm. It was also that my thighs were on the verge of cramping, screaming out from the exertion. When we finally came, I collapsed on his broad chest, my muscles spent.

Sterling rolled me to the side and kissed from my forehead down to my lips. "Go ahead and tell me how that wasn't a workout."

I slapped his shoulder. "Do you have to be right about everything?"

"If it means you're riding my cock, I'd be glad to be wrong." He kissed my nose. "Except I never am. Remember that and remember what you promised."

Nodding with tired eyes, I asked a question I hoped I knew how Sterling would answer. "When we get to Chicago, will I have my own room?"

He leaned back and took me in. "It wasn't in your earlier negotiations. Do we need to open a contract dispute?"

I shook my head. "No. If I can't trust anyone else, I'd like to be with the one man I can trust, as much as possible."

"I like to hear that."

I curled closer to his warm chest and let my eyes close. He'd been right about one thing. It was a workout.

"Next stop, Chicago," I heard him say as I drifted back to sleep.

ARANEAE

I woke to breakfast being delivered to our room. Instead of Rita or the woman whose name I didn't know, my deliveryman was tall, dark haired, wearing low-riding jeans, and shirtless, making me forget what had just happened before my morning nap and considering if food was a necessity.

As he turned around toward the bed, there was a split second of the expression I didn't like. I didn't fear it, but its presence meant he was no longer the man I'd gotten to know in this mountaintop cabin. And then just as quickly as his gaze met mine, it evaporated and his cheeks rose. I didn't think I could tire of his smile. As with the softening of his facial expression, his smile was a gift that I doubted anyone who didn't make his short list of trusted individuals was privileged enough to see.

"Good morning, sunshine. We have plans and you can't sleep the day away."

A glance at my wrist told me I'd slept until nearly noon.

As I took him in, I hoped our plans were either the same as we'd done most of the last forty-eight hours or perhaps another ATV ride to the lake. "I told you. I only sleep late if a man keeps me up into the early hours of the morning. Or apparently awakens me repeatedly. You know, there're supposed be eight uninterrupted hours before getting up."

"I'm pretty sure it was me who stayed up." He lifted the tray from the table across the room where he'd just placed it and carried it toward me. Small collapsible legs fell from the bottom, showing me that it would fit over my lap.

"And therein is the reason for my needed sleep." I scooted up the bed and pulled the sheet higher. "To what do I owe the honor of you delivering my food?"

The gleam in his gaze sizzled as he narrowed his eyes. "Who else would I allow to come in here when you're lying there all naked and alluring?"

My smile bloomed as warmth filled my cheeks. "I'm glad you think so. I think I'm probably a wreck." I lifted my hand to my hair. "I'm sure my hair is a mess and I probably smell of sex."

His nostrils flared as he came closer. "If it were up to me, it would be the perfume you always wore." Sterling placed the tray over my lap and lifted the lid. "You're gorgeous, and I'm not sharing."

The feast before me included a scrumptious vegetable omelet, thick sourdough toast, and a bowl of fruit. Above what had been covered, was a glass of juice, large mug filled with coffee, a small pitcher of cream, and a tiny vase with one of the purple flowers I'd seen growing outside the cabin.

"Are you also the chef?"

"No. I could manage the toast without burning it, but cooking has never been my strong suit."

I took a bite of toast. "Yeah, you probably didn't need to, growing up like this."

His smile disappeared. "I told you, tip of the iceberg. Having cooks, maids, and a big house doesn't guarantee happiness."

"Sterling, I'm sorry."

"Most of my cooking skill came in the army, and I won't feed you the shit we ate...ever."

As he paced about the room, it seemed as though he was giving me glimpses into the man he was, and yet the pieces were all fragmented, a mosaic instead of a portrait. It also seemed that despite Sterling knowing almost everything about me, I would learn his secrets in his time.

No, I'd learn both of our secrets in his time.

Lifting the warm mug to my lips, I asked, "What are our plans?"

His head shook. "It's time to go back to Chicago."

My appetite disappeared as my stomach dropped. "I was hoping that could wait until tonight."

Sterling disappeared into the large closet and came back out with a black dress that appeared somewhat familiar, yet I was certain I hadn't seen it in his closet.

"We have an engagement," he said.

It was hard to tell from the hanger, but the material reminded me of the Sinful Threads prototype I'd worn during my last trip to Chicago. "Where did that come from and what kind of engagement?"

"Where dresses come from," he said noncommittally, "and the engagement is considered formal."

"Am I wearing some other woman's dress to this formal engagement?"

"Of course not."

"We're in the middle of nowhere. Why can't we get to your castle before I dress?"

His hand went through his hair. "You're infuriating."

My eyes popped open wide. "Me?"

"Can't you just do as I say without ten thousand questions?"

"I think the obvious answer is no."

Sterling swallowed as his neck strained. "It was easier to have a dress delivered than the other dress dry-cleaned."

I wanted to mention whose fault it was that the red dress needed dry cleaning, but this conversation wasn't going well and poking the bear didn't seem like a good idea.

"There are shoes and jewelry in there. My house—our home," he corrected, "isn't a castle. My mother still lives in that. When she's done with it, it can burn to the ground for all I care. We live in a penthouse, five complete floors and the best security in the world."

"Why do you need five floors?"

"Only two are the living quarters. You won't need to enter the other three."

"I won't need to enter? Or I'm not *allowed* to enter? Is this like the not talking to people thing?"

"Just eat the damn food and shower," he said as he stepped toward the door and reached for the doorknob.

"Sterling, do not walk out." I was trapped by the damn tray as I lifted it from my lap and threw back the covers, the table setting rattling. Well aware that I was now completely without clothes, I decided to concentrate on the future.

"Why can't I get adjusted to everything before an engagement? I'm..." I wasn't sure what I was.

The expression from before was back, including the dark stare and clenched jaw. "Do you or do you not want to go to work tomorrow? Do you want to continue with Sinful Threads?"

My fists went to my hips. As soon as they connected, I realized that I'd been right. My hips were bruised from the earlier grasp of the man before me. Ignoring the pain, I answered, "You know damn well that is what I want. It was part of my demands."

Releasing the handle, he turned back to me. "Mine is that you do as I say. You're not going out in Chicago, ever, without Patrick or me, and you're not going out at all until the statement is made that you're there and you're mine."

My pulse quickened. "So you're saying that if I want to go to work or to the fucking bakery we have to do this —tonight?"

"I see no reason for you to go to a bakery. The rest, yes."

Closing my eyes, I shook my head. "You're insane." I stalked over to the sofa where the black dress was lying and picked it up. *Holy shit.* "You didn't get this at a store. These aren't sold in stores." I ran my hand over the silky fabric. "It's..." I turned back to Sterling. "I haven't seen this yet, not in full size. How the fuck did you get it?"

He shrugged. "Reid has already been looking into increasing your security."

I gently laid the dress back on the couch as I spun back around and tugged at my own hair. "Gah! I don't get you."

He took two long strides until he was right before me. Wrapping one arm around my waist, he pulled my naked body flush to his partially clothed one. "You do, Araneae. You get me, every damn day for the rest of your life. Get used to it.

"I had this Sinful Threads dress brought to you for two reasons. One, to show you that your design facility is in need of better security, and two, because I knew that in this dress you would slay the room we are going to enter. Every fucking eye will be on you, and as unsure as you are about all that's happened this last week, you are confident when it comes to Sinful Threads. I've watched you. I've sat in large ballrooms and heard you deliver a speech with more emotion and belief in your product than I've heard from the likes of Mark Zuckerberg or Bill Gates. You may not know who to believe or all your own secrets, but there is one thing you do believe in. Sinful Threads."

He's been to my presentations? When? Where?

I didn't get the chance to ask as his deep voice continued.

"I want you to walk into the club tonight like the queen you are." He lifted my chin high enough to stretch my neck and spine. "Head held high, regal, and noble." His lips quirked as he took a step back and scanned my naked form. "That's how I've always seen you. It's how you look now. You're a queen, even here..."

His hand skirted my side, from my breast to my hip, his touch too light to caress, yet too intimate for me not to react.

Shivers peppered my skin with goose bumps.

"It is how everyone in that room will see you," Sterling said, "and when they do, they'll know that if they lay a goddamned finger on one precious hair on your head, I will take great pleasure in watching them die. It'll be my word. A man's word is either his most valuable tool or his most respected weapon. Tonight, it will be a weapon, one I won't hesitate to use."

Letting go of my chin, he ran his finger along my cheek as he shook his head. "It won't take long. My message to every asshole in that room will be short." His stare darkened. "That doesn't mean it will be sweet. No matter, it will come through loud and clear."

Releasing his hold, his hand came down hard on my ass, the slap making me jump as I reached back to my now-stinging skin. "Ouch."

Sterling's stare didn't lighten. "Finish your meal and get ready. I have work to do downstairs. Don't leave this room. I want you to think about what I said about not talking to people—that includes here. We're leaving by five, and I want you dressed to kill. And if you're not ready, it will be more than one slap to your ass."

"Asshole."

Faster than the speed of light, Sterling's fingers pinched my cheeks. I tried to back away as pain flooded my receptors, and once again my mind questioned my safety. I couldn't back away. I couldn't move as his grip tightened. I reached for his hand to no avail. Moisture came to my eyes as the taste of copper floated over my tongue.

His words were slow and weighted. "I enjoy your fire, but if you *ever* speak to me like that in front of anyone—and I mean, anyone—you won't be sitting for a week." He released me.

As I rubbed my jaw, words failed to form. Well, some did.

Asshole.

Bully.

Bastard.

No. He'd corrected that one.

How about son of a bitch?

Before I could voice any of them, he turned and walked to the door. Opening and closing it loudly, he left me standing naked and alone in the middle of the bedroom.

Fuck you, Sterling Sparrow.

ARANEAE

I was dressed and ready before five o'clock. I also decided that if Sterling didn't want me speaking to anyone, I'd start with him. I didn't wait for him to come back to the room. Despite his order to stay inside, when he wasn't there at five minutes before five, I made my way downstairs and out onto the lawn as the helicopter landed. With my arms wrapped around my body and the wind from the blades blowing my new dress and freshly styled hair, I waited for them to stop.

"Ms. Hawkins."

I turned to see Patrick coming my way. Though I wanted to be mad at him too, I couldn't come up with a new reason to add him to my list. He'd done nothing wrong since bringing me to Sterling over a week ago. Then again, that sin could warrant a lifetime membership on my list of people not to speak to.

"Am I?" I asked, having not thought about it much while

in this magical wilderness bubble, the one Sterling effectively popped hours before.

"Ma'am?"

"Am I Ms. Hawkins?" When he tilted his head, I went on. "Please, Patrick, never act uninformed around me. I'm well aware that you know most if not all of what Sterling knows. That's a hell of a lot more than I do. When we arrive in Chicago, will I be Kennedy Hawkins or Araneae McCrie?"

"I believe Mr. Sparrow—"

"Mr. Sparrow can..." I stopped myself. Patrick probably qualified as *anyone* and I wasn't up for more of Sterling's punishments. "...tell me, I'm sure." I added the sweetest smile I could feign. "However, he isn't here and you are."

Patrick turned toward the cabin, no doubt praying his boss would appear.

"I do believe he said to do whatever I said. It seems to me that would include answering this question."

"Ma'am, you can be whomever you like on the plane. In the helicopter you're Ms. McCrie and tonight at the club too. At Sinful Threads, Mr. Sparrow feels it would be better for you and for your business to continue as Kennedy Hawkins."

"So this has already been thought out and discussed without my input?"

Patrick swallowed as he turned again to the cabin. This time Sterling was walking our direction, his expression as pleasant as it had been when he left the bedroom. In other words, he was obviously pissed.

"What is happening?" he asked, his tone matching his grim appearance. Not only that, he was still wearing the jeans from before, and a button-down shirt open at the collar, untucked, and rolled up at the sleeves.

I wanted to ask him why he wasn't ready for a formal engagement and I was, but that would require speaking, and as soon as his rather rudely delivered question left his lips, I turned my attention to the helicopter.

When I didn't respond, Patrick did. "We're ready to leave, sir."

Sterling's hand came to my back as I walked unsteadily in the heels through the grass toward the now-silent helicopter. "You look lovely."

I didn't respond.

"I expected you to still be in the room." His voice was now low, a hiss near my ear.

Instead of answering, I placed the high-heeled shoe upon the step and lifted myself with fucking royal dignity into the helicopter. All I needed was to raise a gloved hand and do my best Queen Elizabeth wave to the staff left behind. Sterling followed closely behind as he and Patrick joined the pilot and me aboard.

As the propellers began to whirl, I placed the earphones over my ears and wondered about Jana. She wasn't with us as we lifted off the ground. I could only guess that my mention of her earlier this morning relegated her to ground transportation back to the plane.

It was another reason to be pissed at the man beside me.

The flight took less time than I recalled. Perhaps it was that it was daytime and I was enthralled with the scenery. Maybe it was that Sterling's show of power in the bedroom continued to play on a loop in my mind and with each rerun, the temperature of my blood rose a few degrees until I was close to the boiling point. Or the fact that I used extra foundation and powder to ensure if bruising occurred on my cheeks, it wouldn't be noticeable—something I never imagined doing or considering.

Truly he was a talented man. In less than five minutes he'd managed to erase every good memory or feeling of desire that I'd experienced over the past four days. Was that his goal?

When it came to Sterling Sparrow, I was at a complete loss.

Thirty minutes later, after the stopping of the propellers, with my head held high, I boarded the plane, nodding to Marianne, Jana, and Keaton as Sterling again walked with his hand in the small of my back. He'd tried to hold my hand, but with a quick maneuver with my handbag, I'd successfully squelched his effort.

As we passed through the first part of the cabin, he successfully reached for my free hand, stilling my steps. "Patrick and I have more work to do. We'll be riding up here."

My jaw clenched as I stared into his eyes. My response was the same nod I'd given the crew seconds before. By the narrowing of his gaze, I was confident he heard my unspoken response—the one I wasn't to say in front of anyone: *Sit wherever the fuck you want, asshole.*

Yep, that was it as I pursed my lips and snapped my head away. This wasn't my first rodeo in this flying mansion. I knew where to go. My heels clipped the flooring as I proceeded to the part of the plane with the television.

"Ma'am," Jana said, appearing in front of me. "May I get you anything before or after takeoff?"

I assumed answering direct questions was acceptable, but then again, I wasn't certain of anything when it came to Sterling. How would it look if I'd suddenly developed laryngitis?

Screw him.

"No, thank you, Jana. I'm good." As she nodded, I reached for her hand. "How was the drive?"

"Better in the daylight. Thank you again for being so kind."

I sighed and leaned back against the plush seat. Her response helped to chip away at a bit of the ice that the man in the front of the plane had caused to flow through my veins.

My eyes opened wide as Patrick appeared with my carry-on. "Ma'am, your laptop is charged, and there's an outlet over there..." He pointed. "...by that table if your battery runs down. It was thought you might like your laptop to respond to emails or check on Sinful Threads."

"Oh." I felt the gratitude shine from my face. "Thank you. I suppose..." I stopped myself from asking if this were Sterling-approved. First, if it wasn't, it wouldn't be here. Second, I hated that his permission even crossed my mind.

If each incident were a strike, Mr. Sterling Sparrow was out. Hell, if I were the umpire, I'd eject his fine-looking ass from the game.

Once we were in the air, I hurriedly moved from the seat where I was to the one beside a shiny wood-looking table that was attached to the interior wall of the plane. As I fired up my laptop, I wondered about internet. The plane had it, or Patrick wouldn't have made the comment about responding to emails. I considered asking Jana to ask Patrick for the necessary codes, but that seemed juvenile. While I debated, the internet connected.

Of course, it did.

That meant that someone had already been on my laptop to add the Wi-Fi code. Maybe in time, I wouldn't be surprised. My shock was quickly forgotten as my email loaded to the hundreds of missed emails.

I'd never been out of touch with Sinful Threads for longer than a few hours while I slept. It had been since Wednesday afternoon and now it was Sunday. I hoped that Louisa had taken care of a few of the fires that had popped up.

Instead of assuming, I began forwarding emails with my inquiry: *Have you seen this? What happened with this order? Did you forward this to Winnie?*

All at once an interoffice messenger bubble popped up on my screen.

Louisa: *"THANK GOD, KENNI. TELL ME YOU'RE BACK IN CHICAGO."*

Me: *"ON THE PLANE."*

Louisa: *"IS EVERYTHING ALL RIGHT? I HAVE A WEIRD FEELING THAT I CAN'T SHAKE."*

Everything except I'm kind of kidnapped by a bossy, arrogant son of a bitch. No, I didn't type that.

Me: *"I'M FINE. READY TO TAKE ON CHICAGO AND ALL OF THE SINFUL THREADS MARKET. HOW ARE YOU? BABY KENNEDY?"*

Maybe I could suggest that she change the baby's name to Araneae, especially if it was a girl.

Was there a masculine spelling?

Louisa: *"STILL HANGING ON. MOM AND DAD GOT BACK TO SUPERIOR THIS MORNING. THEY SAID LINDSEY IS DOING GREAT. SHE HAS A NEW BOYFRIEND. DAMN, I CAN'T WAIT TO SHOW YOU A*

PICTURE. I SWEAR HE LOOKS LIKE A BODYGUARD FROM SOME MOVIE OR SHOW."

Was he? Or was he a threat? Why did I believe everything could be traced to Sterling?

Me: *"AS LONG AS SHE'S HAPPY."*

Louisa: *"MOM SAYS SHE'S OVER THE MOON. THAT'S OLD-PEOPLE TALK FOR HAPPY—I THINK. (laughing emoji)"*

Me: *"NOW THAT I'M GOING THROUGH EMAILS, WHAT DO I NEED TO DO? WHAT HAVE YOU DONE?"*

Louisa and I continued to message as I pulled up emails and sent her questions. She even filled me in a little on the time-stamp blip with Franco, telling me that Jason was concerned that it was an attempt to erase something from the security tape. Since she couldn't reach me, she authorized our security team to review tapes in all our facilities. Looking down at the beautiful dress I had on, I wanted to ask if that included our design facility. At the same time, I didn't want to worry her.

I didn't even realize how much time had passed until Sterling appeared behind me, his dark stare on my screen as his eyes scanned the long trail of correspondence between Louisa and me.

"Emails," he said. "You were given that to catch up on work."

I totally forgot my vow of silence as I swiveled in the seat and turned toward him. "That is what I'm doing. I told you I would talk with Louisa. She's part of Sinful Threads and my best friend. Mostly we've been discussing work and the mass of messages that I missed because of you."

"Mostly."

I lowered my voice. "Get over yourself. I didn't say anything about you."

His chin rose. "Tell her you have to go and turn it off. You're coming with me into the bedroom."

"I'm not done."

His hand reached for the screen of my laptop. "I said you are. Either log off or Patrick will do it for you."

A gust of air left my nose as I huffed in response. That didn't stop me from typing a goodbye message to Louisa as Sterling stood with his arms folded over his chest. I didn't wait for Louisa to respond before I closed out of our messages and my emails, and then shut down the laptop. "There, your highness. It's off."

He didn't respond, yet his lips formed a straight line and he quirked his chin toward the bedroom door.

ARANEAE

*I*t was my turn to fold my arms over my chest as Sterling stripped from his casual clothes. Damn, it was hard to stay mad as he walked around the room naked. Within the closet was what appeared to be a custom suit, different from the one that was there when we arrived. It was light gray with a white shirt and a black silk tie.

"Are you done?" he asked.

"Done with what?"

"With your temper tantrum."

"My temper tantrum?" I followed him into the bathroom as he turned on the hot water within the shower. "You were..." I searched for the right word. Yes, I could call him any one of the names I'd thought of earlier, but I wanted this to be more than about name-calling. "...mean."

Sterling turned my direction, all beautiful six and a half feet of him, completely as he had been so perfectly created. "Mean. That's what you think is mean?"

"Yes. Next time, just tell me what you want. The cheek thing hurt."

With the shower door open, a fine mist splattered onto the floor as Sterling took a step toward me. "I could tell you about mean. I could tell you about pain. I've experienced both from both sides. This afternoon was neither. It's about one thing: keeping you safe. Assuring that tomorrow, you can walk into your new office, distribution center, or warehouse without fear of harm. It's about letting the world know that you are untouchable. Mean and hurt are what will happen if my message isn't received loud and clear."

He reached for my chin, much gentler this time. "Sunshine, I can be mean and I have hurt more people than I remember. You are not on that list."

I closed my eyes.

"Look at me."

Swallowing, I did as he said and opened my eyes.

"I meant what I said about this engagement. We're going to a very private club in the heart of the city. It's so elite that the tenants around it don't even know that it's there. There is a private party taking place. Though I was invited, I doubt they expect me to show. I rarely do. I prefer the club when it's quiet.

"This was too good of an opportunity to pass. I couldn't ask for a better backdrop to show you to the world. They'll be there. Most of them anyway. Those who aren't will get the message. The word will spread like wildfire.

"While there, do not talk to anyone unless I'm by your side and introduce you. If I don't introduce you, you're mute."

My teeth ground. "Fine."

Sterling reached forward, but not to me. He reached for

his growing cock that was bobbing between us. "I have an idea." He didn't let me ask what it was. I honestly didn't want to ask. "There's nothing like my cum on your dress to tell the world you're mine, or maybe..."

I took a step back.

"You could get on your knees right now. When we get to the party your lips will be swollen, and everyone will know it's from sucking me off."

"Go to hell." I turned to leave the bathroom, but his hand on my shoulder stopped me.

"Araneae, turn around."

I didn't. "I'm not getting on my knees for you."

"Turn around."

With more apprehension than I realized I could possess, I did as he said and turned to face him. Did I expect him to do as he had before and jack off on the dress? I wasn't sure. What I didn't expect was what he said next.

"Do it."

My chin rose higher. "Go to hell. I'm not getting on my knees for you or anyone else."

"Good. You're a queen. You were born to be one. Act like it. If you want to call me every name in the goddamned book, do it. Tell me to go to hell. I've been there and back. Do it here or later at the apartment when we're alone. Just don't say or do anything to lessen my power in that room. That includes your fucking silent act. Are we clear?"

I nodded as I spoke, "Yes, Sterling. We're clear."

"And one day..." A bit of a smile threatened to break through his facade. "One day, I guarantee you will be on your knees."

I didn't answer as I turned again and went back to the bedroom.

There wasn't anything I could say because I was certain he was right.

When it happened, it would be on my terms.

ARANEAE

*M*y hand in Sterling's grasp shook as he escorted me from our car, the one that Patrick had stopped in an alleyway. Once inside a building, we moved down a hallway in what, based on the delicious aromas, was the back of an upscale Italian restaurant. Coming to a stop at what appeared to be an elevator, Sterling placed his palm on a screen. Instantly, the screen came to life with green lights indicating that an elevator had been sent.

We were truly a handsome couple, he in his custom suit and me in the Sinful Threads prototype. His suit hugged him in all the right places, accenting his broad shoulders, long legs, and toned torso. The bright white shirt contrasted with his sun-kissed complexion, and the black silk tie complemented my outfit.

This dress was different than the one I'd worn to the dinner on the Riverwalk. This one had a plunging neckline, one that went below my breasts and an open back that forbade the wearing of a bra. The tight waist accentuated my figure, and the skirt clung to my legs, the hem hitting my calves with slits going up each side. The crystal-adorned black peep-toe pumps were from another well-known designer, and I was wearing the jewelry I'd found in the box with the red dress. The only addition to my ensemble was my charm bracelet. I hoped it would give me strength to make it through whatever awaited us above.

Sterling reached for my wrist and turned the bracelet, examining the charms. "I've never seen that before."

"I don't wear it often. I know it wasn't with the things, but it is my moral support."

"That should be me."

By the sound, the elevator had stopped behind the closed doors.

I gave him a sincere smile. "It is now. When I dressed, I was mad at you."

The doors slid open to a man in a uniform, complete with a hat like I'd seen Patrick wear, one with a hard bill.

"Mr. Sparrow, welcome."

"Jamison, it's nice to see you."

"Sir, the event is underway, but I know they're honored that you would take the time to attend."

Sterling released my hand to place his again on my lower back. His warm fingers splayed possessively over my exposed skin. What he didn't do as we rode higher and higher into the sky was to introduce me to Jamison, my clue to stay mute.

As I concentrated on his hand, I decided that maybe following his directions would make this night go easier. Stay quiet, be seen, and get the hell out.

The doors opened to an ornate foyer with dark wood trim,

deep red walls, and a glistening chandelier hanging from the ceiling at least fourteen feet above us. The light from above danced upon the marble floor in prisms of color dominated by the red of the walls.

My high heels clicked as we stepped off the elevator.

"Mr. Sparrow," an older woman, dressed all in black, gushed as we moved forward.

I sucked in a breath as she came closer and Sterling leaned in, kissing each of her cheeks. A bit of green-eyed jealousy reared its head, surprising me at my own reaction in response to her perceived intimacy with my man.

Was he mine?

After all, he continued to say I was his.

When had I started to think that way?

"Evelyn," he replied, his deep tone welcoming, "may I introduce the lovely lady accompanying me, Ms. McCrie."

Her movements stuttered as she offered me her hand, almost as if she knew my first name and feared that perhaps I was a real spider, ready to inject her with my venom. Politeness won as she continued toward me. I offered her my hand as we greeted one another.

"It's a pleasure to meet you, Evelyn."

"And you, Ms. McCrie."

As we stepped toward the larger room, Sterling leaned down, whispering in my ear. "I guarantee in twenty seconds, everyone will know you're here."

I swallowed as a cool chill settled over me. The orchestra's music continued, yet as we stood in the entryway, conversations quelled and head after head turned our way. I scanned the room, unwilling to lower my eyes as each person stared my direction. At a table near the dance floor, I saw someone I recognized. It was Senator McFadden. I'd sat with him and his wife at the dinner at the Riverwalk. However, the blonde woman by his side wasn't his wife. As Sterling led me inside, I tried to remember his wife's name.

There were three empty stools near one end of the bar. He led me to the third, farthest away from others. "Remember what I said. I need to speak to someone. When I return, we will leave."

"You're leaving me alone?"

"You're not alone."

He turned to walk away as I scooted my knees around to the bar.

"Miss, would you like a drink?" the young bartender asked after Sterling was gone. She had her brown hair styled and her uniform was black slacks and a pinstriped vest that covered her, yet left little to the imagination.

Did this qualify as a say-nothing situation?

I thought about answering Jana on the plane.

"A manhattan. Thank you."

Leaving a square red napkin on the bar, she nodded and walked away. Farther down the bar was a younger couple, well dressed for the occasion.

Turning my head slightly the other way, I was able to see Sterling speaking with a man a few years his senior. I recognized Sterling's expression. It wasn't one that I liked.

My whiskey drink arrived in a thick crystal goblet, the maraschino cherry sinking to the bottom of the amber liquid, its stem sticking out. "Anything else?" she asked.

This time I simply smiled and shook my head.

Plucking the cherry from the glass, I bit the juicy fruit before taking a sip. I wasn't sure how much time passed, but during it, a few other men joined Sterling's discussion. They were all well dressed and all listening to whatever he had to say.

Maybe it was nerves or the bottle of water I'd drunk in the car on the way here. Regardless, I needed to excuse myself for a minute. Surely he wouldn't mind if I slipped away to the bathroom. I considered waiting, but his discussion didn't appear to be ending anytime soon.

"I'll be right back," I told the bartender. "Please watch my drink. Where is the ladies' room?"

Another quick peek toward Sterling, and I followed the bartender's directions. For as elegant as the club was, the ladies' room was rather small: two stalls and two sinks. I went into an unoccupied stall, hurrying with my business. Once back out to the sink, the woman washing her hands was the one I'd seen with Senator McFadden.

With a customary smile in the mirror, I went about washing my hands when suddenly the woman gasped.

I turned her way and asked, "Are you all right?"

Her gaze wasn't on me, but zeroed in on my wrist. "That bracelet..."

My pulse kicked up a beat as I quickly reached for a cloth towel from the basket between the sinks and dried my hands.

Her ice-cold, bony fingers that wore diamonds the size of nickels wrapped around my wrist. "Where did you get that bracelet?"

I wasn't comfortable answering this woman even without Sterling's orders. I pulled away from her grip. "Excuse me, my fiancé is waiting."

I wasn't sure what made me use that qualifier. Maybe it was because he'd told me he'd used it earlier to protect me. I hurried from the bathroom. As I reached the door to the club, my steps slowed. It was hardly regal to skid, slip, or fall in front of everyone. I lifted my chin as I walked toward the bar, step by step, as heads again turned. The group of men that surrounded Sterling also turned.

I couldn't identify even one of the other men, yet the dark stare that penetrated the crowd was focused on me. As it had the first time, it stole my breath and increased my pulse.

With an air of the status he said I deserved, I made my way through the people and back onto the tall stool. The liquid in my drink quivered as I lifted my glass. With the rim to my lips, I hoped the contents would ease a little of the strange feeling the lady in the bathroom had given me.

I replayed the scene. She was slender with blonde hair pulled back in an elegant twist, diamonds dangled from her ears as well as her fingers, and her gown was long and emerald green. If I really thought about it, the eerie feeling began before she asked about my bracelet. I felt it as our eyes met.

My neck straightened as the energy around me shifted, telling me he was near even before his hand landed upon my shoulder or voice came to my ear.

"I told you not to talk to anyone."

"I haven't," I whispered back.

"Then how the fuck did you get that drink?"

I turned to face him, my eyes shooting lasers—if only they could.

His large hand grasped my upper arm. "We're leaving."

My gaze went from him to his hand as the pressure on my arm built. "Sterling, you're hurting me."

Instead of releasing his grip, his fingers blanched. His

mouth barely moved as he growled in my ear. "Get down now, or I'll put you over my shoulder. We're leaving."

Since there was nothing I'd put past him, my heels quickly moved from the bar beneath the stool to the floor. "Is everything all right?" I asked as I stood. "Did it work?"

Our words were low. "You're safe."

Was I?

As we began walking toward the elevator with my arm aching under his grasp, for not the first time, I questioned his statement. From whom did I need protection?

"Mr. Sparrow—"

"We're leaving," Sterling said, interrupting Evelyn.

A commotion behind us caused both of us to turn.

"Araneae?" the woman from the bathroom questioned, her pronunciation was like that of the real spider. "Oh my God, is it really you?"

My lips opened as Sterling's grip loosened, and he reached for my waist, pulling me against him.

"Why? How?" she asked, her cheeks red and blotchy and her soft brown eyes flooding with tears. "My God, why? How are you here? And why are you with him? Marrying him?"

The doors to the elevator opened, and the smile on the man inside faded as Sterling escorted me aboard.

"Talk to me," she pleaded.

"Get us downstairs," Sterling barked as the man pushed the appropriate button.

I reached out and stopped the doors from closing. "Who are you?"

"Araneae," Sterling said.

I moved my hand back, allowing the doors to close but not before I heard her answer.

"I'm your mother."

My knees went weak as I collapsed into Sterling's arms.

Sterling and Araneae's story continues in LIES and concludes in PROMISES. You're not going to want to miss the rest of this spellbinding trilogy. Preorder Lies and Promises today.

WHAT TO DO NOW

LEND IT: Did you enjoy SECRETS? Do you have a friend who'd enjoy SECRETS? SECRETS may be lent one time. Sharing is caring!

RECOMMEND IT: Do you have multiple friends who'd enjoy my dark romance with twists and turns and an all new sexy and infuriating anti-hero? Tell them about it! Call, text, post, tweet...your recommendation is the nicest gift you can give to an author!

REVIEW IT: Tell the world. Please go to the retailer where you purchased this book, as well as Goodreads, and write a review. Please share your thoughts about SECRETS on:

*Amazon, *SECRETS* Customer Reviews

*Barnes & Noble, *SECRETS,* Customer Reviews

*iBooks, *SECRETS* Customer Reviews

* BookBub, *SECRETS* Customer Reviews

*Goodreads.com/Aleatha Romig

MORE FROM ALEATHA:

If you enjoyed SECRETS and want more from Aleatha, check out her backlist encompassing many of your favorite genres.

WEB OF SIN TRILOGY (Dark romance trilogy)
SECRETS
LIES
PROMISES

THE CONSEQUENCES SERIES: (bestselling dark romance)
(First in the series FREE)
CONSEQUENCES
TRUTH

CONVICTED
REVEALED
BEYOND THE CONSQUENCES
BEHIND HIS EYES CONSEQUENCES
BEHIND HIS EYES TRUTH
RIPPLES (A Consequences stand-alone novel)

THE INFIDELITY SERIES: (acclaimed romantic saga)
(First in the series FREE)
BETRAYAL
CUNNING
DECEPTION
ENTRAPMENT
FIDELITY
RESPECT (An Infidelity stand-alone novel)

INSIDIOUS (stand-alone smart, sexy thriller):

THE LIGHT DUET: (romantic thriller duet)
INTO THE LIGHT
AWAY FROM THE DARK

THE VAULT NOVELLAS: (short, erotic reads exploring
hidden fantasies)
UNCONVENTIONAL
UNEXPECTED

ALEATHA'S LIGHTER ONES (stand alone light, fun, and sexy romances guaranteed to leave you with a smile and maybe a tear)
PLUS ONE
A SECRET ONE
ANOTHER ONE (free novella)
ONE NIGHT

ABOUT THE AUTHOR

Aleatha Romig is a New York Times, Wall Street Journal, and USA Today bestselling author who lives in Indiana, USA. She has raised three children with her high school sweetheart and husband of over thirty years. Before she became a full-time author, she worked days as a dental hygienist and spent her nights writing. Now, when she's not imagining mind-blowing twists and turns, she likes to spend her time with her family and friends. Her other pastimes include reading and creating heroes/anti-heroes who haunt your dreams!

Aleatha impresses with her versatility in writing. She released her first novel, CONSEQUENCES, in August of 2011. CONSEQUENCES, a dark romance, became a bestselling series with five novels and two companions released from 2011 through 2015. The compelling and epic story of Anthony and Claire Rawlings has graced more than half a million e-readers. Her first stand-alone smart, sexy thriller INSIDIOUS was next. Then Aleatha released the five-novel INFIDELITY series, a romantic suspense saga, that took the reading world by storm, the final book landing on three of the top bestseller lists. She ventured into traditional publishing with Thomas and Mercer. Her books INTO THE LIGHT and AWAY FROM THE DARK were published through this mystery/thriller publisher in 2016. In the spring of 2017, Aleatha again ventured into a different genre with her first fun and sexy stand-alone romantic comedy with the USA Today bestseller PLUS ONE. She continued with ONE NIGHT and ANOTHER ONE. If you like fun, sexy, novellas that make your heart pound, try her UNCONVENTIONAL and UNEXPECTED. In 2018 Aleatha returned to her dark romance roots with WEB OF SIN.

Aleatha is a "Published Author's Network" member of the Romance Writers of America and PEN America. She is represented by Kevan Lyon of Marsal Lyon Literary Agency.